"You cannot *want* to wed me, Giles!

"You would have sought my hand long ere this!" Philippa cried. "And now—how can I marry the man responsible for my father's being struck down?"

His expression hardened, his firm chin lifted. "Even were your accusation true, 'twould be easily done." His voice was dry, implacable. "You will honor the contract exchanged between our families. Your father would wish it."

"He would not! He would help me to break it! Did you not see how he glared at you earlier?"

"Aye," admitted Giles, but neither his stance nor his features relaxed. "His anger will pass. It has no foundation. We will be wed as soon as possible." He unfolded his arms and reached out for her shoulders. "I should have sought my bride sooner, but I intend to remedy the situation with all possible dispatch. Henry is headed for Bristol. We will be wed there."

Loyal Hearts

SARAH WESTLEIGH

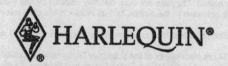

HARLEQUIN®

TORONTO • NEW YORK • LONDON
AMSTERDAM • PARIS • SYDNEY • HAMBURG
STOCKHOLM • ATHENS • TOKYO • MILAN • MADRID
PRAGUE • WARSAW • BUDAPEST • AUCKLAND

ISBN 0-373-30335-1

LOYAL HEARTS

First North American Publication 1999

Copyright © 1991 by Sarah Westleigh

This edition published by arrangement with Harlequin Books S.A.

® and TM are trademarks of the publisher. Trademarks indicated with ® are registered in the United States Patent and Trademark Office, the Canadian Trade Marks Office and in other countries.

Visit us at www.romance.net

Printed in U.S.A.

SARAH WESTLEIGH

Since leaving grammar school, Sarah Westleigh has enjoyed a varied life. Working as a local government officer in London, she qualified as a Chartered Quantity Surveyor. Having married a chartered accountant, she assisted her husband in his Buckinghamshire practice, at the same time setting up and managing an employment agency. Tired of so hectic a life, they moved to Brixham in Devon, where she at last found the time to indulge her long-held ambition to write, publishing short stories and articles for magazines, and a number of modern romances. In writing historical novels, she has discovered a new and enchanting world for her future characters to inhabit.

Chapter One

1399

Philippa crouched in the narrow embrasure, straining to see through the slit, but the sun glinting on steel so dazzled her eyes that details were obscured as the body of some fifty men, all mounted, approached the castle.

They'd been warned of Bolingbroke's unlawful landing at Ravenspur and of his march through England to intercept King Richard on his return from Ireland, so sight of the contingent of men advancing on Alban Castle came as no surprise. The Earl of Tewkesbury and his heir, Roger d'Alban, were prepared.

The drawbridge was already lowered, the portcullis raised. The Earl and his son, both in full harness and mounted on their armoured destriers, their squires a half-length behind, proudly flourishing their lords' banners, led some half-dozen foot-soldiers carrying halberds or pikes from the safety of the castle walls, where all the manor folk had hurriedly gathered at first sign of the approaching army.

Philippa watched anxiously as the portcullis came down behind them and the drawbridge was raised again. No one knew what would happen, and the party setting off to challenge the advancing column looked pitifully small. Her father, for all his present bellicose manner, was not one to retain a large body of liveried men-at-arms to maintain his local rights.

Philippa hated the chamber at the top of the tower. Draughty, chill even in midsummer, it was the last place she wanted to be, but she had been sent up to safety while her father and brother donned their armour and went out to face Henry Bolingbroke's force.

"Can you see what is happening?" asked an anxious voice from behind her.

She glanced over her shoulder at her sister-in-law, Mary, whose round, normally cheerful face was drawn into lines of worry under her fussy, frilly veil. Behind her, watched over by their nurse, Mary's two children, Lionel and Maud, sat on the dusty floor, teasing a kitten with a piece of straw.

"Not really." Philippa peered out of the slit again. "Father and the others have gone out, and the drawbridge has been raised behind them. Father and Roger are riding towards the others. Oh, Mary, I do hope Father keeps his temper!"

"So do I! The lord my husband, too. They're as

bad as one another when it comes to remaining calm!''

''They will spark each other off. How I wish I were with them!''

Mary gave a soft, rueful laugh. ''I can't see you doing much to calm them down, Pippa! All you d'Albans are as bad as one another! Admit it; if you were a man, you'd be out there urging them on!''

''Sitting around waiting for something to happen makes me jumpy. I do get angry sometimes, but I don't have Father's temper!'' protested Philippa.

''Perhaps not,'' admitted Mary with a shrug, ''but you are always jumping into something rash.''

Diverted, Philippa eyed her sister-in-law askance. ''What exactly do you mean by that?''

'''Tis only last week that you risked injury to use your crop on a worthless drover—''

''He was flogging his mules unmercifully! One of them was almost dead!''

''Aye, but you nearly caused a riot in Tewkesbury, and now the beast is in our stables eating our fodder! You never think, Pippa!''

''I did. I knew what I was doing: saving that poor animal from a miserable death!'' She turned back to the slit, indicating what was going on outside with an impatient gesture. ''If I were a man I'd want to be doing something, but that doesn't mean I would want to fight Bolingbroke's men! Surely there's no need to come to blows! All Father has to do is refuse, quite politely, to support Henry. Those men will accept that, and go on their way. I do not think they intend to use force, and they have not come equipped for a siege.''

''I hope you are right. We could not withstand one.''

The two parties had stopped ten paces apart. They exchanged words. Her father was angry, judging by his gestures. Then, so abruptly that Philippa almost missed his action, Hugh d'Alban grasped his battle-axe, waved it wildly in the air and, with a fearsome war cry, charged the leader of the opposing party.

Philippa gasped. Mary gave a cry of consternation without knowing exactly what was happening, and the two children stopped playing, arrested by the blood-curdling shout.

''What was that?'' asked Mary in a frightened voice.

'''Twas Grandsire's war cry!'' exclaimed Lionel excitedly, crowding to the slit. ''Let me see!''

''Go away!'' snapped Philippa, pushing him off.

''Behave yourself!'' ordered his mother hoarsely, wrenching him away. ''Pippa, what is happening?'' Slowly, Philippa turned from her vantage point. Her small face wore a stunned expression. ''Pippa?'' Mary's voice rose to a squeak of anxiety. ''Pippa, what is it?''

''He tipped Father out of his saddle,'' muttered Philippa, her voice strangled.

''Who did?''

"The knight leading Bolingbroke's men. Mary, I think I recognised his banner."

"And?"

"'Tis Giles. Sir Giles d'Evreux."

Mary swallowed, eyeing her sister-in-law carefully. "Well," she observed bracingly, "you knew he was in Paris with Henry. He naturally returned with him. But what of your father? Is he all right? Are they fighting? What of Roger?" she ended anxiously.

Philippa turned back to have another look. "Father is still on the ground," she relayed slowly, a frown of concentration and puzzlement marring the smooth creaminess of her brow. "There's a lot of milling about, our men are surrounded, but I don't think they are fighting—there's no clash of steel. I can't see Roger."

She jumped from the embrasure and ran to the doorway, her unbound hair a black cloud around her determined face. "I'm going down to see. You'd better stay here with the children."

"But Roger—"

"If anything happens to both my sire and your husband, Lionel will be Earl of Tewkesbury. Look after him!" ordered Philippa, darting a glance at the dark-haired boy, who had barely seen five summers yet.

"How can you remain so calm?" wailed Mary.

"They've picked Grandsire up!" reported Lionel excitedly from the embrasure. "I think they are carrying him back!"

"Calm?" snapped Philippa with a scornful snort.

"Stay here!" she warned again and, gathering up her skirts, fled down the uneven stone stairs, round and round, until she emerged, panting, in the Great Hall.

A babble of voices greeted her. She pushed her way through the throng of women and children sheltering there, ignoring the anxious enquiries thrown at her, and passed behind the screens and out of the door. At the top of the steps leading down to the courtyard she halted.

"Lady Philippa!"

The relieved cry echoed thinly across a bailey thronging with manor men arming themselves as best they could. She located its source as the gatehouse. Picking up her skirts again, she sped down the steps, and met the gate ward's messenger halfway across.

"What is it?"

"They are carrying the Earl back, my lady. Gibbon does not know if he should allow them entry."

At that moment a commanding voice rang out from the other side of the moat. "Open up, I say! We come in peace! Earl Hugh needs attention!"

Philippa's lips compressed into a tight line. She knew that voice. If he had harmed her father…"Tell Gibbon to lower the drawbridge. Raise the portcullis and admit them," she ordered.

What else could she do? Her father was now clearly unable to challenge the intruders further, and the forces at her disposal were too weak for her to consider resistance. She would be inviting slaughter. She stood waiting, erect and defiant, as the drawbridge creaked into place and the portcullis rumbled up.

First to enter the yard was a tall man riding a grey horse so light in colour that at first it appeared pure white, though much of its body was covered by a rich caparison of deepest azure embroidered with gold. Neither man nor beast was armoured for battle, though the man wore a breastplate covered by a brilliant scarlet jupon charged with the d'Evreux devices and a bascinet with dependent chain-mail to protect his throat. His long sword was sheathed, his lance held upright, the pennon at its point fluttering idly in the slight breeze created by his movement.

It was Giles. The lean gawkiness of youth had gone, replaced by a more mature breadth of shoulder and assurance of manner; he had grown a beard and developed some interesting lines on his long, tanned face; but otherwise he looked much the same. His deep-set eyes, more blue than grey, met hers with a suddenly arrested expression in their depths.

"Pippa?" he asked in that nerve-tingling voice she remembered so well, frowning as though he was in some doubt.

"Aye. 'Tis small wonder you scarcely recognise me, sir. 'Tis more than five summers since you last honoured this castle with your presence!" The old, familiar sense of dazzlement almost overwhelmed her, but she fought it down. She tore her eyes from his assessing gaze with a distinct effort, directing them towards the figure being carried in by his own men. "What have you done to my sire?" she demanded angrily.

"Nothing untoward."

His voice followed her as she darted across the cobbles and pushed her way through the gaggle of men surrounding her father. They'd removed his helm, and she could see his face clearly. His eyes were open. They shifted restlessly. An inarticulate noise came from his throat. The right side of his face remained wooden, unmoving.

Philippa's stomach lurched. Her hands clenched at her sides "Take him inside," she whispered. "To the solar."

She whirled round on Giles, who had by now dismounted, and was approaching her. "Nothing, you say?" she stormed. "Nothing? When he cannot move a muscle on one side of his face?"

"I did not cause that," declared Giles firmly. "I unhorsed him, but what else could I do? He came at me with his battle-axe. Was I to sit there and be slain? I have unhorsed men times without number in the lists, and been tipped from the saddle myself, without suffering more than a bruise or two. He had a seizure, Pippa. The day is hot, his gorget too tight, and all that armour too heavy. The effort was too much for him."

"What did you say to make him attack you so?" she demanded fiercely.

He lifted his head in an arrogant gesture, his features suddenly taut. His eyes changed from surprised

bluishness to grey ice. "I merely asked him to join
me in supporting the Duke of Lancaster's just cause,
no more. He seemed to take my request amiss. He
yelled that Bolingbroke was a traitor, and I no better,
and attacked. You know his temper, Pippa," he added
on a more conciliatory note. "He was spoiling for a
fight."

Philippa did not deign to reply. She threw him a
fulminating glance, closed her mind to his excuses,
and followed her father's inert body into the building,
leaving Giles d'Evreux to follow or not, as he pleased.

A sigh went around the Great Hall as their lord was
carried in. Philippa cried out for everyone to leave.
"'Tis safe to return to your homes," she told the
women gathered there. "There will be no fighting.
Take your children and menfolk with you."

As the crowd began to shuffle out Philippa trod
heavily up the stairs to their solar, where her father
had been carried and laid on the great bed. "Leave
us, all of you," she ordered tightly. "All except Guy
and you, of course, Sir Magnus," she added, waving
the priest to the bed. "Father looks like to have need
of your holy services. Guy, remove his armour."

The Earl's squire set about his task while Philippa
anxiously watched her father's face.

"Shall I not remain with you, my lady?"

Philippa turned quickly to smile briefly at the
small, round woman who had tended her needs so
well over the last years.

"Oh, yes, Ida. But first run up to the tower and ask Lady Mary to come down, will you?"

"Of course, lady."

As Ida left, Giles entered the chamber, striding purposefully to the side of the bed.

"Go away!" snapped Philippa, attempting to push the knight aside. "Can you not see that your presence is making matters worse?" Her father's eyes were fixed on the other man with a belligerence unusual even for him. His attempts to voice his anger brought the quick tears to her eyes. "He is disappointed in you, Giles," she told the tall figure at her side thickly. "He did not expect his prospective son-in-law to turn traitor!"

"I am no traitor!" grated Giles. "'Tis Richard who has turned traitor! Traitor to all the promises he made his uncle, John of Gaunt. He has confiscated all the Lancastrian estates! Henry but demands his right of inheritance restored."

"So he marches with an army? Oh, go away, Giles," ordered Philippa wearily. "I have too much to do to argue with you now."

"I have sent for a physician."

Philippa looked up at him, surprised by the sudden softening of his tone. "Thank you," she murmured, none too graciously, before returning her attention to the man lying like a log on the bed while Guy attempted to remove the latest in heavy plate armour, which had been its wearer's undoing.

God's blood! What a slough! Giles stood with uncharacteristic indecision, watching the scene before him. He was concerned for the man, who had been a friend of his family for years, but the thing that had totally thrown him was seeing Philippa again.

Was it really five years since he had last set eyes on the child to whom he had been betrothed this eight years since? Certainly, he remembered her as a scraggy youngster of some fifteen summers with little to recommend her in the way of looks, although he had always admired her lively ways and free spirit, and enjoyed her company. In a desultory kind of way he had looked forward to one day taming his young bride and turning her into an obedient wife and mother. But, although at fiteen she had been of marriageable age, there had seemed to be little hurry to burden himself with a wife and family. The women at Lancaster's court were charming, and many had been available. He had felt no desire or need to bed a maid without a hint of womanly softness about her body. There was time enough to produce an heir.

For Giles was the second son, with his fortune to make. His father had served John of Gaunt for most of his life, and had been created Earl of Acklane during the declining years of Edward III's reign, when the nation had been virtually ruled by John, the great Duke of Lancaster.

Giles had joined Lancaster's court at an early age, and been schooled in all the ideals of knightly conduct—of courage, compassion, generosity, honour and courtesy—viewing Henry Bolingbroke, Gaunt's

heir, five years his senior, as a model of chivalry.
When Henry, then Earl of Derby, had sought his allegiance, he had been delighted to join his close band
of followers. Since then Henry had been good to him.
It had seemed both appropriate and exciting to accompany his lord into exile. There had been jousts
aplenty, and he had increased his fortune considerably
in the twelve months he had been abroad.

The thoughts buzzed around in his head as he stood
in a corner of the solar, arms folded across his chest,
watching the scene by the bed.

He wished Hugh d'Alban no harm. Fiery he might
be, but he was also kindly and loyal, though Giles
felt his loyalty to be misplaced in the present circumstances. For the last ten years, until his untimely death
earlier in the year, Lancaster had guided Richard, who
had seemed to respect his uncle's advice. Now, with
Gaunt's wise, restraining hand gone, Richard seemed
bent on pursuing personal policies which could only
lead to disaster.

But it was on Hugh's daughter that most of his
attention was fixed.

How could any maid change so much? Her body
showed signs of delicious curves under the flowing
lines of her gown. The leaf-green colour contrasted
well with the blackness of her long, curling hair. He
was suddenly taken with a longing to see that hair
spread on the pillows, where he could bury his face
in its silky fragrance. He knew it was fragrant, with

a faint perfume of rosemary. He'd caught a whiff as he'd bent over the bed earlier.

"Guy, let me help!"

Her light, musical voice, overlaid by anxiety, penetrated his thoughts, and he watched her quick, capable movements as she helped the squire to divest Hugh of his breastplate and unlatch the heavy gorget he wore around his neck.

Giles took a step forward, about to offer his help in lifting the heavy body, but halted in his tracks. One refusal of his assistance was quite enough. He would not expose himself to her anger and scorn a second time. 'Twas a pity they'd met again under such difficult circumstances. He'd imagined riding peacefully into Alban Castle, enlisting the support of Hugh d'Alban and renewing acquaintance with his betrothed. Even if still reluctant to bed the wench, he knew he could not put off fulfilling his part of the betrothal contract for much longer. At seven and twenty, he must begin to take his responsibilities seriously.

Giles's eyes devoured Philippa's features as she bent over her father. She'd been a plain child. But now her face had taken on an intriguing shape—a broad, high forehead and wide, prominent cheekbones hollowing down to a narrow chin in which the fascinating trace of a cleft caught his attention for a long moment until his eyes shifted back to the dark mole sited near the curving lips of her full, passionate mouth. Her creamy skin held a trace of moist flush as she laboured to make her father comfortable. What colour were her eyes? He tried to remember, and caught an impression of deep, deep black, as fathomless as the night, fringed by equally dark, long lashes which were even now forming lush crescents on the perfect texture of her cheeks.

Her eyes were closed as Sir Magnus said a prayer over her father's still body. As the priest finished the incomprehensible Latin words, she crossed herself and murmured, "Amen."

A stir at the doorway made her turn. Mary bustled in, anxious and out of breath.

"Pippa! Is he recovered? Where is Roger?"

"No, he has not. Though I believe he is breathing more easily. And I do not know what has become of Roger."

Giles's quiet voice intervened. "He disappeared while we were tending the Earl."

"Disappeared?" gasped Mary.

"I fear so, my lady. He was not hurt, of that I can assure you. But he slipped away, and of his present whereabouts I have no knowledge."

Philippa, surprised by his still being in the chamber, sent him a hostile glance. "No doubt he wished to avoid the company of traitors!" she snapped.

Giles's lips tightened. The wench should not be speaking to her future lord in such a manner! But when had Pippa ever minded her words? he mused wryly. In the child such outspokenness had been endearing. But in his wife...She was upset. No doubt she would see reason anon. Meanwhile, a certain sympathy with her plight made him reluctant to add to her troubles.

He bowed. "I will leave you to recover your temper, my lady," he said with sarcastic courtesy and, turning on his heel, left the chamber with a jingle of spurs.

"Really, Pippa! Did you have to antagonise him so?" remonstrated Mary. "He could make life very difficult for us an he willed!"

"Pshaw!" Philippa flounced round to look down anxiously on her father. "He's done that already! With father incapacitated and Roger gone, what are we to do?"

"Manage as best we can until your father recovers and my husband returns!" declared Mary with unexpected spirit.

Philippa stared in surprise, then shrugged. Mary had been châtelaine of Alban Castle since her marriage to Roger almost seven years ago. She was used to being in charge of the household, and found satisfaction in bustling around, seeing to the day-to-day affairs Philippa found tedious.

"Now," Mary began with determined cheerfulness, "we must make the Earl comfortable. Have you discovered what is amiss?"

"He cannot speak, his face is stiff down one side, and I do not think he can move his leg or arm. Giles," said Philippa with a derisive snort, "says it is a seizure."

Mary bent over her father-in-law, taking his hand and judging his response. "I have seen this condition before," she said at last, "in my uncle. 'Tis an apoplexy, I fear."

"Will he recover?" asked Philippa anxiously.

"Probably. I do not think he will die, Pippa. But he may never again be able to use his arm or leg properly."

"Poor father!" Philippa scowled angrily. "It is all Giles's fault!"

"You can't say that, Pippa. If your father hadn't lost his temper—"

"He would not have had cause to if Giles had not come!"

Mary shook her head, but said no more, seemingly too occupied in making Hugh d'Alban comfortable to argue with her tempestuous sister-in-law.

Philippa watched in fretful silence. Mary was so efficient it made her sick. Not that she couldn't do everything that might be required of her as a wife if she had to. Except embroidery. She looked down at her long, tapering fingers in disgust. They would never do what she wanted—the stitches came out uneven, and the cloth ended up a crumpled mess. Otherwise, 'twas just that she preferred wandering the countryside on her palfrey, or practising archery in the butts, or gathering herbs—even snaring conies and other wild animals for meat, or netting fish in the castle stews. Or just sitting in some secluded nook, watching the birds and animals going about their business.

Philippa moved restlessly, feeling sup..fluous in the sick-room now that Mary had taken charge. ''I'll go and see if the physician is coming,'' she told her sister abruptly, and left the solar.

No doubt Giles had sent to Tewkesbury for medical help. Her chamber was on the upper floor of a recently built two-storey wing, flanking the kitchens and stores. Its glazed window would offer an extensive view of the track from Tewkesbury. To reach it she must leave by the Hall and cross part of the bailey. She stood at the top of the steps, irresolute. The physician could not be expected for a few hours yet.

The yard was no less full than it had been earlier. The manor folk had gone, but the fifty soldiers who had accompanied Giles were busy rubbing their horses down in or near the stables. They would want to bed down in the Great Hall with the d'Alban retainers and servitors. Mary would no doubt see to the provision of extra straw for their pallets. Giles, who was nowhere to be seen, would be offered the guest chamber, she supposed. He could share it with any other knights in his party.

Had Mary ordered extra food for supper? Philippa doubted her sister had had time. She sped down the steps, diverting her way to the vast kitchen. The blast of heat almost knocked her backwards as she entered. Sweating scullions, some almost naked, staggered about carrying steaming cauldrons, or bent over the blazing hearths—which made the risk of fire so great that they had to be isolated in a separate building—turning spits on which joints of meat roasted. Cooks and their assistants, scarcely less hot, laboured over chopping boards, rammed huge pestles into enormous mortars, and stirred the contents of huge bowls with large wooden spoons. Someone was rolling out pastry for pies, someone else kneading dough.

The head cook, a Gascon the Earl had brought back from one of his campaigns in Aquitaine, stopped work and moved over to meet her.

He bowed low. "*Ma Dame.*"

"Gaston, have you been told to increase the number of dishes for supper?" asked Philippa.

"Buffey, the steward, suggested more food would be needed, *Ma Dame.*"

"Of course!" Philippa felt foolish. She should have realised that Buffey and Mary between them would not forget to give the order. "There appear to be about fifty extra men," she said quickly, attempting to cover the futility of her visit. "Can you manage?"

"We are baking more bread. Supper may be delayed, but we shall provide sufficient victuals to feed everyone."

"Excellent."

Philippa supposed that the marshal of the horses had received orders to issue rations for the extra animals. Should she make sure? In any case, she would like to see that her palfrey was not disturbed by the

new arrivals. She left the kitchen with a sense of relief
and set off across the bailey towards the stables.

Actually, she just wanted to keep moving, to keep
her mind occupied. Her own thoughts were uncomfortable.

She found Blaze, a five-year-old gelding, quietly
munching his fodder. He greeted her with a soft
whinny, and nuzzled her hand. His glossy chestnut
coat shone, even in the dim interior of the stables,
and the broad white streak running down his face,
which had given him his name, stood out boldly.

Philippa kissed the mark fondly before she left the
animal and made for the stall where the rescued mule
stood. She ran her hands over the animal, feeling its
ribs, the roughness of the hair over previous wounds,
the scabs where the sores caused by the rub of a
wooden pannier cradle were healing.

Several horse-grooms worked near by, and she
turned to the nearest. "Do you think he's better?"
she asked eagerly.

"Aye, my lady," he responded cheerfully. "'Tis
my belief he'll be sound as a bell once his ribs are
covered with flesh. You've got yourself a good pack-
animal there."

"I thought he would die."

The churl grinned. "Small chance o' that now."

Philippa smiled at him. "Thanks to your care."

Looking round, she saw Giles's light grey horse
gleaming palely a couple of stalls further along. The
stallion was called Majesty. She knew that, because

Giles had brought him the last time he had visited
Alban Castle. Then Majesty had been a young colt
under training, showing every sign of deserving his
patrician name. Now he seemed to know how special
he was. His head was held arrogantly high, like his
master's. His eyes held a softness which would disappear in battle, again just like his master's. Philippa
shivered involuntarily as she remembered the ice in
Giles's glare earlier. She wanted him to look at her
softly, teasingly, as he had done when she was a child
and there was no anger between them.

Today his gaze had been either assessing or remote.
But why did she long for Giles to behave as the
charming, playful young man of her childish dreams
when she hated him now?

Would he still want her to marry him? Her stomach
muscles tightened on the thought. They'd been betrothed for eight years; such a contract was not easily
broken. But if both parties were willing...and Giles
had shown little eagerness to make her his bride! He
had left her to fret at being left a maid all these years,
when most young maidens were married by sixteen.
As Mary had been. Why, Mary was scarce two years
older than herself, and already had two grown children!

He must be reluctant to wed with her, or he would
not have tarried so long. As she was reluctant to wed
with him! She would insist the betrothal be broken.
Absently, she stroked the muzzle of the great horse,
and spoke into his ear.

"I will not marry him, Majesty. He cannot force me!"

"You think not?"

Giles stood behind her, his feet planted firmly apart, his arms folded across his broad chest, his features set in a quizzical expression. He had shed his helmet and the attached mail, revealing sun-bleached golden-brown hair and a closely trimmed beard. She fought down the sudden leaping of her pulses.

"You cannot *want* to wed with me, Giles!" she cried, "else you would have sought my hand long ere this! And now—how can I marry the man responsible for my father's being struck down?"

His expression hardened, his firm chin lifted. "Even were your accusation true, 'twould be easily done." His voice was dry, implacable. "You will honour the contract exchanged between our families. Your father would wish it."

"He would not! He would help me to break it! Did you not see how he glared at you earlier?"

"Aye, I know," admitted Giles, but neither his stance nor his features relaxed one jot of their grimness. "His anger will pass. It has no foundation. We will be wed as soon as possible." He unfolded his arms and reached out for her shoulders. "I should have sought my bride sooner, but I intend to remedy the situation with all possible dispatch. Henry is headed for Bristol. We will be wed there."

Chapter Two

Giles's fingers bit into her tender flesh like steel claws, drawing her closer. Philippa knew with dreadful certainty that he was going to kiss her. She squirmed in his hold and beat against his chest with impotent clenched fists. As his mouth drew threateningly nearer she turned her face away with a low cry of protest.

Her desperate struggles made no impression; he simply moved an arm to clamp her against him while his other hand anchored her head so that his lips could plunder hers.

Philippa gritted her teeth and stiffened. Giles had never kissed her before, except her hand in greeting or farewell. Why did he have to do so now? His heart thudded hard and fast under her clenched fingers, trapped helplessly between their bodies. His lips ground against hers, almost as though he was angry. It hurt. She made a protesting sound in her throat, but it was some moments before his touch gentled.

He lifted his head for long enough to take a calming breath. His heart slowed its beat. When next they touched hers, his lips were caressing instead of demanding. The tip of his tongue ran shiveringly along the line of her tightly buttoned lips. Rigid within his embrace, Philippa clamped her jaw shut, startled by the intimacy, afraid of the queer sensations his touch was inducing deep within her body.

Eventually he lifted his head again. His nostrils flared and he drew breath deep into his lungs, as though they had been starved of air. Her eyes seemed locked to his. It was impossible to disengage from that glittering challenge, clear despite the dim light in the stable. Slowly, he released her head, dropping his hand to slide it seductively down her neck and arm.

"We need privacy for this," he growled.

Philippa became aware of the men moving about the stables. Her face flamed. She tore her eyes from his, and concentrated her gaze on one of the silver acorns which dusted the scarlet of a jupon slashed by a broad azure band, bearing the d'Evreux golden castle and fleur-de-lis.

"How dare you touch me?" she spat. "You are despicable! I refuse to marry you!"

"You have no choice, my dear little spitfire." Giles grinned, his composure largely regained, though at what cost only he could tell. "I look forward to our bridal bed," he murmured deeply, seductively, as he loosened his hold on her body and took her by the arm to lead her from the stable.

"Then you have a disappointment coming!" snapped Philippa. "I shall not submit willingly to your animal demands!"

"I believe you will, my love. Sooner or later." His husky voice soothed. "And I can be very patient."

Philippa fought against the strange effect his touch and voice seemed to be having on her system. It must be because she had never been kissed before. Any new experience was bound to affect one so.

"I am not your love!" she spat defiantly. Her hair drifted round her small, flushed face, the sun bringing out highlights like those on a raven's wings; her large, beautiful eyes sparkled from their nest of lashes like twin jewels of so dark a midnight blue they might almost have been jet. Her mouth trembled invitingly despite her determination to keep her lips clamped tightly shut. Giles saw their lush, swollen promise, and drew a deep breath, wishing he had sought to claim his bride before. Wishing fate had not conspired to set her so obdurately against his suit.

"You will be," he vowed softly, as tenderness and admiration fought exasperation and desire for pride of place in his emotions.

He had released her arm. Philippa took a quick step backwards, then, with a cry of annoyance, twitched her gown aside and lifted her foot. Her soft, pointed shoe had landed in a pile of horse manure, and the odour rose pungently between them.

"See what you've made me do!" she wailed as anger and a complete sense of impotence and ineptitude swept over her, bringing unwanted tears to hover tremulously on her lower lids before running foolishly down her cheeks.

Giles quickly grasped a handful of straw from a passing groom. "Let me clean it off," he offered and, not waiting for her answer, squatted down and took her foot in his hand.

Stranded on one leg, Philippa found she had no option but to steady herself against his broad shoulder as he worked quickly and efficiently to scrape off the worst of the offending ordure. His muscles rippled under her fingers. Regardless of her balance, Philippa removed her hand as though she'd been stung.

"There!" He finished his task, let go of her foot, and smiled up into her glowering face. "The worst is off. Your servants should be able to remove the rest."

Philippa swiped at the tears running down her face, and tossed her head. "I suppose you think I should thank you," she threw at him, "but, since 'twas your fault I trod in the dung in the first place, I do not consider thanks due. I will leave you to your offensive duties."

"Wait!"

His harsh command halted her as she began to stalk away. She turned to view him haughtily, her brows arched in interrogation. "Why?" she demanded.

"Why should you consider my duties offensive? I came here in peace, to seek support for a just cause and to claim my bride. 'Twas your father's attitude which caused the problems, not mine."

"I cannot agree," she rejoined stiffly. "You now control Alban Castle. You will doubtless dispose your men to keep it safe for the traitor Bolingbroke. That is what I find offensive about your duties, my lord."

"Henry Bolingbroke is no traitor!" gritted Giles. "I have said it before, and I will say it again and again until I can force some sense into your addled brain!"

Philippa shrugged, feigning indifference. "We shall never agree on that," she told him, "and I am sure you cannot want a bride who is so at odds with your beliefs. Break the contract, Giles."

Her voice had become unconsciously pleading. Giles stared into her mutinous face and saw the vulnerable maid lurking behind the façade of maturity.

"I'm sorry, Philippa," he said gently, smiling with all the charm at his command—which he knew from experience was not inconsiderable— "but I have told you 'tis impossible. We must leave for Berkeley tomorrow. Please be ready to accompany me there, and from thence to Bristol."

Philippa stood and stared at him, fighting the allure of his smile. Of his entire person. Oh, he could charm the cockroaches from their cracks in the walls, but he couldn't charm her. She was immune. But he did have such an unsettling effect on her! If she didn't go at once she might be tempted to return his smile. And that would just feed his overweening ego.

She made one last stand. "You cannot force me."

Giles suppressed a sigh. It seemed his future bride

was impervious to the charm which had served him so well in the past. "I fear I can," he told her with forced cheerfulness. "Since your brother has seen fit to abscond, this castle must be evacuated tomorrow. Your family and retainers will travel to your dower manor of Fishacre. They will be safe there until we are able to join them."

"But Father cannot travel!"

"'Tis less than a day's ride. He will be safe in a litter. But his departure can be delayed if the leech deems it necessary."

"You are so thoughtful!" exclaimed Philippa bitterly.

This was a body blow. If Roger returned he would find the castle deserted. No doubt all their stores would be commandeered. He would have no victuals, apart from anything he could scrounge in the village. The manor folk would not let him starve, but what if he managed to raise an army? The village could not feed many men. He might ride on to Fishacre or another of their manors. But none could either house or support even a small company of men.

She eyed Giles narrowly. He stood, planted solidly, eyeing her in return. For what seemed an eternity to Philippa, they took each other's measure. Giles was definitely planning to thwart any plans Roger might have. Philippa knew it. Just as she knew that if she remained at Alban Castle overnight she would have no choice but to accompany Giles in the morning. If she wanted to escape bondage to him, she must make

her move that night. She could slip away through the
postern, for she had long possessed a spare key. No
one would know, except Ida, who would have to accompany her. Even Philippa could not envisage riding
about the countryside at night quite alone. They
should have a guard, ideally, but who could she ask?
Eadulf, the groom who looked after Blaze, might be
prepared...

Her lips twitched upwards at the corners as she
planned her escape. She dipped her head in apparent
submission. "The physician cannot arrive soon
enough for me," she stated flatly, and when she
turned on her heel and stalked away this time Giles
did not stop her.

He stood watching the graceful line of her retreating back, the swing of her hips as she lifted her kirtle
from the ground. His eyes narrowed. She was planning something. Her apparent submission to his will
rang false. He was used to reading other people's
minds, a necessary accomplishment at any court.

Philippa retired to her chamber without further delay. The young mongrel hound she had fostered from
a puppy followed her. Spot was never willingly far
from her side, and bounded along on long legs,
tongue lolling, his fringed tail waving joyously. Philippa patted his rough, mainly creamy coat absently,
and teased his one brown ear. No one would miss
her. She had no wish to run into Giles again before

supper, and the household ran more efficiently without her interference.

Ida was mending and pressing some of her mistress's older clothes. She looked up with an enquiring smile as Philippa burst into the room.

"There you are, my lady. I wondered where you had gone."

"To the stables," responded Philippa breathlessly. "I wanted to see that Blaze and the mule had not been disturbed. How was Father when you left?"

"Much the same." Ida brushed off Spot's exuberant greeting. "That dog is covered in mire!" she exclaimed in disgust.

"Not much, and so am I," responded Philippa, unlatching her shoes with a grimace. "'Tis all those extra horses in the yard. Lady Mary did not need your help?"

"Nay, she had plenty of other assistance, so I returned here to be about my duties."

"'Tis as well, for I wished to speak with you, Ida." Philippa eyed the older woman keenly as she put her arms around the neck of her dog, evading his eager tongue with a soft laugh of protest. Ida had been born some ten winters before herself, and was surely still young enough to relish a little adventure. "Ida, I am going to run away."

"But you cannot, my lady!" cried Ida, scandalised.

"I can, and I will! Lord Giles insists that I accompany him to Bristol, where he intends we shall be wed. Ida," she cried urgently, "you must help me! I

cannot marry the man responsible for my father's being struck down!''

"Sweeting," began Ida in distress, "you must
think of your future, and that of your family. You
cannot simply break a legal agreement at will. Consider the consequences—''

The wary compassion in her servant's eyes brought
angry spots of colour to Philippa's cheeks. She did
not want pity, but help! She interrupted sternly, "I
am considering the consequences of *not* breaking it!
A lifetime of marriage to a man I hate!''

Ida pursed her lips doubtfully. "You used to like
him well enough.''

"I did not know him then! He is an arrogant dic-
tatorial traitor!'' And a lecher, she thought, remembering uneasily his impassioned kiss and the strange
effect it had had on her. She shuddered slightly.
"How can I possibly marry him, Ida? If you will not
help me, then I shall manage on my own!''

So saying, Philippa rummaged in a coffer for a
huge circular riding cloak, which she spread upon the
bed. On top, she threw a necessary change of smock,
hose and veil, her best comb, her pouch of jewels,
the rosary given her by her dead mother, and anything
else small she thought she might need. As an after-
thought, and because she thought she could manage
to carry it, she included a change of kirtle and a spare
pair of shoes.

Ida watched her furious activity for several minutes
before she spoke again. "If you are determined, then

of course I will come with you, Lady Pippa. But I do not like it. Will you tell Lady Mary?''

''No! It would only upset her, and she has enough to worry about already, with my father's being so ill and her husband's disappearing without a word! Besides, she would try to stop me, and might tell Sir Giles. I do not like leaving my father,'' Philippa added sadly, ''but he is in good hands, and Giles would not let me stay with him in any case.''

''When do you propose to leave, my lady?''

''The moment the castle is quiet. We will slip out of the postern.''

''On foot?'' asked her tiring-woman, aghast.

''No. You must go and find Eadulf. He will saddle Blaze, and a mount for you. If he would come with us, I should be eternally grateful. Will you ask him? And tell him to meet us, with the horses, by the postern, as soon as he can get there without being noticed after the castle has retired for the night. About midnight, I should think.''

''I will tell him to be there. Where are we going, Lady Pippa?''

''To the Priory in Evesham. The nuns know me; I stayed there for a whole year to learn to read and write. They will give me refuge.''

''For a while, no doubt. But I doubt you will wish to stay there for long. I well remember the way you grumbled at being sent there. As I recall, you disliked living at the Priory so intensely that you threatened to abscond on more than one occasion. Are you not

running from a union you wanted above all else to
the kind of life you have always detested?"

"I do not intend to remain there long. Just until I
have made up my mind what exactly to do. And even
the Priory will be preferable to marriage with a man
I hate. Something will turn up," said Philippa opti-
mistically. "Giles will probably change his mind
when he sees how determined I am to break our contract."

"I wouldn't count on it," muttered Ida, but she
offered no more arguments. Instead, she went to find
Eadulf.

"He will accompany us," she reported on her return. "He says he could not allow us to wander the
countryside without protection. Though he is no more
happy about this escapade than I am."

Philippa had given up her preparations to leave,
knowing that Ida would pack for them both, and do
it far more efficiently than she would. She sat at her
window, Spot at her feet, gazing abstractedly at the
track to Tewkesbury, hoping their journey in the op-
posite direction would be accomplished in safety. The
way to Evesham was by no means a main thorough-
fare, and the trees and bushes pressed in close for
much of the distance, though beyond the fringe of
thickets the open fields spread far and wide, their fertile strips growing essential crops or providing pasture
for cattle and sheep. Outlaws or footpads could find
scant shelter there, but attacks on travellers were not
unknown.

Suddenly, her attention was caught by a small party toiling up the slope towards the castle, which was set upon a foothill of the Cotswolds. She sprang to her feet. ''I believe the physician is coming!'' she cried. ''I must go to my father!''

It wanted an hour to supper. It was scarcely three hours since her father's collapse. The messenger must have travelled like the wind, and the leech had made good time. Philippa sped across the sunny court and up the steps to the Great Hall, Spot at her heels, quite forgetting her reluctance to meet with Giles again in her anxiety to reach her father. She wanted to be there when the man pronounced his verdict.

Giles was sitting on a bench with a couple of cronies, drinking ale from an earthenware pot, when she erupted into the Hall. He looked up and rose quickly to his feet.

''Your physician is coming,'' she threw at him in passing, and continued her rush to the solar.

Mary greeted her with a quiet smile, and received the news of the leech's arrival with unfeigned relief.

''Though I don't know what he can do,'' she admitted, ''except bleed him. Mayhap that would prove beneficial.''

Philippa laid her small, cool hand on her father's forehead. His eyes were closed now, and he looked peaceful. Only an unnatural lifelessness in the muscles of his face and a certain sunken appearance about his normally full cheeks indicated that aught was amiss.

The leech strode in, his flowing black gown emitting a great waft of mixed odours: horse, herbs and sweat. Giles followed closely behind. Spot greeted the knight exuberantly, and received an affectionate pat or two in return.

Treacherous beast! He did not like strangers, and avoided Roger when he was home, yet he seemed to have taken to Giles. "Down, Spot!" Philippa growled. "Come here!"

Tail wagging in evident pleasure, the dog obeyed her commands, a stupid grin on his long-nosed, patchy face. The tense atmosphere of the sick-room had not, it seemed, penetrated his thick skull.

"Lie down!" she ordered, and the dog flopped to the rushes, long pink tongue lolling from between large, sharp teeth.

Meanwhile, the physician had begun his examination. He woke the Earl, who had been in a heavy doze, and prodded and poked, seeking reactions. Eventually he confirmed Mary's verdict. "An apoplexy," he muttered.

"Will he recover?" asked Philippa anxiously.

"Only God can tell, Lady Philippa. Pray that he may. He is of a sanguine humour, I believe, and he must be made to sweat. Build the fire and cover him with furs. What was the date of his birth?"

Philippa told him, as nearly as she knew. The man retired to a corner of the chamber and, from somewhere among the folds of his gown, extracted parchments on which horoscopes were charted. He studied them in silence for a long time. Meanwhile, Mary had ordered that the fire be lit and the winter furs be brought. The room became stifling, and everyone except the physician showed evidence of being uncomfortably hot.

He moved at last. "The signs are propitious," he announced. "I will bleed him. That should relieve any pressure on his brain."

The company watched in silence as the slit was made and a small cup filled with the red liquid. Spot whined, disturbed by the scent of fresh blood. The wound was bound, and the physician tied a small model of a man, strung on a length of ribbon, round Earl Hugh's thick neck, before stepping back.

"The patient is not strictly ill," he pronounced solemnly, "merely paralysed. The healing powers will descend into the effigy when the planets are favourably placed, and thence into His Grace."

"Would a journey harm him?"

Philippa jumped as Giles's curt voice asked the question. She glanced anxiously at the physician. Please say it will, she prayed silently. But her prayer was ignored.

"How far?" enquired the leech.

"A day's journey east."

The man puckered his thin lips. "No," he decided. "No, such a journey might be beneficial, provided he is kept warm. It may stimulate his responses. I have known it to happen."

Giles's face broke into a smile of relief. "Thank

you, sir. We are most grateful for your prompt visit, and for your skill. Please accept this purse in payment." He handed the man a pouch which appeared to hold several coins. The leech pulled it open, viewed the contents with evident satisfaction, and pulled the draw-string to close it again.

"Your servant, noble lord. I was pleased to oblige."

"You will remain overnight and examine the patient again on the morrow?"

"Gladly. I shall not return to Tewkesbury before I have assured myself of the Earl's fitness to travel."

"A bed will be found for you," put in Mary practically. "Meanwhile, you will sup with us, sir."

The physician bowed. Giles ushered him from the room, then turned to address Mary.

"My lady, I shall be grateful if you will arrange for the household to be ready to travel to Fishacre tomorrow. I have already dispatched a messenger to advise the steward of your coming."

The blood drained from Mary's face. "You wish us to leave here?" she asked faintly.

"Aye, lady, I fear it is necessary. You will not suffer from the move, of that I am assured. You will be safe at Fishacre."

"But my husband—"

"Departed of his own volition," interrupted Giles tersely, "leaving his sire unconscious on the ground. He must seek his own salvation."

At that moment a trumpet announced that supper

was served. Philippa stood resolutely at her father's side.

"I will remain here. Have my food sent up. You need relief, Mary, if you are to carry out my lord's imperious orders." Her bitter voice echoed round the stone chamber. "I do not come with you. Sir Giles is forcing me to accompany him to Bristol to be wed."

Mary looked from Giles's inscrutable face to Philippa's rebellious features, and sighed. "You will be better wed," she said eventually. "I wish you both happy."

Philippa shot her an anguished look which Mary could do nothing but ignore. She took her young sister-in-law into her arms and kissed her fondly.

"It will work out, you'll see," she whispered.

It certainly would, thought Philippa dourly. But not in the way the others thought.

It was time to go.

A deep hush had fallen over the castle. She picked up her bundle, took hold of Spot's leash, and motioned to Ida to douse the candle and follow her. The heavy door opened without a sound. She stood in the opening, listening. Giles would be in the guest chamber at the end of the long gallery. His door was tightly shut, and no glimmer of light was to be seen anywhere.

With Ida close behind, Philippa crept along to the stairs. The ground floor was given over to wardrobes, store-rooms and other household offices. A churl snored in a far corner of the entry chamber, but they whispered through without waking him.

The deserted bailey held ghostly shadows in the bright moonlight. Philippa was thankful for the light to pick her way, but fearful of being seen, so she led the way around the perimeter, keeping in the shadow of walls and buildings. In fact, the only movement other than their own that she discerned was that of scavenging rats and prowling cats. Spot let out a low growl as they neared the kennels, and Philippa shushed him urgently; it would not do for the hunting pack to be roused.

They passed safely between the keep and the stables to arrive at the postern without incident. A faint jingle of harness in the deep shadow of the curtain wall told her Eadulf was waiting with the horses. She greeted him softly.

"Think you we can move away without being seen?" she asked anxiously. This was something she had been worrying over for some hours. The horses and riders would be plainly visible in the moonlight.

"We must wait for cloud to cover the moon, my lady. Else the watch will surely spot us."

Philippa scanned the heavens, pleased to see a bank of cloud slowly traversing the sky. "It shouldn't be long," she remarked hopefully. "Let us open the postern in readiness."

"I have already removed the bar, my lady. I need but the key."

"I have it here," said Philippa, handing him the

heavy metal object. The lock turned smoothly, with the merest clunk of sound. "Let us mount," she urged eagerly.

"First let me fix your bundles to your saddles," suggested Eadulf.

Philippa thrust hers into his hands, impatient at the delay. Eadulf worked quickly and efficiently and, when he had finished, made a cradle for her foot and threw her up into the saddle.

Queen Anne had introduced the side-saddle some years since, and using it had become fashionable among court ladies. Although Philippa had tried the new riding position, and knew it gave a more dignified appearance, she preferred to sit astride her palfrey, for having the horse between her knees gave her more control. She wore wide skirts for riding and, before settling in her saddle, stood in her stirrups to straighten and arrange the purple fabric of the gown she had chosen. Eadulf spread the slate-grey cloak she wore to cover a trim saffron cote-hardie over the jennet's rump, and she was ready. Ida, less used to horseback, took longer to settle. By the time both women were ready the moon had already disappeared behind one edge of the cloud.

"Quickly," urged Eadulf. "I will close the postern, and follow. But go slowly and quietly. We will attract less attention that way." So saying, he flung open the gate. Philippa urged Blaze through on to the narrow wooden causeway, only then fully realising that Eadulf had muffled the horses' hoofs. Once safely on solid ground, she longed to dig her heels into her horse's flanks and break into a gallop, but she knew the groom was right.

Blaze would have welcomed a good run. He fought against the bit, jangling his harness, though, as well as muffling his hoofs, Eadulf had thoughtfully used a simple headstall without bells or other noisy decoration. Philippa heard the postern close, followed by Eadulf's almost silent progress behind. Soon they reached the main track to Evesham, and Philippa allowed Blaze to lengthen his stride, while still keeping him to a walk. The faint plop of hoofs on the soft ground would not carry far. But the moon threatened to emerge from its cover at any moment, and the nearest trees were still some distance away. On the main track, though, they might be any travellers braving the darkness to reach their destination.

Keeping a firm grip on both the reins and her nerve, Philippa kept Blaze moving steadily towards cover. The three horses entered the shadow of the trees, and still no sound of alarm came from the castle.

"We have done it!" she cried exultantly. "Come, remove the muffles quickly, and let us make haste! We should reach Evesham long before sunrise."

Once Eadulf had removed the skins from the horses' hoofs she let Blaze have his head, the others thudding along behind. Spot's excited barking kept them company as he bounded along beside her.

Now she was free of the castle elation took hold of Philippa. She lifted her black head, her unruly hair carefully braided and coiled in a silken fret for the journey, and laughed aloud.

"So much for my lord Giles d'Evreux!" she shouted to the air. "If he thinks to force me to his will, he may think again!"

Back in his chamber, Giles slept restlessly, aware of the heavy breathing of the others sharing the room. Annoyed with himself, for normally he slept deeply, though he had the soldier's knack of waking instantly alert, he tossed aside his light covering, and wandered to the window. The moon shone brightly, illuminating the bailey and the buildings surrounding it. A shrill whinny from the stables caught his ear, and he was reminded of his horses, probably as restless as their master in strange surroundings.

On an impulse, Giles donned shirt and braies, his padded grey gambeson and azure hose, laced on a pair of cordwain buskins, and crept out of his chamber and down the stairs. He strode confidently across the moonlit bailey, and entered the darkness of the stable. Majesty whickered in greeting, and Giles went to him, fondling and soothing with hand and voice. He stood for some moments before he realised that several of the other stalls were empty, though many of his men's mounts were tethered in the open for lack of space inside.

A rapid investigation brought an oath of anger to his lips. "Is anyone about?" he roared.

A head appeared at the top of the ladder leading to

the hayloft, the liripipe of the man's chaperon falling forwards over one bleary eye. "Aye," said a sleepy voice.

Not one of his own men. They must have bedded down in the Hall.

"Come here, churl!" Giles ordered.

The man threw back the liripipe and descended the ladder with what speed he could.

"Tell me," grated Giles, "which castle horses are missing?"

The groom looked round, a vacant expression on his heavy face. Then a kind of light dawned. "Lady Philippa's palfrey has gone, my lord," he said, "and two of the hacks."

"I thought so," hissed Giles to himself. "Who took them?" he demanded imperiously. "When did they disappear?"

"How should I know, Lord? I bin asleep, like all honest men, and I didn't hear nothing, lord. But Lady Philippa, her wouldn't go far without an escort..."

Wouldn't she? wondered Giles grimly. He'd guessed she was up to something. Why the devil hadn't he had her watched? Because, he thought grimly, he had credited the wench with more sense than to wander the countryside at night!

He stormed back to his chamber to rouse his squire and fellow knights, and on the way unceremoniously threw open the door to Philippa's chamber. Naturally, it was empty. Swearing softly to himself, he roused the men and then rapped on Lady Mary's door.

"Where would she go?" he demanded when he had appraised a bewildered Mary of the facts.

"I do not know! She took Ida with her?" asked Mary in distress.

"Aye, it looks so. And probably a groom."

"Eadulf," guessed Mary. "He is getting on in years, but is devoted to Pippa."

She paused a moment, plucking at the fastening of her hastily donned chamber-gown with nervous fingers. Suddenly they stilled. "She might seek refuge at the Priory where she went for schooling," she told the impatient Giles. "I can think of nowhere else."

"Where is this place?" he snapped.

"Evesham. 'Tis not far—"

"Far enough," growled Giles. "An hour's fast ride." He strode back to the chamber, where the others were hurriedly donning their clothes.

"What is amiss, lord?" asked Wat Instow nervously.

"Nothing that cannot be speedily remedied," Giles told his squire. "My jupon, if you please!"

He addressed the youngest and most personable of the three knights as he climbed into the colourful garment and strapped on his sword-belt. "Sir Malcolm, you will see that half our men are ready to move off to Berkeley by Prime."

"Aye, lord."

"Sir William," he went on, turning to a stout young man, whose sweeping sandy moustache and long beard completely covered the bottom half of a round, ruddy face, "choose ten men, and remain behind to empty the castle of stores. Use the pack-animals, and follow us to Berkeley with any spare mounts."

"You wish me to remove everything, Sir Giles?"

"Everything Lady Mary does not wish to take to Fishacre."

He spoke less briskly to the older knight—a short, stocky man whose weathered face housed kindly blue eyes under bushy brows, and sprouted a sparse, greying beard. "Sir Walter, you have known the Earl for many years. I entrust his safe passage to Fishacre to you. Retain ten men as escort for him and his family and servants. Remain there until you hear from me."

"I shall do as you ask, of course. But will you not be coming back here, Sir Giles?" asked Walter Orpede doubtfully.

"I doubt it. 'Twill be dawn before I can possibly begin to escort Lady Philippa to Berkeley. You have my orders. The castle must be emptied, most of the men must rejoin Henry Bolingbroke, and the d'Alban family must be seen safely to Fishacre." He gestured to his squire, "Come, Wat. We have an unexpected and cursedly inconvenient journey before us!"

Chapter Three

In the moonlight the Priory rose from the fields edging the small town with all the appearance of a ghostly edifice. Philippa shivered slightly, partly from excitement but mostly from superstitious fear. The building had a strange, mysterious aura at odds with its solid, tranquil daytime appearance.

During the journey she had concentrated on the ride, travelling on a wave of euphoria at having evaded detection to escape Alban Castle. But now almost arrived at her destination, the doubts began to crowd her mind. What would she do if the Prioress Mary-Luke refused to give her shelter?

As Eadulf rapped on the great doors, demanding entry, she thrust her doubts aside, sat straight in her saddle, and tilted her chin defiantly.

The nun on night duty gasped in surprise when she slid aside the shutter and recognised the face of her visitor, clearly visible in the pale light of the waning moon.

"Lady Philippa! What brings you here at this hour?"

"I seek refuge, Sister Benedict."

"Refuge, my lady? What possible threat could cause you to travel by night with so few attendants?" demanded the elderly nun, her scandalised tones intimating just what she thought of such irresponsible conduct.

Philippa had no wish to spread news of her difficulties throughout the convent. The sisters found little inside its walls to gossip about, and would seize on her misfortune as a source of endless speculation. She replied with brisk authority.

"Let us in, Sister, and I will explain to Prioress Mary-Luke as soon as she is able to speak with me."

With a disapproving expression on her lined face, Sister Benedict opened the gate to allow the party entry. "Reverend Mother has not long retired after Matins and Lauds. I will not disturb her before the next Office," she told Philippa severely. "Your groom may stable the horses and rest in the men's guest dorter, yonder." Her black habit flapped as she motioned with her hand to an isolated building just inside the gate. "You and your attendant must wait in the women's chamber. You know where that is."

"Aye, Sister, and I thank you." Philippa was desperate to see the Prioress and establish her claim to sanctuary. She slid from her saddle, and handed the reins to Eadulf, turning immediately back to scan the plump features of the nun. "How long before the bell tolls for Prime?" she asked anxiously.

"Dawn breaks early at this time of the year. You will not have too long to wait," replied Sister Benedict, glancing to where her hour-glass stood on a ledge inside the gatehouse cell, the sand running down steadily from an almost full globe. "You must wait until after the Office has been said. Meanwhile, try to obtain some rest."

Philippa nodded. There seemed naught she could do to speed her interview with the Prioress. But Giles would be unable to reach her inside the building. "Come, Ida. Eadulf, we shall need our bundles."

"Your hound would be better in the kennels," muttered Sister Benedict doubtfully.

"Nay, he is used to sleeping with me, and would howl if we were parted. Are there many other guests in the dorter?"

"There seem to be few travellers on the road today, perhaps because of the uproar provoked by Henry Bolingbroke's return. He marched through here early this morning."

"Was his army large?" asked Philippa, unable to deny her curiosity.

"He had thousands of men with him! The column took hours to pass the gate. So many great Lords rode by, and all their retainers and levies! I saw Archbishop Arundel himself!" she said, breathless with awe. "And the Percies and the Nevilles and—"

"Doubtless a magnificent sight," broke in Philippa

curtly. "Take the bundles, Ida. God be with you, Eadulf; sleep well, and my thanks for your escort. We
will decide on your best course on the morrow. God's
blessings, Sister Benedict."

Followed closely by Spot, Philippa and her maid
crossed the courtyard and mounted the stairs to the
sleeping chamber set aside for the use of women travellers. Straw-filled pallets lined the dorter, and, although most appeared empty, snores and snuffles
emerging from the darkness told her several of the
beds were occupied. Philippa trod quietly across the
rush-strewn planks, and sank down tiredly on one
near a window, dimly lit by the last glimmers from
the moon. Ida subsided on its neighbour, and Spot
circled round twice, forming a nest in the rushes between them before settling his long nose on his paws,
though his soft brown eyes remained open, fixed on
his mistress.

Philippa had no intention of sleeping; she wanted
to remain alert to attend chapel and catch the Prioress
as soon as the Office was over. A picture of Giles's
irate face swam before her vision—the last thing she
remembered before she woke to the clang of the bell
calling the sisters to worship.

Philippa sprang up, smoothed her gown, told Spot
to remain where he was and, followed by a fuddled
Ida, who had obviously fallen asleep too, made her
way to the chapel, where the last of the sisters were
filing in from the night stairs.

The voices of the nuns, raised in plainsong, sent a

familiar thrill through Philippa. Despite the hour, despite her uncertainty and anxiety, the swell of the melodious chanting rising to fill the chapel to its vaulted ceiling brought with it a sense of uplift, of peace.

Philippa had always enjoyed the time spent in the chapel, where she could lose herself in the music and her own thoughts. It was the rigorous, austere routine of the nuns' lives, governed by their Rule and the constant tolling of the bell, which sent a shiver of dismay through her. She did not fancy the life of a religious. Yet what other choice was open to her, if she refused to wed with Giles?

Here, in the peace of the chapel, she faced the fact that she would become a social outcast if the d'Evreux family refused to dissolve the betrothal. She had been a full fifteen years old when the contract had been sealed. Only by mutual agreement could she escape her commitment with honour. And Giles had shown no inclination yet to accomodate her wishes.

She had hoped that her determination and obvious dislike would move him to change his mind. Perhaps he would in the end. But in the rational, cold light of all the facts that hope seemed to dim. An ambitious man like Giles would not easily be persuaded to relinquish the rich manors she brought with her to the marriage bed.

What would he do when he discovered she had gone? Would he spare the time to chase an errant bride, not knowing where to look? Philippa squeezed her eyes shut tight and prayed not. Prayed he would be fully occupied by Henry's cause for such a long time to come that his sudden desire to wed her would dim and he would allow the betrothal to be broken. If Henry did not succeed, of course, things could go hard with his supporters, and no one would force her to marry a proven traitor.

A shiver ran right through Philippa. However much she hated him, she had no wish to see Giles tried and executed for treason. Because of his rank he would escape the hanging, drawing and quartering suffered by those of lesser degree. He would be beheaded. She gazed bleakly at the altar, and her hands, clasped on the desk of the prie-dieu in an attitude of prayer, twisted together in sudden agitation. She could wish that fate on no one. Least of all on Giles, whom she had once imagined she loved.

It was suddenly more comfortable to believe Giles's assertions as to Henry Bolingbroke's loyal intentions.

Her hopes that Giles would not know where to look, and that he would not, in any case, spare the time to chase his runaway bride even if he did, were shattered the moment she filed from the chapel after the nuns. She heard a familiar male voice in the outer court.

The Prioress Mary-Luke, alerted by Sister Benedict to her unexpected presence, threw Philippa a shrewd glance and indicated with her black and white swathed head that the girl should follow her. Having spoken quietly to a novice, who scuttled off, Reverend Mother moved swiftly and silently to the chamber, just inside the entrance to the main building, where visitors of both sexes could be entertained. She lit several other candles from the one she carried before turning to face Philippa.

"Well, daughter," she said gently, as Philippa dropped to her knees before her and accepted her blessing, "what trouble has brought you to me this night?"

Philippa swallowed deeply. "I wish to break my betrothal contract, Reverend Mother," she confessed, her voice low and agitated. "I can no longer marry Sir Giles d'Evreux. He has caused much anguish to my family, and is supporting Henry Bolingbroke against our anointed King."

The Prioress ignored the last charge. "What anguish has he caused your family, child?" she enquired.

"My father lies helpless. Had Sir Giles not come demanding his support for a traitorous cause, my sire would not have been stricken by an apoplexy."

Before the Prioress could comment on this statement, they were interrupted by the arrival of the accused himself, shepherded by the novice, who made obeisance and departed. Giles greeted the Prioress, and knelt for her blessing before springing to his feet to give Philippa a cursory bow. The skin stretched tightly over his cheekbones. The muscles bunched round his clenched jaw, and his nostrils pinched in as he drew a long, exasperated breath. An explosive sound made her wince as he exhaled through his mouth.

"Well, Lady Philippa! So you are here. Why did you flee from your duty?" he demanded tersely.

Philippa tilted her chin, her lips compressed. When she spoke, it was from between her teeth.

"You would not listen to my pleas," she informed him fiercely. "'Twas the only way to escape your indecent demand that I marry you with all haste!"

"Indecent? What nonsense is this, Pippa?" barked Giles, momentarily surprised out of his studied formality.

Philippa could find no answer to that. She glared back at him. "How did you find me?" she countered angrily.

"Lady Mary has more sense of duty than you, my lady. She guessed you would seek refuge here. There was nowhere else for you to go."

His remote, formal manner hurt. For some reason she felt doubly betrayed. "Trust Mary to behave with the utmost propriety!" she sniffed.

"My children!" The Prioress's quiet voice broke through their argument, her serene face, in its frame of white linen, mildly admonishing. "Harsh words will not help to resolve your difficulties."

Quietly and rationally, she led them to recount the events of the previous day before delivering her verdict. "I can see no cause for you to break your vows, my daughter," she told Philippa gently. "Go with your affianced husband. He does only what he considers his duty. And go also with God.''

Philippa stared at the Prioress in dismay. In a moment of blinding clarity she realised that the betrothal contract had been sealed by the Church, and was as binding in its sight as any wedding ceremony. Something she had failed to remember when she'd made her decision to run away from Giles. ''You cannot mean it, Reverend Mother!'' she gasped. ''I had thought you would understand, that I could find shelter here until the betrothal contract was dissolved!''

''Which it will never be,'' inserted Giles crisply.

''It is your duty to wed, my child. God grants a great deal of satisfaction to those who execute their duty in an obedient and pious spirit.''

''But I want to take holy vows, Reverend Mother! I wish to become a nun!'' cried Philippa desperately.

The Prioress smiled ruefully, shaking her head. ''I cannot believe you, daughter. I know you too well. You must not be tempted to misuse God's holy calling to escape the trials of life. In a very short while you would be more unhappy here than you will be as the wife of the man chosen for you. You did not settle to the religious life while you were a pupil.''

The smile broadened, became a gentle smile full of understanding. Before she spoke again she glanced from Giles's handsome, determined features, the grim set of his chin belied by the softness lurking in the depths of his eyes, to those of Philippa, rebellious yet lovely, showing all too clearly the uncertainty and immaturity of their bearer. "You have always told me you had a fondness for each other," she reminded Philippa quietly. "With time, respect and affection will return."

Philippa sank to her knees, clasping her hands before her in an attitude of supplication. "Do not force me, Reverend Mother," she whispered.

The Prioress touched the dark, bent head before lifting the girl to her feet. "I cannot force you, daughter. I can only advise. But neither can I allow you to remain here. Your unwarranted presence would unsettle the prayers and the work of the sisters. And before long you would become restless, causing more disruption. God has ordained your path, my child. Obey his will with faith."

Philippa knew she was beaten. A sickness settled in the pit of her stomach. She ran her tongue around dry lips, and raised her eyes to Giles's stern face.

"It seems, my lord, that you have won," she choked bitterly. "I fear you will find little joy in your victory."

Giles bowed. The muscles in his jaw bunched anew. "It gives me little joy to win my bride in this way," he told her grimly. "I regret that you made such a confrontation necessary. Be ready to ride as soon as may be. We must make up the lost time. We travel straight to Berkeley."

"We do not return to Alban?"

"Nay, my lady." His voice softened, and he no

longer used her title as though it were a weapon. "I fear that will not be possible."

"But I have so few of my things with me!"

"Enough for several days, I warrant. And Sir William will have your possessions with him when he joins us. Your further needs can be supplied when we reach Bristol."

She sought wildly to delay the inevitable. "I have barely slept—"

"Neither have I. But I doubt we shall fall out of our saddles with fatigue."

"Ida—"

"And Wat. Both are suffering needlessly as a result of your escapade. Eadulf had better accompany you, since he is here. My grooms are quite busy enough without other horses to see to."

So she would have two familiar faces with her. For an instant a feeling of gratitude almost overcame Philippa's resentment. She stiffened her resolve. "Blaze and the other horses will barely be rested. We travelled fast."

"As did we. Stop making excuses, Pippa." He grinned suddenly, showing the slight irregularity in his gleaming white teeth. "We must not keep the lady Prioress from her duties. I will see you in the courtyard as soon as you have recovered your possessions. And, I believe, your hound," he added, then turned to Mary-Luke to execute a courtly bow. "My apologies for disturbing your peace, my lady. And my gratitude for your wise counsel."

The Prioress smiled benignly. "Take time to break your fasts before you depart. I will order food brought here from the frater." She lifted her hands in benediction. "God be with you, my children."

The sun was well above the horizon by the time they left the Priory. Philippa rode between Giles and his squire, knowing they were expecting her to bolt.

She also knew escape was not possible. Giles was not riding Majesty but Panache, a spirited bay stallion led in his train by a groom, and bred to carry him swiftly wherever he wanted to travel. Blaze would never be able to outrun him. And, as Giles had pointed out, where had she to go? Fishacre? A possibility, but she knew in her heart that she would never survive that journey on her own without mishap. So she rode on proudly, back straight, head held high. She would not give him the satisfaction of chasing her and dragging her back.

Thought of escape being futile, she concentrated on reminding herself how much she hated Giles d'Evreux. A sidelong glance told her that he had removed his cap to allow the breeze to cool his scalp. The rays of the fiery orb rising in the east shone through his sun-bleached hair to form a golden halo. He looked like a Greek god, she thought disgustedly, when he should resemble the devil. To think that she had harboured childish romantic dreams about her betrothed for all those years! He was naught but a cold-hearted, arrogant churl without a grain of honour or chivalry in him!

But an unexpected *frisson* of excitement shook her nerves when he turned his head and caught her gaze with his. For it was the old Giles who looked at her from laughing eyes, turning her stomach. "Cheer up, my love! 'Twill not be so bad, you'll see! Prioress Mary-Luke spoke the truth. We were meant for each other."

"Everything you do and say makes me hate you the more!" cried Philippa recklessly, fighting down the treacherous lift of her spirits occasioned by his wicked, infectious smile.

It vanished like the sun behind a storm cloud. Bushy, gold-tipped brows met over suddenly bleak eyes. "If that is the atmosphere in which you wish to conduct our affairs, then so be it, my lady. I would have preferred a more amicable relationship, but I am entirely ready to reciprocate your ill-feelings," he informed her coldly. "Your behaviour since we met again yesternoon has been nothing if not childish and offensive. I have no reason to feel kindly disposed towards you."

Philippa felt a qualm of regret for her hasty declaration. True, she did hate him, but she could have been more circumspect. She was entirely in the man's power, and to lose his goodwill might mean that she would feel his displeasure. And she had the feeling that Giles's displeasure might be rather alarming.

After that, she rode in silence. Giles and Wat conversed over her head. Ida and Eadulf exchanged idle chatter behind. Spot gambolled alongside. Philippa stared fixedly at the track ahead, wondering what she had done that God should treat her so.

As the great shell keep of Berkeley Castle rose above the Gloucestershire countryside ahead of them, the ancient stonework glowing warmly in the late afternoon sun, Philippa marvelled at the vast, uncountable numbers of Henry's supporters encamped outside the castle's defences. Lords' gay silken pavilions jostled with makeshift shelters erected by men-at-arms, archers and camp followers: the servants and tradesmen, not to mention the women ready to accommodate the needs of the men for a fee. The red rose of Lancaster and the Lancastrian version of the Royal Arms fluttered from almost every pole, counterpointing the splendidly charged pennons of the impressive array of magnates whose support Henry had enlisted.

Young Wat Instow had ridden ahead to discover the situation, Giles's personal badge—an acorn—painted on the arms of his leather jerkin making his allegiance plain for all to see. The party from Alban Castle, under Sir Malcolm de Boyes, had already pitched their tents, and it was from Sir Malcolm that Wat had elicited his information.

"The castle is almost full, lord," Wat reported, riding out to meet them as they approached. "Edmund of Langley, the Duke of York, is here!"

"Is he indeed? As Keeper of the Realm, he has

come to meet the King on his return from Ireland, no doubt. How did he greet Henry?''

"Amicably, I gather. They are in conference now. Room can be found for Lady Philippa and her woman in one of the domestic dorters in the eastern bailey, but we shall have to camp here overnight. Sir Malcolm already has your pavilion erected.''

"'Twill be no hardship in this weather. I thank you, Malcolm,'' he added as the knight strode over to greet them. "Did all go well at Alban this morn?''

"Aye, lord, as far as I know. We left before Sir Walter and the Earl and his family were—''

"What was my father's condition?'' cut in Philippa anxiously.

Sir Malcolm bowed in her direction. They had not dismounted, and he lifted his rather nice brown eyes to her face. "Much the same, my lady. Though I believe he had articulated a word or two, and was able to move the fingers of his hand. The physician gave his permission for him to travel.''

"What of Sir William?'' asked Giles. "He has not arrived as yet?''

"Nay, lord. He expected to be a day at least carrying out your orders.''

Giles frowned. "So long? Were the stores so vast?''

"I do not know, lord. I left, as ordered, before he had properly taken inventory.''

"No doubt he'll catch up ere long. Meanwhile, I will escort the Lady Philippa to the castle.'' Giles turned to Philippa with formal courtesy. "Come, my lady. You should rest comfortably again tonight."

Philippa followed obediently as he prodded Panache forward through the embattled entrance and, having ascertained the direction, threaded his way through the throng to cross one bailey to reach the other.

Her thoughts were far from comfortable. Her father seemed to have improved slightly, but, although the journey might not harm him in itself, he would resent having to make it. Her stomach turned and the sickness returned. Frustration at his helplessness might bring on a relapse. Still, she consoled herself, forcing down her panic, Mary would be well able to cope, and was fond enough of her father-in-law to do her best. She herself could have done little apart from offering her presence, but she would have given much to be with him.

Memories of home filled her momentarily with nostalgia. Alban was small compared to this vast edifice. Thrusting her anxiety behind her, Philippa eyed her surroundings with growing interest, noting the frenetic bustle of all the officials and serfs as they carried out their orders, while tired Lancastrian retainers lounged idly by. The farriers' hammers rang around the yard, horses stamped and neighed in impatience or protest. Pigs, chickens and geese scattered at their approach. There seemed hardly room to move within the castle walls.

Ignoring the ancient tower and passing the more

recently built Great Hall, Giles drew rein before the entrance to the newish building containing the living quarters. He called a servant, who showed them the way to a small, bare, closet-like chamber which contained two pallets crowded together to leave a small space for movement near the doorway.

"You are fortunate," remarked Giles drily. "You will have privacy here."

"Except that there is no door to the chamber, which, being designed for the use of servants, leads directly from that used by the ladies of the castle," returned Philippa sharply.

"You have an arras to shield the doorway. I will find you better lodgings in Bristol," promised Giles. "We will meet again shortly in the Hall, at supper. Farewell, Philippa."

Philippa shifted uneasily and voiced an awareness which had been growing on her since entering the castle. "Is this not where the King's great-grandfather was murdered?" she asked, and cleared her throat to free it of a sudden thickness.

"Aye." Giles met her eyes steadily. "Edward II met his end somewhere in this castle." He smiled grimly. "Richard should have learned from his ancestor's mistakes. The second Edward was extravagant, and attempted to rule through favourites, rather than through Parliament. Richard has not only been profligate and taken bad advice from his cronies, but has tried to take all power into his own hands. He thinks he is above the law, a law unto himself. He must be shown that he is wrong.''

"And you and Henry Bolingbroke are appointed by God to show him the error of his ways?" scorned Philippa, suddenly angry again. It was better than being scared.

"Henry has been wronged. The duty of every true knight is to see all wrongs righted, be it with or without the King's writ. Richard must answer to Parliament. He has no real power without its consent."

"Richard is King," stated Philippa flatly.

Giles bowed. "On that at least we are agreed, my lady. We meet at supper."

Ida found a page to send for water, which arrived in pitchers carried by a file of churls. The fact that it was cold did not matter, since the weather was warm.

Sponged down, changed into her spare kirtle, her hair freshly braided and held in the silken frets, Philippa began to feel better. She would see Henry at supper. And the great Duke of York, Henry's uncle. Richard's uncle, too. How must the old man feel, she wondered, caught between his nephews? Yet he owed duty to Richard, who had left the Realm in his uncle's safe-keeping while he himself went to Ireland to put down a rebellion by that troublesome and elusive chieftain, Art MacMurrach.

Philippa had led a sheltered and uneventful life, seldom venturing further from Alban Castle than Tewkesbury or Evesham, though once a year the whole family travelled to one of the Earl's other castles or manors while Alban was sweetened. These expeditions had seemed like a holiday, and Philippa had made the most of them. Once she had travelled to the beautiful manor house of Acklane in Oxfordshire to meet Giles's parents. But she'd only been twelve at the time, and memory of that important occasion had dimmed.

She didn't want to be here at Berkeley, of course, but she could not help a feeling of importance, of excitement, of destiny, almost, at being caught up in great events. How many women would be able to tell their grandchildren that they had actually seen Henry Bolingbroke on his way to confront his cousin?

If she ever had grandchildren. The knowledge that if she did they were likely to be Giles's too brought a flush to her cheeks and a pout of rebellion to her lips.

Philippa felt quite lost in the vast, lavishly decorated Hall, and was betrayed into a feeling of gladness when Giles strode to her side, and escorted her to a seat beside his own—not at the high table, but well above the salt cellar.

Trumpets flourished. Lionel, Duke of York, strode in, followed by a procession of men which included his nephew Henry Bolingbroke, the Henry Percys— father and son, Ralph Neville, Earl of Westmorland, Archbishop Arundel, and others who had been with Henry in Paris. Philippa had the feeling that, had it not been for her presence, Giles would have been among them.

"See young Thomas Fitzalan, Archbishop Arundel's nephew?" he shouted in her ear. She would not have heard him, else.

"The one in red brocade?" speculated Philippa in return.

"Aye. He, too, is out to regain the inheritance taken from him two years ago when his father was executed for treason. Did you hear of that disgraceful episode, and of the even more disgraceful murder of Richard's other uncle, Thomas, Duke of Gloucester, in Calais?"

"I heard something of the scandalous accusations made against the King," muttered Philippa.

"They were not made without just cause. Richard swore by John the Baptist that his uncle's exile would bring good to both of them, and that no harm would come to the Earl of Arundel. Both men are now dead. Do you wonder that others now lack trust in his assurances?"

"Mayhap not," admitted Phillipa reluctantly.

"You may not remember—you were only a child at the time—but some ten years ago the Earl of Arundel dared, with Gloucester and others, including Henry Bolingbroke, to attempt to limit Richard's excesses. And succeeded, for a while. They became known as the Lords Appellant. Despite appearances to the contrary, Richard never forgave any of them."

Philippa digested this in silence. Politics had never previously touched her life.

Despite his advanced age, Lionel was still a handsome man, his easy-going nature evident in his face. Lavishly robed in purple velvet and ermine, a chaplet of gold set with glowing jewels resting on his sweating brow, he had escorted his nephew to the table and, with the utmost courtesy, placed him next to himself. Before Grace was said, he ordered a flourish of trumpets, and rose again, commanding silence by the lifting of his hand.

"Most here support my nephew Henry Bolingbroke against his cousin, our Sovereign Prince, King Richard, in the matter of his inheritance," he began. "Let it be known that I, too, render him my support. I believe the King has been led into error. I will use my utmost endeavours to bring peace between my nephews, and thus to this Realm."

A great cheer rang around the vast Hall. Men sprang to their feet, lifting their mugs and goblets to drink to the Duke, Giles among them.

"Even he has deserted the King," scowled Philippa in disgust.

"Not deserted. You heard him. He hopes to mediate between the cousins. No one can deny the justice of Henry's cause. And remember, Thomas of Gloucester was York's brother. No doubt he feels as insecure as the rest of the great lords under Richard's capricious rule."

Philippa's head began to whirl. Only yesterday life

had seemed so black and white, right and wrong so clearly distinguished. Suddenly, there were vast areas of grey in between which she did not wish to examine too closely.

She fixed her eyes on the source of all the confusion, admitting to herself that Henry was an agreeable surprise. Another handsome man—but which Plantagenet was not, according to popular acclaim? Not as tall as his uncle, rather stocky in fact, but reputedly an able soldier, strong, agile, an accomplished jouster and swordsman. Red hair curled into his nape from under a golden chaplet, a serpentine moustache and neatly trimmed beard edged his mouth and chin. His chaplet and robes were simpler than those of the Duke, though the high collar of his houppelande was studded with costly jewels. There was definitely something about him...

A charisma. An innate air of command which York lacked. No easy-going face, Henry's, but one full of determination and authority.

He would be no easy man to defeat.

Chapter Four

The calvacade moved off early the next morning. Philippa found herself more towards the front than the rear of the column, still riding between Giles and his squire. Young Wat proudly carried his knight's lance for him, the azure, twin-tailed pennon with its silver acorn streaming from its head.

Progress was slow. The lords and knights rode heavy destriers, who plodded purposefully forward, bearing the enormous weight of both man and armour. Since they were marching on Bristol, all were prepared for battle. Giles wore his haubergeon under his breastplate, with his bascinet and its dependent chain-mail. His arms and legs remained unprotected, the plates designed to armour them still strapped to Wat's horse.

Pikemen and archers, sweating inside their mailed vests and steel helmets, grooms leading strings of spare horses, servants—some driving meat on the hoof—and many of the whores walked, though a few of the latter rode donkeys or mules. Philippa, although aware of the straggling mass of humanity and beasts stretching for miles behind, was more interested in those who preceded them.

York, Bolingbroke and the magnates, with mounted retinues in attendance, snaked ahead in a brilliant panoply of scintillating armour and colourful surcoats overflown by heraldic banners and pennons borne on a forest of bristling lances. Eadulf travelled well behind, among the grooms, but Ida rode in attendance just ahead of Sir Malcolm de Boyes, who followed Giles closely, leading the men under his command. Of Sir William Grafton there was as yet no sign.

Philippa hoped he would catch up before they reached Bristol. Giles spoke confidently of obtaining necessities there, but supposing the city closed its gates against them? Her riding gown had become dusty and stained, her saffron surcoat crumpled. As for the spare kirtle Ida had packed, that seemed plain and dowdy set against the splendid gowns the ladies at Berkeley had worn. It would be nice to dress up and take her place with pride…

At Giles's side—aye, there lay the rub. It was because of him that she was in a position to shine. As an Earl's daughter she was entitled to a place at court, but what with her being betrothed to Giles, and her father's disinclination to have anything to do with court circles, the opportunity had never before arisen. She sighed gustily, earning an enquiring glance from Giles, which she studiously ignored.

After a long and tedious progress, enlivened only by the constant to and fro of heralds and marshals, Bristol appeared before them. Henry, an experienced general, had already made plans to deploy his forces. By the Priory of Saint James, part of the advancing column split off to the west, seeking to seal off Pyttey Gate and the other gates and bridges in that direction, while the second arm of the pincer moved off to the east, to cover the castle's Nether Gate, Temple Gate and the Redcliffe Gate to the south of the city. Henry and the main force continued ahead, making straight for the New Gate and the castle. The front of the column halted at the crossing of the Frome. Those behind caught up. Philippa eased her aching back. A tense hush fell over the ranks.

Suddenly a cheer went up. The townsfolk had flung open the gates of the city! Word flew round and back from mouth to mouth as the columns began to move forward again.

"What will Courtenay do?" wondered Giles aloud.

"Courtenay?" asked Philippa.

The frigid silence of yesterday had been broken long since. Travelling in such company had brought with it a sense of comradeship which had affected even Philippa's prejudiced mind.

"Sir Peter Courtenay, the Constable of Bristol Castle," Giles told her. "'Tis one of the greatest strongholds in the land. I doubt he will surrender it easily, since he holds it for the King. It is his duty to defend it, and 'twould be difficult to reduce."

Philippa bit her lip. "Will Bolingbroke fight?" she asked apprehensively.

"Only if he must," opined Giles with an expressive gesture of his hand. "He does not seek open confrontation, and must tread warily, for Richard holds his heir, young Harry of Monmouth, hostage."

"Hostage?" This was news to Philippa.

"Aye." Giles's face expressed disgust as he shortened his rein the better to control his mount. "Not officially, of course, but the King refused to allow Harry to leave Court when his father was banished, and took the boy to Ireland with him." He lifted his shoulders in a dismissive shrug. "Henry can as well wait for Richard without the castle's walls as within," he concluded.

The narrow streets of houses which had sprung up outside the city walls seethed with bodies as the column swarmed past. They moved forward only a pace at a time, and Philippa was glad of her stalwart protectors, for once or twice it seemed likely that she would be jostled from her horse's back, so great was the press.

She caught a glimpse of the great keep of the castle, framed by buildings at the end of the narrow lane. York and Bolingbroke had crossed the Frome and halted on the far bank, out of arrow range.

With a flourish of trumpets, York and Lancaster heralds rode slowly forward to state their masters' business. Philippa could just hear the distant voices, enough to grasp the gist of their message: allow their lords entry or be besieged until the King returned.

"I wouldn't come here if I were the King," muttered Philippa.

"Nor I. But Henry will have thought of that. He has spies out to discover the King's intentions."

Philippa glanced sharply at Giles, surprised he had caught her words in the noisy confusion of their progress. "He is exceptionally well organised," she commented sourly.

Giles grinned suddenly. "Henry Bolingbroke is no fool, and an outstanding soldier. Have no fear, Pippa. He will achieve what he desires."

Philippa wished she knew with certainty what that might be.

The wait seemed interminable. The bell of the nearby Dominican Priory tolled the hour of Nones, and its notes were echoed by every Church and Monastery in the city—and there semeed to be many. Philippa filled the time of waiting by eyeing enviously the brilliant bolts of cloth and other goods being snatched to safety from the merchants' stalls lining the narrow, noisome road. At the moment Bolingbroke's following was under control, but, if tens of thousands of men rampaged through the town bent on pillage, it was best to have one's merchandise—and one's womenfolk—safely locked away.

Spot, who had gambolled alongside, keeping well away from the horses' hoofs whenever possible, now forged ahead, foraging among the filth collected in the doorways, where he met up with an aggressive town cur. The snarling animals were well joined in battle before Philippa noticed. She gave a cry of angry alarm.

"Spot! Stop it! Come here at once!"

Not that Spot took the slightest notice, and Philippa was helpless to intervene. Fortunately the other dog's owner appeared to part the combatants. Spot, still bristling, his nose bloodied, eventually obeyed Philippa's anxious calls, and edged near, creeping obediently under the dangerous hoofs.

Giles snorted. "Stupid hound! That cur was twice his weight."

"Spot does not lack courage," Philippa defended her pet hotly.

"Nay. Just sense," grinned Giles.

Luckily, at that moment those in the front surged forward. The horses tossed their heads and strained against their bits. Everyone, including Spot, was diverted from his escapade.

"Hear that, d'Evreux? Courtenay has yielded," shouted a young and comely knight, of around Giles's own age, who was riding just ahead under a pennon bearing his portcullis badge. Triumph rang in his voice.

"Just like that!" exclaimed Giles joyously. "I could not believe he would do such a thing! 'Tis against all precedent! What think you, Beaufort? Was it the presence of York that influenced him?"

"Aye, perhaps, but more likely the fact that Richard took away his office of Chamberlain and gave it to his own half-brother, John Holland. Courtenay, like so many others, bears a grudge against Richard. He has long been Henry's friend, and the castle sits in the centre of an insurgent city.'' John Beaufort smiled and urged his mount forward through the press. Giles followed, taking Philippa with him.

"You wouldn't think he was born a bastard, and owes his present honours and fortune to the King,'' remarked Philippa acidly.

Giles glanced at her sharply. "Nay. He is every inch a Plantagenet, and very like his father, John of Gaunt. He is half-brother to Bolingbroke, do not forget, who has played the elder brother from the first. Henry knighted John Beaufort long before Richard legitimised him and his siblings as a favour to his uncle of Lancaster. Beaufort's first loyalty is to Henry, and always has been. He was devastated by Richard's arbitrary banishment of his brother.'' He paused and, if possible, straightened his straight back even more as he gently prodded Majesty forward. "No man can help his birth,'' he reminded her coldly.

Philippa coloured. For the moment she had forgotten that her future father-in-law had also been base-born, though now he was an Earl.

"No. I suppose not,'' she agreed ungraciously, her knee touching Giles's again as Blaze edged closer to Majesty.

"And Gaunt defied convention to marry his leman, once free of his political alliance with Constanza of

Castile. He had loved Katherine Swynford, John's mother, since shortly after Henry's mother, Blanche, died. As she loved him. 'Twas more than just an affair, Philippa," he told her gravely. "Katherine was more his wife than ever Constanza was. She bore him four children, all legitimised now. The youngest, Joan, is wife to Ralph Neville. Be careful whom you label bastard."

Philippa shifted uncomfortably in her saddle, and patted Blaze's neck to cover her disquiet. After just one evening in Court circles she had sensed the danger lurking in any ill-considered word. Old enmities and treachery seethed beneath the surface. All were united behind Henry Bolingbroke for the moment, but for how long could the present comradeship hold?

"Aye, I will," she promised grudgingly.

"Katherine was with John right to the end," Giles told her quietly. Somehow they seemed to be moving forward in a private enclave within the cheering, milling masses. Wat had been forced to drop behind. "When he died, God rest his soul—" he crossed himself quickly "—she retired to her manor at Kettlethorpe. She did not seek position or riches. Only love."

"Why is it," wondered Philippa bitterly, "that love seems to exist only outside marriage?"

"Not always, Pippa." Giles's voice had softened, and his jewelled gauntlet came out to touch her thigh. "'Tis often so because men, as well as women, are forced into unsuitable alliances to secure a family's wealth and power. But love can grow, even from a marriage such as that. On occasion, lovers evade the demands of family aggrandisement. My parents were such lucky ones.''

Philippa edged Blaze away from the unsettling reach of that hand as soon as she was able. ''Yet they did not scruple to promise us to each other when I was but a child,'' she pointed out bitterly.

''I could have refused, Pippa. As could you. But if you remember, we rather liked each other. Neither one of us was averse to the match. Had you expressed a dislike—''

''I was too young to know!'' protested Philippa hotly.

''Young, but always very opinionated, my love! As for me—I always believed we would deal well together. Such love is rare, and not necessary to a successful marriage. Mutual respect and tolerance are far more important.''

''You think so?'' Philippa stared at him, disappointed. With his background, she had imagined he would have a more romantic attitude to marriage. His lean face was serious, his almost-blue eyes reassuring as they rested on her doubting features. Their horses collided, and her knee touched his for the umpteenth time. Philippa ignored the peculiar sensation the contact seemed to engender. She could not avoid it, so she must endure.

She was saved further response and speculation, for at that moment a new surge carried them through the

gateway and into the castle enclave. Never had she
seen such confusion. Knights, men-at-arms and
Cheshire archers of the garrison, wearing the White
Hart badge of the private army Richard had been recruiting and retaining for several years past, were being herded into a corner of a courtyard already
crowded with an assortment of buildings, there to
throw down their arms. The chaotic invasion of
prancing horses and jubilant knights looked likely to
crush all before it, so eager were they to remain close
to their leaders.

There could never be room for all Henry's supporters, of course—even the inner bailey would hold
only so many pavilions and men. Most retainers
would have to find lodgings elsewhere in the town,
or even, mayhap, camp outside its walls. But Giles
was privileged, and, because of him, so was Philippa.

There were few ladies in Henry's train; most men
had left their wives and families behind. But there
were a few intrepid women who had decided to follow their husbands, and Philippa was to share a bed
with two of them.

"I am here to make sure the Earl does not
weaken," Helen Cooksey, Countess of Butterwick,
told her as they settled into the chamber allotted to
them. Lady Helen, a forceful woman of around five
and thirty years, attempted a rather brittle smile with
her thin lips, as her tiring-woman fixed the wrought-
gold, jewel-encrusted bosses into which her lank hair
had been coiled to either side of her angular face. "He

wavers between a misplaced loyalty to the King and a desire to regain the offices taken from him and given to Richard's cronies. What do you here, wench?''

"I am to be wed," replied Philippa grimly, concentrating on smearing salve on Spot's damaged nose.

"Wed? To whom? When?" asked Isobel Fortescue, wife to one of Lancaster's tenants, eagerly. Younger than Helen Cooksey, and pretty in an insipid way, she had admitted to accompanying her husband for selfish reasons. "If I am with him," she had confessed, a tide of red sweeping up her neck and face, "he will not be tempted to seek his pleasure elsewhere."

"Pshaw!" Helen had exclaimed. "What matter if he does? All men go a-whoring to slake their lust and find their pleasure; they bed their wives only to get heirs."

"Not all," Isobel had protested with quiet insistence. "Miles says I give him more pleasure than any of the lewd women he knew before we were wed. And I... I enjoy receiving him in my bed." The blush had deepened, and a secret smile had curved her shapely lips. Now Philippa eyed her warily as she let Spot go, and rose from her knees.

"I have been betrothed to Sir Giles d'Evreux this eight years past." She flung out a hand in helpless bewilderment. "He suddenly insists I honour the contract, and is arranging for us to marry within days.

But I do not want to!'' she burst out, unable to hide her rebellion.

''Oh, but Sir Giles!'' Isobel regarded her as though she had been given the pot of gold at the end of the rainbow. ''Why would you not wish to wed with such a renowned knight?''

''Renowned?''

''Aye. Did you not know?'' enquired Helen Cooksey curiously.

Philippa shook her head. Her heart began to beat faster than usual. She really knew very little about her future husband.

''He is famous for his prowess in the lists, and is one of the best swordsmen in the world,'' Isobel informed her eagerly, her eyes shining with enthusiasm.

''I knew he jousted,'' muttered Philippa. '''Tis how he makes his fortune.''

''And a goodly one, I'll warrant! I well remember a tournament at Windsor several years past when he was acclaimed the most worthy knight to take the field! All the ladies were at his feet. He could have wed any maiden there, yet you protest yourself unwilling! Why so?''

''Because he—'' Philippa cut herself off short. These women were on Giles's side in this. She had better not call him traitor. Discretion came hard to her, but she was learning. ''He has neglected me for nigh on five years,'' she growled instead. ''Now he suddenly wants to wed me in haste, without family or friends present, with my father lying sick, and with no time to prepare a gown…''

''I cannot say that I blame him,'' observed Helen with a cynical smile. ''I dare say he got a surprise when he saw you again, my dear. You must have been full young and undergrown when last you met. Perhaps you did not excite his manhood then, but I'll wager my last gold noble you stir it now!''

It was Philippa's turn to blush. She was not used to such crude talk. ''I cannot think why,'' she retorted stiffly.

''Don't be stupid, wench! You have the face of a dark angel and the body of a goddess. What more is needed to excite a man? Of course he desires you. Make the most of it while you may. His passion will soon die.''

''You speak from experience?'' asked Isobel, with a chilly disdain which surprised Philippa. Isobel did not like Helen Cooksey. Neither, actually, did she.

''I shall have to see that it doesn't, shall I not?'' she returned tartly. Not that she meant to do anything of the kind. She did not want Giles's passion. The thought of his touching her sent shivers of fear down her spine. But she would not admit that to anyone, least of all to the worldly Lady Butterwick.

''I will help you,'' offered Isobel shyly. ''You have enough apparel here to make a goodly bride.''

''Thank you,'' murmured Philippa, not ungrateful for the offer, since it was made in good faith. Sir William had arrived with her coffers, and Isobel had delighted in examining their contents. Philippa suspected the knight had stripped Alban Castle of its entire contents, for all her clothes were there. Something else to hold against Giles.

"I'll vouch the bridegroom would not protest an the wench turned up naked," sniggered the Countess, bringing a new surge of colour to Philippa's pale cheeks.

"Will you wear your chaplet this evening, my lady?" enquired Ida loudly, emphasising her mistress's title with great deliberation.

Philippa smiled gratefully, thankful to feel her blush subside. "Aye, Ida. I must dress as befits my rank."

Helen Cooksey lifted an arched brow and grinned crookedly, passing no comment. But Philippa noted that the older woman subsequently curbed her patronising tone.

The following morning Philippa was woken by the sound of banging in the bailey below. In the pale light of dawn, she slid from the edge of the bed she had shared with the other two women, stepped round the pallets of their servants, and gazed down from the window embrasure.

Men were erecting a scaffold. Her stomach muscles tightened. She knew that some of Richard's officials had been inside the castle, waiting anxiously to meet their King on his hasty return from Ireland to confront his cousin. Surrender of the stronghold had delivered them into Henry's hands, and they had been imprisoned in the Great Dungeon tower.

She looked out across the embattled wall which divided the old Norman castle, where she had been lodged, from the massive keep where the men must be awaiting their doom. There had been talk last evening of their treachery to the realm they had plundered in Richard's name. William Scrope, Earl of Wiltshire, the Treasurer, had come in for the most severe vilification, for he had raised the extortionate taxes and imposed the forced loans so hated by nobility and burgesses alike. But his henchmen, John Bussey, Henry Green and Thomas Bagehot, upstarts of the Royal Household, were scarcely less universally hated.

Philippa gripped the edge of the embrasure so tightly that her knuckles showed white. Could hate warrant a summary execution? The others were awake now, and crowded to the window to see.

"I thought so," said Helen Cooksey with satisfaction. "Those men have ravaged the land with their financial chicanery. They deserve the scaffold."

"Without trial?" demanded Philippa bitterly.

"Oh, they will have been tried by their peers," said Helen carelessly.

"But how can they execute them?" whispered Philippa. "Without the King's sanction 'twould be murder."

"Would the King easily condemn his cronies? Or those who have filled his coffers? Nay, lady, 'tis for the magnates of this land to decide their fate. The great lords have too long been denied their rightful powers."

"It seems they have already decided," observed Philippa indignantly.

For some reason not clear to her, Bagehot was to be spared. The executions of the other three were to take place immediately after dinner. Nauseated by the prospect, Philippa ate little, sitting in silent protest throughout the lengthy meal.

Giles attempted to divert her thoughts. His cheerful announcement that he had obtained a licence from the bishop, and that they would be wed before Vespers and make supper their wedding feast, brought nothing but frigid silence and a look of such loathing from Philippa's dark, eloquent eyes that Giles stopped trying to humour her.

Insensitive fool! raged Philippa inwardly. To fix their wedding to follow so closely upon the executions! Could he not understand her revulsion?

Apparently not. With consummate composure and complete disregard for her feelings, he worked his way steadily through a pottage of venison broth pungent with herbs, a dish of succulent lampreys, thick slices from a roasted ox and a solitee which consisted of mixed berries cooked in honey. The whole was accompanied by soft white bread and fine Bordeaux wine, and he conversed the while with others at their board.

The executions were on everyone's lips. Philippa found herself the only one with doubts as to their legality. The sentences were considered well deserved, and the sooner carried out the better.

After the meal almost everyone trooped to the bailey, where the scaffold had been erected. It would be fine entertainment to see the detested oppressors' heads roll. Philippa could not bear to watch. Her chamber overlooked the block, so she could find no refuge there. Instead, she found her way to the King's orchard, which was across the moat and bordered the river, though the great defensive wall denied her any view of that, except for the tops of the masts of ships moored in the port beyond the bridge.

Insects filled the arbour with the sound of their lazy drone as they searched the blossoms for nectar. Fruit trees provided shade, roses, herbs and pink gillyflowers filled the summer air with fragrance, masking the stink from the polluted river. Although the waterway sounded busy with small boats plying between the ships and the town, ferrying goods and people under the low arches of the bridge, and shrill cries fractured the peace, Philippa found the place restful. She sank down on the hard turf under a small apple tree, and rested back against its trunk, swatting half-heartedly at a worrisome fly.

Bells throughout the town tolled the hour of Sext— the hour appointed for the executions. Philippa buried her head between her knees, attempting to shut out all sound, knowing cheers would greet each death. But she could not shut off her mind. It was midday. She had so few hours of freedom left. By Vespers, she would be married to Giles.

There was still time to escape. She eyed the steps

leading up to the allure. This stretch of curtain wall was unguarded. From the wall-walk she could climb into an embrasure and plead for a ride in one of the passing boats. If she jumped into the river she should escape injury, though the thought of immersing herself in the filthy water made her shudder with distaste. And mayhap there would be too much bank, too many boats lining it...

If she did risk it, and was successful, most probably someone in the town would give her refuge, for a price. But she had nothing with which to buy such services. She had scant money with her, and what little she had was in the chamber overlooking the executions, together with all her most precious jewellery.

Besides, Giles would find her. Even if he did not, what future did she have? With no money or posessions she would have to beg—or worse—to eat. Much as she hated Giles and all he stood for, marriage to him seemed the lesser evil at the moment. Prioress Mary-Luke had virtually denied her any chance of escape, and had commanded obedience to God's will. Tears squeezed from between her shut eyelids. Why was His will so difficult to accept?

Something touched her downbent head. She jerked upright, instantly defensive.

She looked ready to hiss and claw like a startled kitten, thought Giles ruefully, noting with compassion the tears drying on her cheeks. Poor maid! He wished he could have arranged things otherwise, but wed him she must, and to leave her longer under her father's influence would be to pile up worse trouble for the future. Better that she knew what was happening to their land. Eventually she would see that Richard must be bridled. Enlightenment would end the discord between them. His pulses quickened at the thought of Philippa soft and pliant in his arms. The day would come, he vowed. And soon.

He dropped to the turf beside her. She ostenchtatiously snatched her skirt aside, tucking its voluminous folds under her knees. "I thought you would be enjoying the executions," she remarked icily.

"I do not enjoy such spectacles, Pippa. Whatever you may think of me, I am not a vindictive or sadistic man. Justice must be done, but it can be done without my presence. I would rather talk with my bride."

A shudder ran through Philippa's body, which Giles noticed with a dismay he was careful not to show.

"If you call that justice, we have nothing more to say to each other," she responded flatly.

Giles drew in a deep breath. It seemed his task might be more difficult than he had thought. "Philippa, you are ignorant of the world and of politics," he pointed out reasonably. "You cannot judge such things by what you have seen at Alban Castle. Your sire has been a great knight, but no courtier or politician. How can you know what is right and what is wrong when the nation's future is at stake?"

"I know treason is wrong," muttered Philippa.

"Much depends on your definition of that word."

"Those men," she choked, "they are not traitors! They served the King loyally!"

Too loyally, he thought grimly. But if he admitted that they had only been carrying out their Sovereign's

orders, criticism of their actions could be construed
as treason. He must temporise. "And right badly,
too." He shrugged. "Their greed has made him hated
throughout the realm."

"I hate you!"

The words seemed torn from her throat, and echoed
hollowly in Giles's gut. She would not listen to reason! Had that episode at Alban really killed all hope
for their future together? He eyed the girl's mutinous
face, the enmity in her eyes, the heave of her tender
breasts under the layers of kirtle and cote-hardie, saw
the nervousness she tried to hide, and prayed that it
should not be so.

He had once declared patience as one of his virtues,
but in truth it was wearing thin, and he wondered at
his determination to wed the maid in the face of her
fierce opposition. Why not allow her to go her own
way? To flirt with danger, as her brother seemed determined to do?

His lips tightened. He could not allow this wench
to dictate to him! For her own safety she *would* wed
with him, and he would teach her to become a loving
and obedient wife.

But how? Charm did not work. He could not cajole.
There seemed only one way left. He would have to
demand, to order.

"Very well—" he met her hostile gaze coolly
"—hate me. Make things difficult for yourself, Philippa. But I swear by the Holy Rood you shall wed
with me, and this very day, as arranged." He watched
the panic flit across her expressive face, and his voice
softened by an almost imperceptible fraction. "I sug-

gest you go to ready yourself for the ceremony. Henry Bolingbroke and all my friends and brothers-in-arms will be present. I feel sure you will not wish to discredit your family by appearing either reluctant or badly attired.''

"My family and friends are not here to see me wed," she pointed out shakily.

"My people will not be present, either. When this crisis is over we will throw a feast and invite all our relations and friends to celebrate our union. But it is important that we wed immediately, Pippa. I want you under my protection.''

"Why should I need your protection?" she demanded frostily. "Your arrogance is overwhelming. It seems to me it is you who are running into danger. When the King hears you supported Bolingbroke—"

"When peace is made between the cousins, Richard will not move against Henry's supporters. They are too powerful."

"I still cannot see why I need your protection."

Giles sighed. "'Tis too complicated to explain, Pippa." He did not want to tell her that if peace was not made there could only be one winner. Richard would be forced from the throne. With the following Henry had already amassed Richard must compromise or lose his kingdom. Mayhap he had lost it already. But in her present mood he could not burden her with that knowledge. "Believe me," he told her quietly, "you will be safer married to me."

"I suppose," she observed scornfully, "you need to find an excuse for your autocratic demand."

At that moment the first cry of approval—triumph, glee, satisfaction—carried above the edifice of the castle towers from the bailey beyond. Philippa shut her eyes and fingered the beads at her waist, her lips working in agitated prayer. Giles hastily crossed himself. Watching her anguished face, pity such as he had never known before surged through him.

She was still so young, with so much of life's harshness and hardship yet to face. She could not be expected to see the risks her father and brother ran in opposing one as powerful as Henry Bolingbroke, rightful Duke of Lancaster. Especially now that Henry was backed by the King's own Regent, Lionel, Duke of York. How could she be blamed for not seeing things through his own more experienced and somewhat jaundiced eye?

On an impulse, he reached out for her and drew her to him. Her resistance was nominal. With a choked, piteous cry, she buried her face in the fine velvet of his cote-hardie, and wept.

How long she poured out her grief and uncertainty, her ears closed to the echo of repeated cheers by the sound of her own racking sobs, she never afterwards knew. But the feel of strong, gentle arms holding her had never been more welcome. Giles might have been her father, comforting her in some childish hurt.

He held her cradled against him, her head pressed to his breast by one tenderly caressing hand. She nestled in his arms, soft and infinitely sweet, like a frightened kitten. He held her so until the last cries of triumph from the executions had long died away.

Eventually her sobs quieted, her grief spent. She

felt empty, drained. It took her some moments to realise where she was. She gazed up into Giles's intent
face with eyes whose lids were red-rimmed and swollen with tears.

What she saw there brought a strangled sound from
her throat. She tore herself from his protecting arms
and jumped to her feet. "You need not think—" she
began chokingly, only to be interrupted by Giles's
calm voice.

"I would not presume, my lady." He, too, had
risen. He bowed with faultless formality, his gaze
tender behind the cool façade of his face. "We will
meet again, in the chapel."

Philippa did not see the expression in his eyes. She
only knew that she had allowed her need to overcome
her principles, and that Giles's arms were treacher-
ously seductive.

Chapter Five

Isobel had taken charge, insisting Philippa wear her best gown for the occasion; and Ida, entering into the spirit of the thing, had shaken out and pressed the costly samite of which the kirtle was fashioned. The material's shimmering silken threads, interwoven with silver to form an intricate pattern of drifting leaves and flowers, flowed softly over Philippa's slender hips to the narrow band of miniver fur edging the full, slightly trailing hem. The patterned sleeves and bodice of the kirtle emerged from the miniver trim of a short, sleeveless cote-hardie made from a silvery material and fastened down the front with silver buttons. Ida had lovingly sponged and brushed all the fur to a pristine, snowy whiteness.

Philippa made no protest at the choice. Since leaving Giles in the pleasaunce she had stopped pretending that she could avoid the marriage. She just wanted it to be over quickly. The emotional outburst had left her drained. She had become no more than a puppet for others to manipulate.

Feeling abruptly returned to swamp her in a new wave of panic as she smoothed down the tightly buttoned sleeves of the kirtle, which extended beyond her wrists to cover her knuckles. In less than an hour Giles's ring would rest on the finger she had touched, a sign of his loveless possession. She gripped her hands together, thrusting down her dismay with fierce determination.

He knew she was reluctant to be his bride, but he did not have to know how greatly she feared becoming emotionally ensnared by one she could only think of as an enemy. She had told him she hated him, and she did, most fervently, for the grief he had caused, and yet...and yet, hard as she might try, she could not deny his attraction, the masculine magnetism which intimidated as well as seduced her. His embrace held an allure, a promise of security, of something more fundamental to which she could not put a name.

"We picked forget-me-nots and gillyflowers for your chaplet," Isobel explained, placing the carefully woven, fragrant pink and blue circlet on the drifting black curls which hung around Philippa's shoulders and down her back as a sign of her maidenhood. "You look like a moon princess!" she declared happily. "Dark, pale and silvery."

"Sir Giles would prefer something warmer—a

sun goddess, I'll warrant,'' opined Helen with a derisive laugh.

She had taken little interest in the proceedings so far, confining herself to interjecting a trenchant or ribald comment from time to time. Philippa had hoped she would absent herself from the unwelcome ceremony, but the Countess was already dressed in some splendour for the occasion. Her gown of crimson brocade and cloth of gold completely overshadowed that of the bride. One side of her kirtle had been embroidered with the chevrons and crosslets of her father's coat of arms, the other charged with the swans and battle-axe of Butterwick. The foliated golden coronet set above the jewelled and enamelled boxes covering her ears allowed no trace of hair to mar the perfection of a high, smooth brow. Hard, sharp eyes went with a thin, discontented mouth to impair what could otherwise have been a handsome visage.

Isobel's soft pliancy was hidden beneath the folds of a simple kirtle of saffron flurt silk, most of which was concealed by a rather old-fashioned green damask sideless surcoat, though the hem of the latter was caught up to show the buttercup-coloured skirt beneath. Her fair hair was bound in simple cauls topped by a silver circlet, her cheeks were flushed with pleasure and expectancy, her blue eyes alight with goodwill. The contrast between the two women could not have been greater.

Impulsively, Philippa hugged the younger woman.

"Thank you, Lady Fortescue," she murmured huskily.

"Call me Isobel, do."

"My friends call me Pippa."

Isobel smiled. "I will gladly count myself your friend, Pippa. Don't be nervous. All will be for the best, you'll see."

Philippa straightened her spine and firmed her trembling lips. "I cannot imagine how, but I will try to believe you, Isobel. In any case, there is naught I can do to evade my duty."

"So you will meet the challenge with courage," nodded Isobel bracingly. "I would expect nothing else from you, Pippa."

Courage was something Philippa did not normally lack. Physical courage was no problem, and she could express her opinions with a heat and conviction which amused her family. But to be caught in a trap from which there was no escape...that was different. And to Philippa her enforced marriage was just that.

A page came to summon the bride to the chapel. Ida fastened a heavily jewelled necklace around Philippa's bare throat. "There, sweeting," she whispered, giving her mistress a reassuring hug, "you will shame no one this day."

Philippa followed the page wordlessly, escorted by the two ladies and Ida. Spot roused himself to trot at their heels, tail waving uncertainly, as though he sensed something amiss and was not sure of his welcome. Philippa did not have the heart to bid the dog to stay. Her pet's presence would give her comfort, and she needed all of that she could get.

Giles waited for her by the door of the chapel, his face inscrutable until his eyes lighted on the gossamer figure of his bride, so dainty, so ethereal did she appear in her silvery finery. Warmth and, yes, admiration leapt into his heavily lashed eyes as he extended his hand in welcome.

Something in Philippa's breast contracted painfully at sight of him, tall and straight, his knightly jewelled belt and the glittering baselard in its golden scabbard resting on the azure velvet sheathing his lean hips. His lighter-hued hose clung to his thighs, betraying every movement of the muscles beneath. He, too, wore a chaplet, though his was mostly woven of foliage, with a few marigolds to add the illusion of gold.

Two priests, with a following of youthful acolytes, waited with him. The ceremony proceeded immediately. Philippa promised to take Giles to be her wedded husband, to forsake all other, to hold only unto him in sickness and in health, in riches and in poverty, in well and woe, until death parted them, her throat so tight that the, "Yea, sir," demanded of her would hardly come out.

Giles had made his responses in a firm, determined voice. When directed, he placed a wrought-gold ring on her finger. Philippa wondered where he had got it from. Her thumb found and investigated the strange, intrusive object. Too large, it hung heavy as an iron shackle.

They moved to the altar for the nuptial mass. At the end of the service Giles helped his bride to her feet, and leaned forward to kiss her, as was expected of him. Only Philippa knew that his lips, for all they had appeared to linger, barely touched hers. Even so, the effect had been devastating. Revulsion, she told herself, grimly enduring the tremors coursing through her body.

Outside the chapel the guests crowded round. Philippa found herself being embraced by Henry Bolingbroke. He kissed her heartily and beamed with avuncular goodwill.

"We look forward to the bedding, Lady Philippa," he told her, winking broadly.

Her heart thudding painfully at the reminder of a future ordeal, her face aflame, Philippa forced herself to meet his shrewd eyes, and saw strain in their depths. She could feel the tension emanate from the man's body—a tangible thing, matching her own. For all his apparent confidence and ease of manner, Henry Bolingbroke was strung taut as a bow-string. The shock of this discovery made her forget her own screaming nerves for a moment. It must be costing this man dear to confront his cousin to demand his rightful inheritance. One thing was certain: right or wrong, he did not act lightly. His very life was at stake, not to mention the lives of his children and those of many of his friends.

His impact faded as others claimed the privilege of saluting the bride, and she forgot Henry Bolingbroke in the doubtful pleasure of being kissed by divers men—old, young, rough, courteous, clean, malodorous, sober, drunk.

Giles kept an arm possessively round her waist, a restraint she almost welcomed, but even so some of the more boisterous knights made a meal of it, laughing and chaffing Giles on his good fortune in acquiring so delightful a bride. The touch of some was bearable, of others definitely not.

But none of their kisses produced in her anything like the sensation Giles's brief salute had done. It had not been revulsion she'd felt. She knew exactly what *that* felt like now, having suffered so many unwelcome embraces.

When the party trooped in to the Hall for supper, Philippa was given a place of honour at Henry's right, with Giles on her other side. A festive atmosphere pervaded the company. Three executions and a wedding in one day were worthy of hearty celebration.

Philippa had, to some extent, relaxed. The deed was done. For good or ill, she was Giles's wife. No brooding, no rebellious thoughts could alter fact. As for the bedding… She crumpled a tiny piece of fine white bread between clammy fingers and chewed it round to stop her teeth from chattering, washing the resultant stodge down with a gulp of wine. Her empty stomach rumbled.

She replaced the silver-rimmed maple-wood mazer on the table with shaking hands. Giles lifted the vessel and raised it to his own lips before putting it down and reaching for one of her hands. Philippa wriggled her fingers, trying to escape his firm clasp without making it too obvious. He squeezed the harder.

"Eat, wife," he commanded softly. "You refused dinner. I cannot have my bride fainting from hunger before the night is through."

"You—you brute!" she spat, her cheeks scarlet.

"'Brute'?" He lifted the captive hand to his lips in a courtly salute, the only one present able to see the reckless defiance in his bride's dusky eyes. One shapely, golden-tipped brow lifted in tolerant amusement. "You tempt me to teach you what brutish behaviour is, Pippa." His thumb stroked the palm of the hand he still held seductively. Philippa's arm jerked uncontrollably as the sensation leapt up it, and he laughed softly. "Eat, my love," he murmured huskily. "Here, let me…"

His voice trailed off as he used his knife to cut a piece of roast mutton from the thick slice on the trencher they shared, picked the morsel up in his fingers, and carried it to her mouth. Philippa pressed her lips shut, but Giles merely chuckled and began to tease them with the meat.

She wanted to turn her head away, but his bluegrey eyes in their nests of tawny lashes held hers. Why was she incapable of breaking the spell cast by his gaze? Philippa didn't know, nor why her mouth opened and she accepted the piece of flesh, but she chewed greedily once the taste of the succulent morsel began to stimulate her juices. The moment she swallowed, Giles offered another titbit for her consumption.

To those around his actions were those of a charming, attentive and lover-like bridegroom. Only Philippa knew that it was sheer force of an overwhelming personality which kept her accepting the food from his fingers.

"Thank you, Giles," she managed at last in a strangled whisper. "I can feed myself."

"An you have the will," he agreed dubiously.

"I promise."

He smiled, brilliance lighting his handsome features as he gave her fingers a final squeeze before releasing them. "Courage, my wife," he whispered. There it was again. The admonition to have courage. Why the devil did they all believe she lacked it? 'Twas plain, straightforward inclination she was short of.

Mummers and dancing followed the meal, and the sun had disappeared beneath the horizon before anyone made a move to escort the bridal couple to their chamber.

The men led Giles off while Isobel, Lady Butterwick and a number of other women took Philippa to the State Chamber, loaned to them for the night by an expansive Duke of York. The huge state bed, raised on a platform and draped with purple hangings embroidered with white harts—an uncomfortable reminder that this was the King's bed—intimidated Philippa. She could not look. Nor could she bear to gaze at the royal arms and banners glowing colourfully against the stone walls in the light of myriad candles.

The women fluttered about her, though it was Ida who washed her and rubbed in a liquid, made from rosemary, mint, rose and lemon peel distilled in grape spirit, to perfume her skin. With her hair freshly combed, Philippa was led to the expansive bed and ensconced on a swansdown-filled mattress under a heavy silken coverlet.

"You will not need a blanket tonight," remarked one of the ladies, wife to a member of the castle's garrison.

"They will doubtless indulge in enough exercise to keep them warm," chuckled Lady Helen, with a malicious glance at Philippa's white face.

Isobel leaned forward and whispered in Philippa's ear. "Take no notice of the ribaldry, Pippa," she advised. "Greet your bridegroom with modesty and joy. With Sir Giles to husband, your marriage bed will be a wondrous place, an you will allow it."

Philippa tried to smile acknowledgement. Isobel's romantic dreams and her own were very different. Or—were they?

July had been warm and stormy, and that evening was hot and humid. The silk clung to Philippa's clammy body as she alternated between hot and cold sweats engendered by the temperature and apprehension. She drew the cover up under her armpits as she sank deeper into the mattress and leaned back against the pillows to await the arrival of the groom.

Giles was brought in by a group of boisterous knights, many far from sober, led by Henry Boling-broke. Her husband wore a long, fur-trimmed gown, which was torn from his shoulders as he reached the bed.

Philippa knew what a naked man looked like; she had caught forbidden glimpses of her father and brothers—though two of them, Daniel and Hugo, had died of the plague four years since—living as they had in the close confines of Hall and solar until more recent years. She was no innocent about mating, ei-ther. Dogs, cats, horses—the farm animals too—she had witnessed them all. As a child, before her mother's death in childbirth, she had heard her par-ents, seen the heaving bulk of shifting bedclothes... heard her father's grunts and her mother's cries...and wondered whether they were of pain or pleasure until she had heard the woman's soft laugh and the man's whispered endearments.

'Twas natural, normal and nothing to be shamed about. So why did her face grow warm, her hands sweat at sight of Giles's lean, broad-shouldered body, his flat belly and the bush of golden-brown hair be-tween his thighs only partially hiding his—?

The part was whisked modestly under cover as Giles slid in beside her. Thanks be to the Holy Virgin, the bed was so large that he seemed a safe distance away. There was space for two others where the demanding swansdown rose like a protective bastion between them. But that did not stop the colour seeping from her cheeks, the cold, clammy damp of apprehension prickling her skin. Courage! she admonished herself sternly. Seeing, knowing and doing were such vastly different things.

No one troubled themselves over a trembling bride, one moment flushed as though in a fever, the next pale as death. This maid might be older than most, but such a reaction was only to be expected of a virgin.

Sweet herbs and flowers were strewn over floor, and those thought to induce fertility over the bedcovers; the priest present blessed the bridal bed and the couple in it, praying for their fruitfulness and the gift of many lusty sons and daughters. Flasks of wine were brought in, cups filled and passed around. Henry Bolingbroke raised his and gave the toast. With jovial shouts and great ribaldry, everyone drank to the success of the coming nuptials.

At length it was over and the noisy company filed out, leaving the bride and groom in conspicuous privacy to consummate the union. The instant the heavy door closed behind the last reveller, Philippa struggled up from the shifting swansdown's clutching embrace, swung her legs over the side of the bed, and reached urgently for her chamber-gown.

Before she could grasp it, Giles had moved and, in a swift tangle of silken covers and undulating feathers, gripped her arm in a clasp like a band of steel.

"Where do you think you are going?" he demanded with a wicked lift of one expressive brow.

"To—to…" Philippa ran her tongue round leaf-dry lips, seeking moisture. Giles's eyes darkened to a deep slate-grey at the unconsciously provocative action. "Away from you!" she finished breathlessly, alarmed anew by the expression she read in those vibrant eyes.

She tried to wrench herself free, but Giles simply tightened his grasp, turning her tender flesh white and bloodless where his fingers bit. "You are hurting me," she protested hotly.

"Your own fault, my wife," he murmured. But his grip slackened, though not so much as to set her free.

"Pippa." There was determination, tenderness, a kind of resignation in his voice and expression as he sighed and pulled her closer to him. The silk was swathed about them, the mattress billowing, but, even so, in places she could feel his bare flesh against hers. The comforting bastion between them had disappeared as though by magic.

His now guarded eyes looked down on her intently. He had drawn her so close that the sensitive tips of her breasts rubbed against the fine mat of golden-brown hair covering his chest. Philippa trembled. In her heart she knew that, if Giles had married her sooner, before her father's seizure, before she had branded him traitor, she would have welcomed him as her husband. Already she could feel the tendrils of attraction twining around her heart and emotions, threatening to blot out every other consideration.

She could not allow that to happen! She must hold to her principles! She pushed at his chest, putting space between them.

"'Tis no use, wife," murmured Giles deeply. "Whether you are willing or not, our marriage will be consummated this night. I want no threat of annulment to come between us in the future. You are mine, and what is mine, I hold!"

"You are welcome to my dowry," spat Philippa. "'Tis my person I wish to deny you—"

"I have little interest in your dowry, Pippa. Else, despite your youthful interest in manly pursuits rather than in men themselves, I would have wed you years ago, bedded you and left you, while taking your undoubtedly rich manors into my keeping. But I chose to wait, hoping…" His voice trailed off, and Philippa frowned, wondering exactly what he had hoped. He quickly gathered his thoughts and went on wryly, "But I waited too long, I see that. However," he added softly, his voice a tender threat, "I will not now be denied the delights of your sweet body, my wife. I shall demand and take my husbandly rights."

"Very well." Philippa knew when further resistance was useless. Wives were expected to be submissive and obedient to their wedded lords. No cry for help would be heeded, and Giles was far too strong and agile for her to escape him for long. "Take your pleasure, my lord," she invited coldly.

She flopped back into the swansdown's embrace, massaging the angry red weals which had appeared where Giles had first grasped her arm, and shut her eyes. Men had the right to treat their wives as they willed, could flog them into submission. She doubted Giles would be as ruthless as that. Not, at any rate, the youthful, lively, kindly Giles she had known since childhood. But this new, mature, domineering Giles, the Giles who had become a traitor to his King? Whatever, she preferred not to put his ruthlessness to the test. Indignant, reluctant submission was her best course now.

"'Twould give me greater pleasure—and you, too, Pippa—were you a willing partner, my love.''

Giles's voice had become deep, vibrant and coaxing. Like the soft touch of his hands on her breast and neck. Like the tickle of his beard, the whisper of his lips as they brushed her closed lids and then moved down, trailing over her high cheekbone, her hollowed cheek, to find the small mole at the corner of her tightly clamped mouth. There they lingered for a moment before travelling along the line of her jaw to the sharp angle below her ear. His tongue found the nearby hollow, flicked her lobe, probed the orifice itself.

Philippa lay rigid, striving to ignore the persuasiveness of his overwhelming male presence, the heady odour of clean male flesh scented with thyme, the trickles of excitement dancing along her nerves. Determination not to enjoy what had been forced upon her grew. Even when the sudden darting of his tongue made her stifle a gasp, when his clever fingers brought her nipples to stand proud and erect, ready for…for…

She could not help the moan that escaped her as Giles abandoned her face and neck and brought his mouth down to claim one of those treacherous hardened peaks. The hair on his face caressed the tender flesh surrounding it. At the same time his hand inserted itself between her thighs and his fingers began exploring parts of her anatomy previously entirely her own preserve. Her moan became a cry of protest at his invasion of the secret centre of her womanhood.

With a sense of shock she recognised the sensation his probing fingers wrought. 'Twas only of recent years that the sight of animals mating had brought unease to her, strange reactions to assail her womanly parts.

"No!" she moaned.

"Yes." Giles lifted his mouth for just long enough to emit the one breathless word. Then his lips descended again, on the other breast, and the exquisite pain of his sucking shot straight to the place his fingers probed.

Hot, hard, throbbing flesh pressed against her thigh. She felt her muscles weakening. Her limp arms shifted, instinctively seeking to clasp to herself the man giving her so much unexpected pleasure.

Just in time her brain cleared and she remembered. She hated him! She was an unwilling victim! She stiffened in an utter rejection all the more determined because she had almost succumbed, and brought her thighs sharply together to stop her husband's delicate, arousing caresses.

"Get on with it!" she spat. Or would have spat, had her throat not been so closed with emotion that her voice came out in a croak quite unlike its normal self.

Giles stopped his wooing. He had felt her momentary surrender, knew that her rejection was one of will, not of distate. So be it.

"As you command, my lady," he returned icily, his tone quite at odds with the fierce anger which threatened to overwhelm him because of her stupid, wilful rejection and of the hot demand of the blood pulsing urgently through his veins.

He heaved his body over hers, pinning her rigid, resistant form to the bed, his mouth a thin line of determination as he clamped it over hers. His teeth ground against her lips and then her teeth, forcing both apart until he had gained the entry his tongue demanded. Even in his anger he remembered she was a virgin still, and moderated his first thrust, exploring her readiness, thankful to find that her body was still partially prepared to receive him. Once past the slight barrier of her maidenhead he waited a moment, expecting a cry of pain which did not come. Only then did he unleash his body, driving again and again, hard and fast. His release came swiftly. For a moment he lay supine; then, with a single great shudder, he rolled from his still and silent wife and, turning his back, composed himself for sleep.

Or so it seemed to Philippa. She did not know that her husband lay staring into space, ashamed of his punishing outburst while still believing it fully justified.

His mouth had suffocated her, his body crushed her, while his hard tongue and…and other thing had invaded her. She clenched her teeth against the indignity of it all. Hate boiled up and spilled over into the clenched, impotent fists digging into the mattress on either side of her. The knowledge that it could all have been so different, that, had she allowed her muscles to relax as they'd begun to do, had she not angered Giles with her rejection of his tenderness, things would have been very different, did nothing to ease her sense of violation. She ached down below, her thighs were stuck together with something wet. Blood, she supposed disgustedly. The women would be back in the morning to examine the sheets for evidence of the success of the union. Giles would have that one satisfaction, at least. There would be no question of an annulment now.

Some new-born, womanly instinct told her it would be the only true satisfaction her husband would reap from the night's work. He had eased his body, but, she recognised, he had been seeking more than that.

She ought to feel that it served him right. But she did not. Why had she denied him the pleasure he sought, forced him into treating her the way he had? Because she wanted to be able to justify her hatred?

Tears welled in her eyes, rolled down her temples and into the tangle of her hair. Deep down she did not hate her husband at all. She had been fighting a rearguard action against liking him too well, and thus becoming a traitor to her family loyalty.

Chapter Six

Giles had gone when Philippa woke the next morning. The hollow where he had lain felt cold to her touch.

Ida was pottering about the room, filling a small tub with warm water from a row of pitchers just inside the door. The arrival of those had probably wakened her. The tiring-maid turned as she heard her mistress stir, and smiled enquiringly. "You slept well, my lady?"

Philippa blushed. "Er—yes."

"Good." This time the grin stretched Ida's round face into a mask of satisfaction. "Your bath is almost ready."

The dried tears still stiffened her face. Soon after becoming Giles's wife in the flesh as well as in law, Philippa had dropped into the deep, dreamless slumber of emotional exhaustion, from which she had only now emerged.

She moved carefully, flung back the coverlet,

reached for her chamber-gown, slid her legs over the side of the bed, and escaped the soft clutches of that awful bed. Sun streaked through the eastern-facing windows.

"What hour is it?" she asked, slanting a surreptitious and embarrassed glance at the dark stain where her hips had been, as she stepped from the platform to the floor.

"'Tis after the hour of Prime, my lady. You have slept late."

"When did—?" Philippa gulped, swallowed and began again. "When did my husband rise?"

"I do not know, my lady. He had already gone when I arrived, a full hour ago."

He had not sought to linger. To waken her and... Depression settled on Philippa. Nothing would ever be right between them again. She could have loved Giles, she acknowledged, there could have been laughter and happiness and caring in their union, had it not been for Bolingbroke and his quest.

All her pent-up resentment focused, not on Giles himself for some reason, but on the man he followed with such unswerving loyalty, her reluctant sympathy of the previous evening quite gone. Henry Bolingbroke was a threat to the peace of the entire nation! He had ruined their marriage before it had begun. Yes, it was Henry Bolingbroke's fault that she felt abused, deserted and alone.

Isobel and a bevy of other ladies arrived at that moment, greeted her with cheerful cries and exclaimed over the evidence of her lost virginity as they stripped the bed. They soon departed, carrying their booty—all but Isobel, who remained.

She looked intently into Philippa's eyes. "'Twas so bad?" she demanded abruptly.

Philippa met her new friend's puzzled gaze grimly, determined not to admit her new vulnerability. "He used me brutally, Isobel," she declared. Her voice shook on the half-truth. "Look!" She bared her arm and showed the blue bruise-marks left by Giles's fingers.

Isobel frowned, shaking her head in bewilderment. "I would never have thought...but, if you resisted, 'twas his right," she pointed out. "Did you?"

"Only at first." Philippa made the admission reluctantly, her head lowered as she stepped into the steaming tub. Her knees came up under her chin as she sat down, but the herb-scented water was warm and soothing about her hips. "He was taking an age. I told him to get on with it."

"And he did!" exclaimed Isobel, enlightened. "How could you, Pippa?"

"I did my wifely duty," said Philippa defensively. "He should have had a care—"

"Duty makes a cold bedfellow, Pippa. Had you welcomed him... I am certain he did not wish to use you ill."

Philippa shrugged. "It hardly matters now. I fear we shall never find the joy of which you speak so beguilingly."

Isobel looked into the girl's mutinous face and saw some of the true emotions she was trying to hide. Hurt, disappointment and regret lurked in those dark, defensive eyes. She smiled encouragingly. "I would not be so pessimistic, Pippa dear," she advised. "Only those who cast horoscopes can tell what the future holds."

Bathed and refreshed, gowned in a simple kirtle Ida had fetched, Philippa returned with Isobel to be greeted by an exuberant Spot.

"He whined all night," Isobel told her wryly.

"I hope he didn't keep you awake! Poor old boy!" Philippa took his narrow face between her hands, inspected his healing wound with satisfaction, and kissed the top of his head, avoiding his eager tongue with a laugh. "Did your mistress desert you, then?"

Once she had weathered the dog's boisterous greeting, she peered from the window, relieved to observe that the scaffold had already disappeared from the yard beneath.

The State Chamber had been theirs for the wedding night only. No one had mentioned further arrangements designed to provide the newly-weds with privacy. The castle was over-full, space for such a luxury an impossible dream, even had they desired it. So she would continue to share her bed with Isobel and the Countess, all three women separated from their spouses at night. Philippa assured herself that this was for the best. The less she saw of her new bridegroom the better. He aroused too many conflicting emotions in her for comfort.

Giles appeared to share her sentiments. She saw nothing of him all that day. He did not appear for dinner. Neither did his squire, Walter Instow. Philippa deduced they had gone off somewhere together. She sat with Isobel and her knight, Miles—a shortish, well-mannered man not above thirty years, whose brown eyes seldom strayed far from the delicate face of his wife.

Philippa found their obvious delight in each other painful. It reminded her of earlier, carefree days when she and Giles had been friends, when tenderness and caring, understanding and harmony might have been possible between them. Now, although husband and wife, they were further apart than they had ever been. They had been at odds over the last days, but not completely estranged. Last night had driven a huge emotional wedge between them that it would be well-nigh impossible to remove.

If she wanted it removed. Did she really want to be close to a man so opposed to her family's loyalties? Her father and brother were both prepared to fight for the King. While Giles was equally ready to take up arms against his Sovereign, if doing so became necessary to Bolingbroke's cause.

Impossible to change her own loyalties overnight. Just because she was surrounded by a vast army of people ready to challenge the King and force his hand, that did not mean she had to acquiesce in an act of treachery which would enable her sire and sibling to brand her traitor. It was far better by far to remind herself of her reasons for hating her husband.

Giles appeared late for supper, tired, hot and sweaty. He sought out Henry Bolingbroke and spoke earnestly with him for some moments before he joined her at their board.

He greeted her courteously enough. "You are well, wife?" he enquired, not quite meeting her eyes.

"Well enough, I thank you, husband." Philippa spoke stiffly, covering her embarrassment, which seemed greater than her resentment. The aura of sheer animal strength emanating from him in a mixture of odours—hot steel, leather, horse, fresh manly sweat—stirred her newly awakened senses, made her too conscious of his nearness. She fiddled with the girdle at her hips and tried to make amiable conversation. "I see you have just returned from abroad. You have been far from the castle?"

"Some distance. 'Twas a hard ride. But I was glad of the exercise, which has made me hungry as a wolf!" exclaimed Giles, helping himself to a large crust of bread, and allowing Wat to pile his trencher with a mixture of roast meats. He had indeed welcomed the vigorous physical activity to relieve both his lingering frustration and his irrational sense of guilt.

"You went on Bolingbroke's business?"

He glanced at her sharply. "Aye."

"He was quick to deny us our bridal days."

"Did you wish them, wife?" This time his eyes did meet hers, a startled, enquiring expression in their depths. "I thought you would be content, relieved of my company," he added with a cynical laugh.

Philippa shrugged. She could not allow him to know that she had missed him. That in some way she couldn't understand his absence had hurt her. "In truth, lord, it makes no difference to me," she assured him coolly. "But such days are usually obligatory. I wondered what guile you had used to avoid spending unwelcome time with your bride."

"These are stirring and unusual times, wife." Giles chewed deliberately and swallowed, his expression remote. "Henry had need of my services. I could not refuse to do his bidding." He lifted more meat to his mouth.

Philippa smiled provokingly. "Mayhap you volunteered?" she suggested.

He stopped chewing and his brows arched up until she thought they would disappear into the sun-streaked hair sweeping back from his high forehead. "And if I did? Would that have mattered to you, Pippa?" His voice challenged. He began to chew again, slowly, his questioning eyes on her face. Philippa concentrated on cutting up the portion of roast boar on their trencher. What had possessed her to needle him? But she had discovered that he was not as indifferent as he would like her to think. The knowledge cheered her considerably.

"Not at all," she declared, a little too positively.

"But after last night you would scarce have wished to face me until forced."

They were speaking low. Giles had bent his head, the better to ensure the privacy of their conversation. His eyes were very near hers when she looked up to see the impact of her words. They were opaque, as though he had pulled a veil over them. His Adam's apple shifted as he swallowed his food. His shapely lips twisted into a mocking smile. "You did not enjoy your bedding, my love?" he enquired smoothly. "But then, you have much to learn of the art of ensuring your husband's pleasure, of being a submissive and obedient wife. I look forward to giving you further instruction."

Philippa gasped. His last words had been spoken in a tone that left her in no doubt of his intent. She took a grip on her courage, and tossed her head.

"I warned you that you would find little joy in our union," she reminded him grimly. "You should not have forced me, Giles."

This time he gave a shout of genuine laughter, though he still spoke low enough to keep their conversation private. "Forced? My love, you stated your willingness."

Confused, Philippa said nothing for a moment. He was right, she had… "Only because you insisted on making me your wife against my will," she came back sharply. "I but bowed to my duty."

"As did I. I did but insist on your honouring our

contract immediately." He hesitated. "Don't hold it against me, Pippa. I felt I had no choice."

Was there just the suggestion of pleading in his voice? Philippa glanced up from under a fringe of long black lashes to catch the frown between his eyes. "I trust," she said coldly, "that, now you have proved your virility, you will leave me alone. There are plenty to attest the fact that I am no longer a virgin."

"That fact, I believe, is in no doubt." The male arrogance in his voice set her teeth on edge. "But unfortunately I cannot promise what you wish, wife. You forget, you have yet to prove your fruitfulness. But—" he paused to take a draught of wine and wipe the back of his sinewy, sensitive hand across his lips "—I shall not trouble you here. There is scarce a private corner to be found in Bristol."

"For that small mercy I give you most hearty thanks!" cried Philippa furiously, and jumped to her feet. "I have eaten my fill. I will leave you to enjoy your repast alone."

Giles disappeared again the next day, and for several days thereafter. Philippa began to suspect that he was out gathering information for Henry Bolingbroke, for he invariably reported to his lord immediately upon his return.

Her suspicion was confirmed when, on the first day of August, Henry Bolingbroke gathered everyone in the Great Hall to make an announcement. This Lammas-tide was the twenty-eighth anniversary of Giles's birth. Travel-stained and weary, he stood at his lord's shoulder as Bolingbroke addressed the throng.

King Richard, Henry informed his audience, returning from Waterford in Ireland, had landed at Milford Haven in Wales two days after they had entered Bristol. As soon as he had landed the King had, of course, heard of the defection of his uncle of York, the fall of the castle and the deaths of his officials. He, Henry, had been waiting to see what the King would do.

Now it seemed that Richard had abandoned his initial intention to come to Bristol. According to the latest intelligence, brought by Sir Giles d'Evreux in the last hour, King Richard had ordered the army he had brought back from Ireland to march on Bristol while he himself set off across the mountains of Wales to join John de Montacute, the Duke of Salisbury, in Conway. Salisbury had previously been dispatched there to raise men, some from North Wales, but most from Richard's stronghold of Cheshire.

Philippa knew by now that Cheshire had been a fertile recruiting ground for the King in past years, providing not only his personal bodyguard of formidable Cheshire Archers, but also a large number of men who wore the badge of the white hart as a sign that they had sworn themselves ready to answer his call to arms. If the King could reach them, he would have power at his back. He must be attempting to match his cousin's military strength in the conflict of wills ahead.

"Therefore we march at first light and must make all speed to Chester. A forced march, sirs," announced Bolingbroke in ringing tones. "Let the faint-hearted remain with those who must defend Bristol, should the King's army decide to attack. Who is with me?"

The resounding shout of support almost lifted the thatch high above their heads. The smoke-blackened beams rang with the sound of cheering.

Giles left the dais and strode through the throng, making purposefully for Philippa's side. He bowed. "I march with Henry, of course, and you, my wife, will travel with me. You will need Ida, of course. Bring with you only such things as can be carried by one pack-animal."

"Will Eadulf accompany us?"

Giles grinned, looking suddenly young now that the long days of riding to meet with the agents Henry had sent to scour the Welsh valleys for news, the anxious waiting and watching, were over. And his wife had so far raised no objection to the proposed journey. "Aye. He is one of my company by now, an excellent groom, and he will guard you faithfully should I be otherwise engaged."

Philippa looked him straight in the eye. "Do I have a choice in this?" she demanded. "I would prefer to travel to Fishacre, to be with my father while I wait for my wedded lord's return."

The smile left Giles's tanned face. "Pippa, your father is recovering well; you heard Sir Walter's messenger deliver this welcome news yestereve. You have no need to fear for his welfare. But your family is headstrong, and I do not want my wife tempted to act unwisely in the wrong cause." He reached out and took her hand, folding it between his toughened palms. "Trust me?" he asked her softly. "I want no ill to befall you. Remain with me. 'Twill be an interesting experience for one as fond of action as you are, my love. The ride will not exhaust you, of that I am certain, or I would not ask it of you."

"You are asking it of Ida, too," Philippa reminded him.

"Aye. But she is still young and fit enough to enjoy an adventure. Else she would not have been so ready to accompany you to Evesham," he pointed out slyly.

Philippa nodded. Mention of Evesham brought with it a vision of Reverend Mother smiling and ordering her to go with her betrothed. Were she here, she would now be persuading her it was her duty to accompany her husband.

"Very well." She inclined her head in graceful acceptance of the inevitable. "I believe, husband, that today you celebrate the anniversary of your birth. I wish you well and happy."

For an instant Giles looked taken aback. He had not expected her to remember, let alone mark the occasion with good wishes. In quick response, he squeezed the hand he was still holding. "I thank you,

Pippa.'' He gazed deeply into her dusky eyes. ''Much of my future well-being will depend upon my wife.''

Philippa saw the ardent light glowing in the depths of his beautiful eyes, the eager curve on his smiling lips, and caught her breath sharply. She had not wanted to arouse his carnal passions! She tugged her hand from his hold.

''We will be ready to ride at first light,'' she promised stiffly.

Giles, disappointed, let her small hand go as it squirmed in his hold. A sigh of weariness escaped him as he watched her graceful retreat. Her small gesture of caring had led nowhere. But at least it had been made.

Ready at dawn they were, but the logistics involved in getting an army the size of Bolingbroke's on the move meant that they waited interminably to move through the castle gate, and then endured another lengthy delay outside the city walls.

Giles had been trotting around on Panache, helping to organise order out of chaos. He brought the roncey over to where Philippa sat on a low wall awaiting her turn to move off, while her palfrey and Ida's hack both nibbled contentedly at the grass, and Spot sniffed excitedly at every coney warren or badger set he could find.

''We travel with the men-at-arms and archers on foot,'' he told her, dismounting. ''They must be kept moving at a smart pace if they are not to lag too far behind. 'Tis my job to see that they do not.''

"Does that mean we can set off at last?" asked Philippa, pointedly looking at the sun, which had risen high in the heavens.

"Aye." He ignored her sarcasm. "The last of the soldiers are on the road. We travel behind them, but before the camp followers. If *they* lag, 'tis no great loss, though others will keep them moving, else we shall be short of farriers and food. Are you ready to mount?"

"I have been ready since dawn." He grinned at her tone and, catching his amused gaze, Philippa flushed, while her heart knocked diconcertingly in her chest.

"Then give me your foot."

She did so reluctantly. She did not want him touching her.

Wat, who had joined them, held the palfrey's head while Giles helped her to mount. Giles smiled up into her set face, one hand on Blaze's neck, the other lingering on her calf. Even through the layers of her riding gown his touch disturbed her breathing. "Eadulf and my grooms have ridden ahead," he told her, "so our camp will already be made by the time we arrive. Enjoy the ride, Pippa."

She made no reply, but put Blaze into a trot to join the departing column. Giles and Wat took up their stations on either side of her, Ida as usual following closely behind her mistress, her round face beaming. Philippa scowled as she caught a glimpse of her tiring-woman's enjoyment. Ida seemed to have discovered a taste for change to match that which normally drove her mistress. But Ida didn't have to make her pleasure so obvious.

The journey along the Severn valley passed without great incident. For most of the time Giles rode steadily at her side, now and again spurring ahead to join those of his men riding alongside the foot soldiers to chivvy the marching men along. Stops for rest and refreshment were short. By the time they reached the camping place chosen by Henry's scouts, the sun had already set. The van had been established in position for some hours. Pavilions stretched for mile upon mile beside the river. As the first appeared, Giles scanned the camp for sight of his pennon.

Eadulf came running out to meet them, greeting Philippa with a dutiful flourish and a broad smile which disclosed his blackened and gappy teeth.

"Follow me, my lady!" he shouted, and set off at a good pace to lead them to the d'Evreux encampment.

Several tents had been erected. Giles dismounted, and turned to his wife, who, helped by Eadulf, was already out of her saddle. "Come, wife." His smile held intimate invitation. He indicated the largest tent, formed of scarlet silk dusted with golden acorns. His shield, charged with his coat of arms, hung over the entrance, and his pennon fluttered from the central pole. "Our pavilion is ready."

Philippa hung back. "I do not wish to share your

pavilion,'' she told him bluntly. "Ida and I will lie elsewhere.''

"Where do you suggest?''

The icy fury latent in his voice almost diverted Philippa from her purpose, but she rallied in time. She was perilously near forgetting her hatred of her husband in a reluctant return of her old liking. To share his pavilion would endanger her fragile hold on antipathy still further. His cold anger was preferable to that seductive charm he knew how to wield so effectively.

She stiffened her spine. "You have several tents here. There must be room in one of them for us.''

"You would share with other men?'' he enquired dangerously.

Philippa tossed her head. "They can move in with you,'' she told him haughtily. "Otherwise, I will sleep under the stars. 'Twill be a warm night.''

Giles's lips tightened into a thin line. The flesh around them was white. His fists clenched and unclenched. For an instant she feared he would drag her, kicking and screaming, into his tent. But suddenly he relaxed. The smile he gave her was indecent in its suggestiveness.

"Afraid you will succumb to my virile charms?'' he enquired silkily.

"No!'' denied Philippa instantly. "My fear is of having to endure your brutal advances!''

"Well, my dear, you have given everyone much entertainment with your quite unjustified reluctance to submit to your wifely duty. But—'' he shrugged expansively ''—I can be a tolerant husband. For the moment. Wat!'' He turned to his squire. ''Bring your pallet into my pavilion, and those of the men sharing with you. Then perhaps you will so good as to show Lady Philippa to her quarters.'' He turned on his heel, and the ring of his spurs jangled on Philippa's nerves. Without a backward look, he disappeared into the glowing crimson pavilion.

Philippa glanced around at the circle of curious, amused faces, felt her own flame, and took a deep breath.

''Come, Ida. Wat, show us which tent is ours.''

Philippa spent a miserable night in a small tent with few comforts, and the following day did little to cheer her.

Apart from a courteous greeting Giles ignored her, choosing to ride alongside the ranks of the foot soldiers rather than behind them with her. Wat accompanied him. Without their presence to restrain the camp followers in the rear, she and Ida were soon overtaken by those loose women possessed of donkeys or mules who wanted to establish contact with their prospective clients before nightfall. Philippa rode in aloof silence, though her curiosity was keen. Although tawdrily dressed in sometimes filthy finery, on the whole they seemed a cheerful and not ill-favoured company.

One of them, riding a mule—a buxom, fresh-faced but wordly wench younger than herself, as far as Philippa could judge—had her eye on Giles.

"There be a bonny one!" she remarked to a companion, pointing ahead to where Giles rode on Niger, his spare black charger, man and beast splendid in heraldic jupon and brilliant horse-trapper. She rubbed her thumb across the tips of her fingers in the age-old gesture of greed. "He'll be good for a nice bit o' siller. He'm mine!"

"Good luck to ye, Miriam. Me, I prefer a bit o' rough wi' me siller. Like that un ower there."

She pointed to a hairy archer, and the girls giggled. Philippa watched the one called Miriam sidle up to Giles whenever opportunity allowed, making ribald pleasantries which he returned with an unconcerned aplomb and chaffing good humour which made Philippa squirm. He was flirting with the lewd wench! How dared he? And within sight of his wife, too!

When they halted for the night she was not surprised to see the girl standing outside Giles's pavilion, crowded close to the knight, laughing up into his face. Giles, grinning, chucked her under the chin, said something which made her pout, and sent her off with a playful smack on her round behind. As he turned from sending the woman on her way, Giles caught sight of his wife's fulminating glare. The suggestion of a smile twitched the corner of his mouth.

Eadulf brought them supper, as he had the previous evening and Philippa settled down for another uncomfortable night. And now she had vivid pictures of

Giles and the whore to plague her mind. Had the wench returned? Or had Giles gone to visit her in the privacy of her own tent?

Her body ached and her mind rebelled. She seemed to be in the grip of some nightmare from which she could not escape. She would not attempt to run away. Some force greater than her own will seemed bent on keeping her with Giles. And, in a strange way, despite all the discomforts of body and mind, she was quite enjoying herself. She'd been lifted from her safe, restricted little world and thrown into the midst of turmoil.

Fleetingly, she wondered how Isobel was coping. She hadn't seen her friend since leaving Bristol. Isobel had joined her knight near the front of the mounted column, and no doubt spent her nights happily sharing his pavilion. As for the Countess of Butterwick, she had decided to follow at a leisurely pace, riding pillion behind one of the Earl's grooms. No camping out for her. She would seek civilised shelter overnight.

Not that her pavilion was that uncivilised, Philippa had to acknowledge. Her discomforts arose more from unaccustomed exercise and a restless mind than actual hardship. Her pallet was well stuffed with straw and the one coffer she had brought was placed in the tent each evening. Eadulf drew water for her and Ida ministered to her needs. In fact, she thought as she turned over with restless energy, the pallet on the ground was infinitely more comfortable than the billowing down-filled mattress on which she had spent her wedding night.

The memory of that occasion brought a sudden and devastating reaction in her body. Her nerves tingled and a peristent throb began between her thighs. She groaned inwardly, bit on her bottom lip, and buried her hot face in one arm while she tried to quell the uncomfortable feeling by cupping her free hand over its source.

It died at last, and Philippa fell into an exhausted sleep aware that her bridal night had changed her in a way she had not anticipated. However reluctantly, she had become a woman, and now she had a woman's needs.

On the second day they crossed the Severn at Gloucester and turned north-west towards Hereford. Richard had created Bolingbroke Duke of Hereford before his banishment, so he had adherents in the area. Men flooded to join him at every stage of the march. As the days progressed, they turned from the city of Hereford itself, heading north for Leominster and Ludlow.

Ludlow Castle, set on high ground in an angle between the rivers Teme and Corve, was bounded on two sides by high cliffs descending to the flowing waters. The east and south approaches were defended by concentric walls, with the outer bailey between. Most of the travellers camped in the meadows lining the banks of the rivers, where rocky outcrop gave way to gentle slopes, but Giles had been allocated accommodation within the castle itself. Wat escorted Philippa through the outer gatehouse into the vast yard, where the grooms had already erected the d'Evreux pavilions. Philippa would rather have been down by the river, and told Giles so when he punctiliously came to see her safely installed.

"The bailey is noisy and none too clean," she complained. "The grass by the river would have been soft and sweet-smelling—much preferable."

"But then, my lady, you would have been without protection, for my following has been invited within the castle curtilage. I sup with Henry this evening—something of a banquet, I believe. You will not be joining me at the board. Supper will be brought to you in your pavilion."

Philippa stared at her husband. "And who," she demanded quietly, "made that decision?"

"I did," he owned, unabashed. "You have declined to undertake your duties as my wife. There is therefore no reason why you should enjoy the privileges of your position."

Philippa shrugged. "You do not discomfit me, sir. I shall enjoy my supper the better for eating it away from your presence."

"That is what I thought," responded Giles blandly. "Sleep well, Philippa. We have another long march ahead of us on the morrow." He strode away to his sumptuous feast, and Philippa stood watching his retreating back, biting her thumbnail as he strode across the drawbridge and through the inner gatehouse.

Supercilious beast! Had she really imagined she liked him? And as for wanting him… No! Those feelings were no more than her natural womanly desires. She needed to be wed. But not to Giles d'Evreux. Never to Giles d'Evreux!

Chapter Seven

They did not linger at Ludlow, moving off next morning as the first streaks of day lightened the eastern sky. Now they were in hilly country near the border with Wales. That night they camped beside the ancient Roman road just short of Shrewsbury, where the broad way and wide grassy banks of the King's highway wound between distant silhouettes of wooded hills, with the bulk of the Wrekin towering near by.

The Cound Brook provided their water and, after another long day in the saddle, Philippa felt the urge to splash her hands and face in the clear, clean water, mayhap to dip her hot and aching feet in its cooling depths.

Ida was busy about their pavilion, Eadulf away currying the horses. With Spot for company, Philippa decided to make her way to an isolated stretch of the narrow stream and indulge her fancy.

Soon she left the bustle of the camp behind, not

far, but far enough to be alone. Blessed solitude! How she had missed the chance to roam free, to sit idly watching the wild creatures as they went about their daily business. Darkness had almost fallen, but the rustles in the grass, the twitters and hoots in the branches of trees spaced at irregular intervals along the river's banks told her that the nocturnal creatures had begun to emerge as their daytime brethren retired for the night.

A band of long grass and wild flowers interspersed with low bushes edged most of the stream, and Philippa headed for a gap beside one of the trees, where the bank sloped gently to the water. Spot ran off to one side, intent on routing out unsuspecting otters or water voles.

Philippa picked up her skirts and hooked the hem into her belt before squatting to remove her shoes and hose. Her laces were barely untied when she heard heavy footsteps approaching, and looked up to greet whoever had come to intrude on her privacy.

A stout knight approached, made heavy and ponderous by the mailed vest and breastplate under his yellow jupon.

"Good even, sir," She greeted him cheerfully, despite her annoyance at being disturbed. "'Tis a fine evening, is it not?"

He did not answer immediately, but stood watching her. In the dusk it was difficult to make out his features, but something in his manner alerted Philippa to

danger. Instead of removing her shoes, she hastily re-
tied the laces and sprang to her feet.

He put out a hand to detain her as she began to
walk away, and his words confirmed her worst fears.

"So, my pretty," he chuckled, eyeing her tucked-
up skirts. "preparing yourself to receive me, I see.
How much?"

"No, sir!" gasped Philippa, terrible fear clutching
at her vitals. "You mistake me for someone else. I
am no lewd woman of pleasure—"

He thrust aside her protestations with a snort of
anger. "Don't like the look of me, huh?" His tone
had turned nasty. He crowded close enough for her
to smell the ale on his breath, see his rotting teeth,
his raddled, pock-marked face. "My money not good
enough for you, eh? Here!" He threw a silver penny
on the ground at her feet. "I saw you among the
whores today. You can't fool me with your haughty
ways! Come here, woman. I'm eager for my sport."

He grabbed at her, and Philippa let out a small
shriek. "Spot!" she screamed.

The dog responded with a warning growl as he
burst from the bushes, fangs bared, back bristling. He
hunched for a spring. Snarling, he leapt at the man
who was threatening his mistress.

The knight had been warned by that growl. Had
had time to wrench his sword from its sheath. And as
the dog leapt he caught it on its point, spitting it
through with one deadly thrust.

Philippa watched in horror as her pet yelped and

dropped to the ground, whining and writhing in a pool of blood. "No!" she screamed. "Oh, Spot! Spot! What has he done to you?"

She gave no further thought to escape, but made to drop down at the dog's side. The unknown knight gave her no chance. He grasped her arm and swung her to him, pinning her struggling body against the unyielding, chafing metal which the thin material of his jupon did little to soften.

His hot, repulsively wet lips closed over hers, and Philippa felt her senses reel under the assault of stinking breath laden with the stench of stale ale and rotting teeth. She managed a despairing wail as she felt herself flung to the ground.

"No!"

The bump as she landed, with that evil bulk on top of her, brought fierce anger to clear her brain. She would not submit to this brute! She kicked and writhed while her fingers fumbled in the folds of her gown, searching for the small knife hanging from her belt. The man was holding her down with one hand and the weight of his body, the other hand fully occupied fumbling with his breech-belt. Philippa brought out the knife and stabbed wildly downwards. The blade danced off his armour. He did not even notice the strike. In a new fury, Philippa lunged again, seeking to find the vulnerable spot above his steel gorget, for he wore no helmet.

This time she succeeded. He let out a bellow of pain and anger and blood spurted over her from his neck, just as the weight of his body was miraculously flung aside.

"Giles!" She croaked his name in a burst of disbelieving joy. And next moment her husband's sword had finished the work she had begun.

"Pippa!" He was on his knees beside her. Anxiety made his voice hoarse and somewhat shaky. "Did he harm you?"

Philippa shuddered. "No. Not much, anyway." She rubbed a breast bruised by the armour. "But Spot! He killed Spot!" she wailed, and burst into tears.

Giles muttered an oath under his breath, and issued crisp orders to Wat and others of his retinue who had come running with him when her anguished scream of Spot's name had told them who was calling. No one would have bothered about a whore in trouble by the river. But Giles had been galvanised into action by the cry from his wife.

The man was dead. Would like as not have died of Philippa's stab, but more slowly. Giles almost wished he had not dispatched the brute in such a hurry. But he could no more have prevented himself from striking out at his wife's attacker than he could now help picking up her shaking body and cradling it in his arms as he carried her tenderly back to his pavilion.

Philippa made no demur as the red silk closed about her. In the warm glow reflected by the horn lantern hanging overhead, held fast in her husband's arms, she felt safe and secure for the first time in days.

Giles laid her on his pallet and supported her shoulders while he held a wine-skin to her lips. She drank greedily.

"Better?" he asked tenderly.

"Oh, Giles! Did I kill him? I meant to!"

Giles hesitated. Would it be best for her to think she had, or to believe him responsible for her attacker's death? She was a fierce little thing, who liked to fight her own battles. He told the truth.

"You gave him a mortal wound, Pippa. I but put him out of his misery."

"I'm glad! He deserved to die!" she choked.

Suddenly, the floodgates opened. She flung her arms about his solid, reassuring body, buried her face in the hollow of his shoulder, and wept as though her heart would break.

"What is it, love?" he questioned. "He didn't…?"

"He killed Spot," she gulped. "Spot is dead! What shall I do without him? I—I loved him so much…"

All this grief for a dog! thought Giles grimly. Would she have been as shattered had it been he who had died? He thrust the thought aside. It was reaction, too. Reaction and grief together could very well produce a storm of emotion like this.

He signalled Ida and Wat, who stood enquiringly by the opening, to remove themselves. Then he stretched out beside Philippa, and drew her into his arms. She nestled closer. Giles smoothed down her tumbled hair and composed himself for a long night of discomfort and self-denial.

* * *

Philippa woke next morning to find Giles standing watching her. She sat up abruptly.

Realising where she was, and how she had spent the night, colour flooded up her neck and brought spots of bright red to her high cheekbones. "Oh!" she gasped. Then she remembered why she was where she was. "Spot," she whispered. "Is he really dead?"

"Aye, and buried." Seeing her about to burst into new floods of tears, Giles's compassion found its outlet in anger. "What the devil were you doing down by the river alone, Pippa?" he barked roughly. "You must have realised the risk you ran!"

"No, I didn't! And anyway, I had Spot..." Her voice trailed off and Giles made an exasperated sound under his breath. "He thought I was a whore," shouted Philippa defensively. "Small wonder, since I was left to travel alone among their company!"

"So this is my fault, too, I suppose?"

Giles's scathing anger cut Philippa to the quick. Last night he had shown nothing but tenderness. That had soon disappeared, like his first tenderness on their bridal night. She scrambled to her feet.

"Well, isn't it?" she demanded, equally angry now. "You ignore me, so how was a stranger to know who I was?"

"I ignore you because you deserve to be ignored, wife. But from now on I will brook no more disobedience from you. You will share my pavilion and wear my badge on your horse's trapper. That way there should be no further misunderstandings!''

''So I am to be branded your property!''

''Which you are,'' he reminded her silkily, his first anger turning to admiration at her show of spirit. God's bones, but taming this wench would bring reward past imagining! 'Twould be a tough task, but how he would enjoy the doing of it!

He smiled. ''And now, my lady wife, if you would be so good as to ready yourself, we must move off within the half-hour. I believe you need to change your gown. Your coffer has been brought here for you. I will call Ida.''

Philippa, seething, looked down to see the bloodstains spattered across the front of her kirtle. Memory of the previous night's terror returned to send a shudder through her. ''Where did they put Spot?'' she enquired tightly. ''I will not leave without first seeing his grave. I have no defender now,'' she added plaintively.

''You have me,'' Giles reminded her quietly.

Philippa met his level, intent stare, and remorse overcame her. He had charged to her rescue, dispatched her attacker and then held her while she spent her tears. Twice now he had shown a tenderness and understanding she would scarce have expected from any man.

''Aye.'' She gave him a watery smile. ''I believe I have to thank you for coming to my aid so promptly.

And for soothing my sorrow. I am not ungrateful, husband.''

''Then let us cry truce.'' His smile caused her stomach to lurch. ''When you are ready, I will show you where your dog lies.''

''And—there was no trouble over the knight's death?'' she asked rather breathlessly.

Giles shook his head. ''There were witnesses enough to his attack. His sword was drawn and bloody. His squires are taking his body home for burial. There will be no further questions asked.''

Philippa drew a bolstering breath. ''Then send Ida to me. I will be ready in good time.''

''That,'' said Giles softly, ''is more like it, wife.'' And dropped the softest of kisses on her startled mouth.

The cavalcade reached Chester on the ninth day of August at the beginning of the twenty-third year of Richard's reign. The town had fallen without resistance by the time Giles and Philippa arrived. Like the Bristol burghers, those of Chester had no love for Richard. And the royal border castle's garrison, faced with the immense hordes Bolingbroke had brought with him, could see that resistance was useless.

Henry could cry checkmate on the King.

North Wales was now Richard's only source of support. Henry immediately ordered most of his forces across the border to Flint, to challenge the King, who had reached the safety of Conway. With

Chester secure, most were already on their way. So the town and its castle were relatively empty.

Thus Philippa discovered that she and her husband had been allocated a small private chamber in the tower of the castle, which had been built in an angle of the city walls. The windows were little more than arrow-slits commanding a view over the encircling river, the straggling suburbs and the surrounding countryside.

A box-bed, high and relatively narrow, had been fitted into one corner of the chamber. She eyed it disparagingly. And with a certain amount of guiltily pleasurable anticipation.

She had shared Giles's pavilion since Shrewsbury, but not his pallet. Ida and Wat had kept them company. But there could be no escape from sharing this bed. And their attendants had already laid their pallets elsewhere. A shiver of perverse excitement ran along her nerves. She had come a long way, not only in miles, since Bristol. Giles was liked and respected among his peers, almost venerated by his inferiors. She could not help a feeling of pride in being his wife.

And Henry? Never had any leader appeared so popular. Cities and castles fell before his mere presence. Men, great and small, flocked to support his cause. As for Richard…it seemed that men were less ready to rally to his side. Already the southern army, left to march on Bristol, had disintegrated when its leader, Edward of Rutland, the Duke of Albemarle, had declared for Bolingbroke. The Chesire force had failed to materialise. Henry's intelligence was that Richard had reached Conway to find the Welsh army scattered, on a rumour of his death. He had retained the support of Salisbury, but without an army he could no longer challenge Henry.

Most strangely, Philippa found that what happened between the two cousins mattered to her less and less. Whatever the outcome, her future lay with Giles d'Evreux. If Henry prevailed, Giles was likely to prosper. If Richard, by some masterly stroke, regained the upper hand, and Henry's banishment—or worse— was reimposed, Giles would suffer the same fate. And she wanted to be with him.

When the change had come she couldn't truly say. Perhaps during that night spent in his arms after Spot died. Whatever else, she could see things now in a longer perspective. Whoever ruled England, for good or ill, Giles was her husband. She might as well accept the fact. And make the most of it. For he was certainly not repulsive to her.

They mounted the stairs together. Giles went through to the tiny wardrobe with Wat, leaving the bedchamber to Philippa and Ida. "I wish you a good night, my lady." Ida had not been too happy with her mistress's behaviour since leaving Alban, but was too fond of the girl to show it. Sympathising with her situation did not blind Ida to the fact that Philippa's lot would have been eased had she not antagonised her new husband from the first. So, as she helped her mistress to climb into the bed, she patted Philippa's small hand and smiled. "Were I ten years younger I could wish myself in your place," she confided, speaking low because the men were close by with only a skin arras between. "Bed is a lonely place without a man to warm it," she added wistfully.

Ida had joined her service as a young widow. Philippa studied her tiring-woman with new interest. Ida had always been more friend than servant, yet they had never before spoken of such intimate matters. Perhaps I was too young, if not in years, then at least in mind, thought Philippa ruefully. "You miss your husband?" she asked curiously.

"Aye, my lamb. But mayhap, now, I shall meet another." Her face, like her body less round after a week of intensive travel, flushed. "I have enjoyed this march, meeting so many new people. Alban was an isolated spot."

"You have met someone special?" asked Philippa, illumination flooding in. She had been so wrapped up in her own passionate resentment that she had barely noticed Ida's new animation, or taken trouble to wonder what her woman did in her limited free time.

"Mayhap." Ida blushed even more rosily. "He is man-at-arms to Harry Hotspur."

"So you would leave me to travel north?"

"Nothing has been settled as yet, my lamb. Do not fret yourself. Wolfram has not spoken. But I think he finds me to his liking."

"And so he should! He would be a wise man to take you to wife, Ida. I wish you happy."

"As I wish you, my lady. I must leave you now." She hesitated. "Be kind to your lord husband, my dear. He is a good man. You would look far for a better husband."

Philippa bristled at her maid's well-intentioned admonition. Knowing her words to be true did not make them easier to accept. From another. But had she not been thinking much the same thing? So she controlled her irritation, and nodded dismissal. "God keep you, Ida. I'll not need you again until morning."

When Giles came through Philippa was huddled under the cover, lying near the wall. Wat passed through and out. Her husband strode quietly towards the bed, his face grave. He wore naught but his shirt, which he drew off as he walked.

He stood beside the bed, naked, and Philippa peeped up at him from shadowed eyes. Giles reached out for the extinguisher to pinch out all the candles but one, then slid into the bed beside her. No billowing feathers separated them this time. The mattress was stuffed with fresh straw and herbs, clean and firm, so narrow that Giles could not avoid touching her as he stretched out beside his wife. And the wall blocked off her last chance of escape. But she no longer had a wish to escape.

He inserted an arm under her shoulders and drew her to him. "So, wife," he murmured deeply, "at last we have a chamber to ourselves." His other hand came up to smooth the freshly-brushed curls from her high forehead. His fingers trailed down her face and fingered the slight cleft before taking hold of her chin, turning her small face to his.

In the almost-dark his eyes glittered in the strong silhouette of his face. A small sound escaped Philippa's throat, part anticipation, part anxiety, part pleading. Giles seemed to read her mood, and made a soothing murmur in return. "Just relax, sweeting," he murmured. "'Twill not be so bad, that I promise you. You may even enjoy yourself; who knows? I intend to be gentle, and gentle I will be—an you do not try my temper beyond endurance!"

Philippa was not prepared to accept the implied criticism without protest. "So your ill-usage was my fault, was it?" she hissed indignantly.

"As much as your stupidity and Spot's death was mine," came the immediate, sharp riposte. His voice thickened again. "But we have a truce, Pippa. Don't spoil it now."

She pouted in the darkness. "Very well. I am quite ready to do my duty as your wife."

"Mmm." Giles shifted his weight, turning into her and throwing a long leg over her thighs, pinning her to the bed. She presented a challenge, this delightful, difficult, passionate wife of his. He had felt her initial surrender that first night, and knew that if he could wake her dormant womanhood successfully he would win himself a responsive and worthy bed-partner. Silently, he acknowledged his debt to all those women in his past on whom he had practised the art of seduction. They had not mattered. This woman did.

"You are a true beauty, my wife," he murmured, interspersing his words with small kisses on her forehead, her eyes, her nose. "And you have a desirable body—" he ran his palm the length of her arm and torso, on down over her swelling hip until it came up against his own leg "—soft as a kitten, yet beneath your velvet flesh lie steely muscles which can control a lively mount and draw a heavy bow." His hand travelled up again, coming to rest on her ribcage, just below the tender swell of one breast. His fingers splayed beneath it, his thumb caressing the valley between it and its twin, his fingers resting in the warm fold beneath. "Lovely," he growled seductively.

Philippa's eyes were shut, her breathing shallow. One of his hands cupped her head, the other rested intimately upon her body. His breath was soft and sweet on her skin. His lips were feather-light as they explored every crease, every feature, traced the line of her jaw and found the fluttering pulse where neck met shoulder.

Giles raised himself on one elbow and lifted his head the better to see the pale oval of her face, defined by black arching brows, the dark, sweeping fans of lashes resting on her cheeks, the shadow cast by her rather long nose, the curves and depressions of a generous mouth. And the mole at its corner. She wasn't truly beautiful. Yet his wooing words had been no lie.

So absorbed was he in the contemplation of the individual, imperfect, utterly charming parts that gave the overall impression of beauty, that he remained still for some moments. Philippa, missing the intimate touch of his lips, the grazing of his beard on her skin, opened her eyes.

Immediately, in the flickering shadows cast by the single candle, their gazes locked. Giles drew in a sharp breath before he lowered his head again, this time to claim her mouth.

For a long moment he seemed content to savour her lips. But then his tongue began to probe, to demand entry to her mouth. Philippa, swimming against the tide in a sea of sensation, was powerless to resist, though part of her wanted to. She had determined to be submissive, but she had not intended to co-operate quite so enthusiastically. Her mouth opened involuntarily, and as his tongue thrust fiercely into the sweetness of the cavern Philippa felt her whole body respond. She tasted the wine from supper, mingled with the extract of calendula flavouring the chalk he had used to rub his teeth. A low growl broke from her throat.

With a soft chuckle that ended in an answering growl, Giles shifted position again. His hands moved, each claiming a breast. He pushed them upwards, holding the plump flesh in his palms, guiding first one nipple, then the other, to his mouth. As he suckled, the shafts of painful sensation she had come to know speared to the centre of her womanhood. Philippa moved restlessly, not knowing what she wanted—for him to stop or to go on to something else, something more satisfying.

He began to concentrate on one tender peak, releasing a hand to search out the secret places between her thighs. Pleasure flooded her body. As it must be flooding Giles's, if the heated, hard, throbbing flesh pressed against hers was any indication. She had needed to summon up all her hatred and resolve to deny Giles pleasure on their wedding night. She could still do it, she told herself as she let the waves wash over her, but she had decided not to...

Her hands, which had somehow become tangled in the thickness of Giles's hair, dropped limply to her sides as strength drained from her limbs. She began to take deep, gasping breaths, as though she was struggling for air. Giles emitted another low growl, and abandoned her breasts as he rose above her, poised to enter her flowering, expectant body.

"Pippa, sweeting," he whispered, "I want you so much." Gently, he lowered himself. She felt him slide into her sheath, and then lie still, controlling his own ragged breathing. She gasped at the unexpected pleasure his entry brought. Her arms came up and held him, demanding closer union.

He began to move again, thrusting slowly, gently, gradually probing deeper and deeper into the core of her. And Philippa moaned under the onslaught of ravishing sensation. She didn't want him to stop. There was no soreness this time, no true pain. She could have borne his soft stroking of her womanhood for ever. When he stopped to gather his control, she uttered a small cry of protest.

Giles chuckled, and the undisguised triumph in his tone brought a measure of sanity rushing back to Philippa. Her arms slackened as he began the last phase of his journey to completion. She could not let him enjoy complete victory over her traitorous body. Not yet.

He had lost her. Giles groaned inwardly, but maintained the steady, erotic rhythm for as long as he could. When at last he could bear it no longer, he unleashed his body. A few fierce thrusts, and he collapsed over his silent wife as the shudders of fulfilment shook him.

Her arms tightened again. He felt the faintest of soft kisses touch his shoulder. Yet when he regained control and rolled from her she did not seek to restrain him. He gathered her into his arms and pressed her head into his shoulder. She was so quiet. He feathered a kiss on her white forehead. "Thank you, my wife," he murmured softly.

Philippa did not answer. She could not. Overwhelming emotion had deprived her of the ability to speak. Tears choked her throat and threatened to course down her cheeks. She blinked them back. She must not let him see. For these were tears of sheer joy. And of tenderness for the man who had brought it to her.

Chapter Eight

Several days passed without great incident. Giles was kept busy during the day, but the nights were theirs. Philippa began to revel in the sensuous delight she found in her husband's arms, but some part of her refused complete abandonment to her new-found passion, fearing it would be the final act of treachery to her family.

Bolingbroke had sent Henry Percy, Earl of Northumberland, as emissary to the King at Conway. Bolingbroke's terms for a peaceful solution to their quarrel were reasonable. Richard would, of course, remain King. Henry continued to maintain that he had no intention of threatening the throne. But Richard must bow to the wishes of his magnates: clear Henry's name and return John of Gaunt's estates to his rightful heir; rescind the sentence of banishment and appoint Bolingbroke hereditary High Steward; and surrender five members of the council for trial for treason, since they had abused their powers so wretchedly.

Henry could dictate what terms he chose, since the King lacked effective support. Rumour had it that Richard had reacted to his cousin's challenge with a mixture of self-pitying despair and furious defiance, swearing that Bolingbroke should die a death that would make a noise as far as Turkey.

Philippa wondered what he would do. There must be ships in Conway harbour. But if he sailed to some other land to raise an army, he would be abandoning a throne Henry had promised he would retain. Yet that Henry was now in a position to make such a promise made that throne glaringly insecure.

And what was her brother up to? she suddenly worried. She realised rather guiltily that she hadn't given Roger more than a passing thought in days. She frowned, deeply disturbed now that she did think about him. Any army he could muster would be puny beside that of Henry Bolingbroke. Roger would be risking ruin, even death, if he dared to go to the assistance of his sovereign lord. A shiver of apprehension ran through her. He would as likely try. And, she admitted ruefully, she would once have encouraged him in his loyal defiance.

But the last weeks had taught her things she hadn't dreamt of in her sheltered life at Alban. And since she could do nothing to prevent whatever happened, to Roger or to the King, she did her best to thrust all her uncomfortable thoughts to the back of her mind.

It took ten days for the negotiations to be completed, for Henry to receive word that Richard was prepared to leave the safety of Conway and risk all on a meeting at Flint.

Jubilation in the Bolingbroke camp was reserved. Giles, like everyone else, was fully aware of the magnitude of the events taking place. The future prosperity and safety of England depended upon their outcome. Richard might yet have a trick or two up his embroidered and jewelled sleeve. And if he accepted the terms, could he be trusted not to go back on his word? Richard had a long memory for injuries, and never forgot a slight. His quick wit, physical courage and trickery had brought him victorious through crises in the past. There could be no guarantees where King Richard was concerned.

So it was with severe reservations that Giles collected his wife and followed his lord to Flint.

There, Philippa found herself housed in a pavilion once more, though this time Giles took care to ensure their privacy at night. And she discovered Isobel Fortescue in the same part of the camp.

"The Countess Helen?" laughed Isobel once their glad greetings were over. "Aye, she is here, sharing a pavilion with the Earl. Why?"

"She arrived at Conway some days ago, and was most affronted not to be given accommodation within the castle walls!" chuckled Philippa. "But every inch of space was taken, and her husband here, so she was

sent on to join him! I did not speak with her, but I
heard her voicing her strong disapproval!''

"But you and your lord husband were given a
chamber within the tower, you say?'' Isobel paused,
glancing at Philippa's blooming face quizzically.
"Have you settled your differences, Pippa?''

"Mostly,'' admitted Philippa reluctantly, suppress-
ing a sigh. "I have come to accept—nay, I must confess, enjoy, my wifely duty.'' She lowered her eyes
as colour rose in her face. "But there is still the question of my father's illness, of our conflicting loyalties,
to be settled. I cannot feel truly at peace in this alien
camp.''

"But you are not as unhappy as you were,'' observed Isobel with a smile. "And this despite the loss
of your hound. I heard of that tragedy, though I found
no chance to speak with you then.''

Philippa's face dropped into lines of sorrow. "Aye,
poor Spot! He died trying to fend off my attacker. I
do miss him terribly, though I have had small chance
to mourn his loss. Even in Chester there always
seemed to be something to take my attention.'' She
shuddered. "Thank the Virgin I had time to replace
the gown ruined by that awful man's blood.''

"By the time you settle down to real life again,
you will be over your first grief,'' soothed Isobel.

"True. Giles has promised me another puppy. It
won't be the same, but I'll have something of my own
to love again.''

"Mayhap, by then, you will have a babe," suggested Isobel gently.

"Mayhap." Philippa pushed the thought aside. A small Giles to love? The idea confused her. "But have you no children, Isobel?" she suddenly thought to ask.

"Aye, a bonny boy, safe with his grandmother. And I believe another babe is growing in my belly," confided Isobel shyly.

"I am glad for you," said Philippa sincerely. "Look!" she exclaimed. "See, Bolingbroke's herald is riding out again!"

"Heralds and messengers will ride busily back and forth between the two camps until all is finalised!" prophesied Isobel.

And so it was. Eventually it became known that Richard would arrive at Flint on the nineteenth day of August. The denizens of the castle scuttled about making ready to receive him.

Philippa had not expected to find a place in the Great Hall for his reception, but Giles pulled a few strings, and she found herself at his side as Henry Bolingbroke awaited his moment of triumph. His rather heavy but good-looking face looked calm enough under a high-crowned felt hat.

Distant fanfares and the echo of muted cheering announced the King's approach. A bustle at the door, and Richard strode in, high-collared houppelande billowing around him. All dropped to their knees except Bolingbroke, who prostrated himself three times in

the traditional act of submission before kneeling at
his Sovereign's feet.

Richard's face was pale, perhaps paler than usual,
but it was true what they said: he did not lack courage. A tall man, he carried his head high, wore a
coronet on thick, long hair the colour of ripe corn,
and an imperious expression on his rather womanish
face. Exquisitely barbered tufts of beard protruded on
either side of his chin, and a slight moustache shadowed the extremities of his lips as though to belie the
essential delicacy of his features. As those present
began to rise to their feet he looked around and, one
by one, as his frosty blue gaze rested on them, men
and women dropped again to their knees.

Obeying Giles's urgent tug, Philippa sank back to
hers as Richard eyed her carefully braided head with
complete detachment. She realised that he was im-
pressing his majesty, calling on the elaborate ceremonial and acts of deference he had instituted at his
Court to bolster his exalted notion of his own importance. Giles had warned her. She had scarcely believed it possible that a mere man, even God's
anointed King, could demand so much servility of his
subjects.

The meeting progressed. Richard graciously acceded to all Bolingbroke's demands as though he
were granting favours. Philippa occupied herself observing this King who, over the years, had managed
to alienate himself from the vast majority of his subjects, both great and small.

He was thirty-two years old. Had lost his beloved Queen Anne and, though still lacking an heir, married Isabelle of France, a child of eight years, who even now was not old enough to bed. Rumour had it he preferred men. Yet he had truly loved his first Queen, and been desolate after her death, ordering the destruction of their favourite palace of Sheen, where she had died.

He appeared all scarlet and gold. Philippa eyed his costly garments and priceless jewels with reserved envy. 'Twould be wonderful to afford such luxurious adornment, but to pay for these and other extravagances Richard had levied his forced loans and intolerable taxes, had invented the iniquitous fines which came to be known as *La Plesaunce*—payments demanded from any who had even remotely supported the Lords Appellant—those nobles, including Bolingbroke, who had challenged his powers in 1387. Ten years after the event, with unrestrained power in his hands, he had executed some of his old enemies, banished others, and demanded payment from the unspecified remainder in order that they should regain his good pleasure. Individuals and the people of seventeen shires had paid up, submitting themselves to him as traitors rather than suffer the consequences of his grave displeasure. But this stratagem to extort money had endeared him to no one.

The King waved an imperious dismissal which only Bolingbroke and the assembled magnates ignored. Next day they were all to ride to Chester, with Richard in their midst.

From Chester, Richard sent out letters patent and writs to summon a parliament to meet at Westminster at the end of September. He also sent to Ireland, at Bolingbroke's request, to summon young Harry back, to be reunited with his father after their long separation.

Then began the lengthy journey to London. Philippa was beginning to long for the quiet life she had known at Alban! Yet she also knew that she would not have missed the excitement of this eventful journey. She felt intensely alive, fit and well, the days seemed brighter, the birdsongs sweeter, the scent of new-mown hay more pungent than she remembered, especially after one of the increasingly frequent showers. And the nights were filled with delights she had never imagined.

The King travelled with Bolingbroke, well guarded but separated from his own small retinue of servants, and from Salisbury, his only real friend in that assembly.

As the cavalcade passed by, reapers stopped work on the harvest to stare. Because the three visitations of the great pestilence had halved the population since 1348, whole villages on their route lay abandoned. Sheep grazed where once crops had grown, for there were not enough labourers to till the land. But from villages and towns where people did still live, crowds appeared to cheer their progress. Philippa couldn't help but notice that the name cried out the loudest was that of Bolingbroke. There were few enthusiastic cheers for the King.

Giles had been relieved of his duty of shepherding the marching men, for this was a more leisurely progress. They rode amid the main body of mounted knights, just behind the King and his immediate bodyguard.

Day succeeded day. At Shrewsbury they turned east, following the King's highway to Lichfield, from there dropping down to Kenilworth, one of the Lancastrian castles now returned to Henry's hold.

The stone walls glowed softly rosy in the sunlight, the ancient keep, known as Caesar's tower, and the extensive assemblage of other towers, walls and buildings seemingly rising from the centre of a shimmering lake. The weather had been kind during the entire expedition, with just those light, refreshing showers and the occasional dull day to mar their enjoyment of a ride through a countryside where green was mingled with gold, where spikes of purple loosestrife grew from beds of yellow creeping cinque-foil to paint the way with colour, and travellers' joy laced the hedgerows to fill the air with the heady scents of summer.

Only those of knightly rank were admitted within the walls, the remainder left to camp on the banks of the mere which defended the approach to the castle from west and south. As she queued to cross the long,

embattled causeway which dammed the lake at its
eastern end, separating it from the defensive pool to
their right, Philippa gazed in delight at the wide
stretch of water, at the small barges tied up along its
banks.

"Giles!" she exclaimed. "Could we go out upon
the lake? 'Twould be wonderful to drift lazily in one
of those boats...mayhap we could catch fish!"

Giles smiled indulgently. His wife was full of
youthful enthusiasm for the simple pleasures of the
countryside. "Aye, mayhap. Henry plans to rest here
for two nights, for he wishes to meet with the Lancastrian stewards and check on his inheritance while
he is able. Few will question the delay in such a delightful place! But if you require fish, the stews are
yonder, beyond the Brays!" he told her with a grin,
nodding over his shoulder.

"I just want the fun of catching one!" She laughed
joyously, happy to have won such a hopeful response,
though that grin had left her unaccountably breathless.
"Have you been here often, Giles? Do you know it
well?"

"Tolerably well. 'Twas Katherine Swynford's favourite home, and John of Gaunt had much of it re-
built. The kitchens, the Great Hall and all this nearer
wing, including a garde-robe tower. Henry spent a lot
of time here in his youth, and later visited quite reg-
ularly. I accompanied him more often than not."

"Lucky you!"

She kept the envy, even the resentment, from her

voice with a considerable effort. But Giles read it, and voiced the thought she was trying to suppress.

"I am sorry, Pippa. I was selfish. Had we wed five years since, you would have been made welcome here, too. But then again, mayhap you would not have been so happy to live in exile."

"But yours was voluntary! You did not have to go, and could have returned at any time!"

"And been suspected of spying for Henry? No, once the decision to go with him was made, it would have been difficult to return."

"So you did not intend to honour our contract?"

Giles shifted uncomfortably in his saddle. Niger tossed his great head, and the harness jingled. "I had not given it much consideration."

"Nor how your family would feel."

"My father served and followed John of Gaunt for most of his life. He was with him at Najera—he met my mother in Spain—and later joined many of his campaigns. So he understood my need to support Henry. And at the time we thought it was for ten years only. Richard went back on his word there, too, in extending the banishment to life."

"I," said Philippa deliberately, "would have been nigh on thirty years old by the time you returned. An old and sour maid. Almost too old to bear a child."

"Nay, Pippa, I would have sent for you within a while. The choice would have been yours. I would not, then, have insisted on your honouring the contract. You would have been free to find another husband.''

''Mayhap, then, 'twould have been better had you not returned!'' She couldn't keep the snap from her voice.

''Did you have a candidate in mind?'' enquired Giles mildly as, at long last, they began to pass through one tower gateway and traverse the causeway towards a second.

Her knee knocked against his. She glanced sideways quickly. Caught the devilish gleam in his dancing eyes, and knew that he was teasing her. Mother of God, but he was an attractive devil! Her nerves jumped with the sudden shock of the contact, of his possessive, self-assured smile, of his arrogant—and entirely accurate—assessment of her new dependence on his favours.

''No,'' she retorted haughtily, ''but no doubt my family would have found little trouble in securing one.''

''But none more devoted and amiable than I, my love.'' He hauled on Niger's bit to stop the eager destrier from forging between two horses ahead. ''I fear we shall have to pitch our tent in the outer court,'' he went on casually. ''There will be no chamber to spare in the castle, and I do not fancy spreading a pallet in one of the halls. I have come to treasure the nights in my pavilion spent with my delightful wife.''

Philippa realised she was having a hard job to keep

up the antagonism which had come so naturally at
first. All her emotions, her beliefs, seemed to be in
some vast melting-pot, and she no longer knew exactly how she felt or what she thought. Only that she
no longer wanted to be separated from the strange
mixture of security and stimulation she found in
Giles's company.

Their pavilion was pitched in the outer court, not
far from the chapel of St Mary. Eadulf took Blaze
and Niger off to the stables while Ida and Wat saw
that their mistress and master had everything they
needed.

They ate that evening in the Great Hall. Climbing
the flight of steps to the finely decorated doorway,
admiring the intricate carvings on the arch and jambs,
Philippa caught the rich aroma of roasting meat, the
sharp tang of spices, the mouth-watering waft of
freshly baked bread coming from the adjoining kitchens. Ventilation shafts from the undercroft beneath
the Hall emitted a faint, vinous whiff of oak casks
and a fine vintage to mingle with the cooking smells.
She realised she was ravenous.

The westering sun glowed through the high, tra-
ceried arches of the Hall windows, throwing a golden
sheen over trestles laid for a banquet. Grooms, servitors and pages scurried everywhere, carrying laden
platters and steaming cauldrons, heavy flagons and
slopping pitchers. The carver was at work on the dais,
the sewer stood near by ready to taste everything before the King or nobles ate.

Trumpets flourished from the gallery above, and Henry led Richard to the chairs of state at the high table in the centre of the dais. People bowed and made deep obeisance. Richard swept the chamber with his haughty gaze, but no one cringed to his knees. Somewhere along the road he had lost his regal authority to become little more than an honoured noble. A noble who was not free to leave the cavalcade.

He had proved that, yesterday, by attempting to ride off at a tangent. He had been prevented. For his own safety, naturally.

Failing to receive the deference he considered his due, Richard sat back, his face flushed and angry. He extracted an elegant square of fine linen from the folds of his jewelled and embroidered houppelande, and wiped his sweaty forehead before delicately dabbing at his nose. Philippa had never seen such a thing before. People used their fingers, or their sleeve, mayhap a piece of rag. She glanced at her husband. By the sardonic smile twisting his lips she judged he considered the carrying of a hand kerchief unmanly. And so must everyone else, for this innovation of Richard's had not caught on.

Philippa still had sympathy for the King, but she no longer felt deeply indignant at his humiliation. By all accounts, and by what she herself had observed, he deserved no less, anointed Sovereign or not.

She gnawed the last piece of flesh from the leg of a pheasant and licked her fingers. "The King does not appear to be hungry," she remarked to Giles, who was busy dealing with the remnants of a haunch of venison.

Giles glanced to where the King sat, staring morosely at a trencher laden with meat. "The food is not to his liking," he told her with a shrug. "He prefers his meat ground and spiced, mixed with wine and sugar. 'Tis then fit only to be eaten with a spoon. The cooks here are not accustomed to his tastes."

"And have not been instructed to accommodate them," observed Philippa. "Giles, what will become of him?"

He shot her a sharp glance. "What should happen to him?" he demanded. "He will remain King."

"Will he? Have you not noticed, he is virtually a prisoner? Henry has him in his power."

"But Henry means him no ill," affirmed Giles stoutly. Then he shrugged again. "The only problem is, can he trust his cousin to keep his word? At the slightest sign of Richard's wishing to renege..." He let the sentence die, a deep frown between his golden-tipped brows.

"The King will find himself without a throne."

Giles opened his mouth and immediately compressed his lips over the sharp reprimand. "Do not even think such a thing, Pippa!" he urged, looking round apprehensively to make sure no one else had heard his too astute wife voice thoughts best left unspoken. "Who would succeed? Richard named the Earl of March, as grandson of his eldest uncle, although Mortimer's descent was through his mother. But he is dead, his son but a child…''

''And can hardly be looked upon as a desirable monarch,'' Philippa finished for him. ''But Henry…? Next in the direct male line—?''

''Shush! Enough, Philippa! What are you saying? Mind your tongue lest you speak treason!''

Giles's voice was low and harsh. He glared at her, his eyes hot with suppressed anger. And anxiety.

It was Philippa's turn to shrug now. ''I but repeat what others say,'' she told her irate and worried husband unrepentantly. But she kept her voice to a murmur, so that it would not carry to others sharing their board.

''Pippa!'' exclaimed Giles in exasperation. ''What am I to do with you? You must not listen, must not gossip…''

''You could send me home,'' she suggested, the picture of innocence, her dark eyes narrowed seductively to linger on his.

Giles was forced into a chuckle. Saucy wench! ''Where I am unable to keep an eye on you? Never, sweetheart!'' he returned, equally innocent. But his eyes flirted with hers.

Darkness had fallen. With it had come the ladies of the night, flitting from pavilion to pavilion in the intermittent flare of scattered torches. They no longer troubled Giles.

Philippa grinned with satisfaction at the thought as

she threaded her way back to their tent to prepare for the night. Giles was still closeted with Henry, but had promised not to be long. She hummed softly under her breath as she walked, Ida a step or two behind. She never wandered the camps alone now. One bad experience was more than enough.

When a man's voice came from the darkness to accost her, she therefore jumped with both apprehension and surprise. Ida was beside her in an instant.

"Who is it? What do you want?" she demanded, keeping her voice crisp and authoritative despite its attempt to squeak.

"Pippa!"

Her name was repeated, and she belatedly registered what had been said before. Few people called her Pippa. And the voice was familiar!

"Roger?" she gasped. "What do you here? Have you joined Bolingbroke—?"

Her brother stepped from behind the sheltering pavilion, and Philippa saw that he wore a plain black jupon, the distinctive green lozenge of Alban, even his badge—the alban knot, twisted into a fancy capital "A"—missing from his clothing. Her nerves tensed as she realised the implication. She felt slightly sick.

"Roger?" she repeated.

"I'm glad to see you well, sister. Mary told me how d'Evreux pursued you in order to carry you off on his traitorous errand. Like so many others, I have joined Bolingbroke's truimphal procession." His voice dripped scorn. "They allowed me entry here because I am a knight, though no one knows my true identity. I am come to see you."

"To see me?" Philippa grasped at the one sensible thing he had said.

"Aye, sister. I need your help."

"What for?" asked Philippa apprehensively.

"To get a message to the King. You must be able to reach a page with access to him. Give him this."

He held out a small piece of parchment. Philippa eyed it as though it were a viper. "What is it?"

"A warning of our plan to rescue him from his captors." He suddenly realised that she had thrust her hands firmly behind her back. "Here, take it," he ordered brusquely.

"No."

"Now see here, Pippa—"

"No, *you* see here, Roger." She gulped down a bolstering breath and prepared to defy the brother she had respected and somewhat feared all her life. Roger could be frightening in a temper. And, by the look of his square face, the beard at his chin silhouetted against a torch and wagging in outraged aggression, his spleen was rising fast. "I am wed now," she told him firmly. "My first duty is to my wedded lord. I cannot go against his wishes. I cannot do as you ask. I am no spy."

"Would you desert your King? Your father and brother?" demanded Roger bitterly. "Why so? Do you love the churl who forced you to marry him?"

"That," shot back Philippa, ignoring the thrust of some new, agonising sensation in her chest, "has naught to do with anything! 'Tis the law. And besides," she added more quietly, "'tis dangerous to attempt to help the King. You would do well to return to your family, Roger, and let affairs of state take their course."

"I never thought to hear such words from you, Philippa," said Roger harshly. "It seems I needs must find some other way to deliever my message. But make no mistake. Deliver it I will. And if a warning is given," he added menacingly, "I shall know who gave it. I shall know how to revenge your disloyalty, sister."

Philippa brought her hands round and clasped her arms across her chest. Her teeth had begun to chatter, and she clamped them tightly shut. She felt as though she were being torn in two. She did not want to deny her brother, yet she wanted no part in his plots. She did not want to betray him, either, could not. Yet to keep silent over what she knew would amount to betrayal of Henry's cause, which was also her husband's...But she had no choice.

"I will not speak of this. Neither will Ida," she told Roger d'Alban at last. "But do not let me see you here again, or riding in Henry's train, or I may change my mind. Go, Roger. Leave Henry's army, for here you are a spy."

"I'll go, readily enough, once I have found the means to deliver my note. I will see you anon, sister.

I shall ask the King to be lenient with you. I know you do but follow d'Evreux's lead.''

Philippa lifted her stubborn chin. "And I pray you will not have to lay your head on the block, Roger," she retorted tartly. "Your attempt at resistance is useless, pathetic. Cannot you see that all the great lords of the realm are behind Bolingbroke? Richard threatens them all with his imperious, extravagant ways, and it will take more than your puny efforts to overthrow so many powerful men.''

Roger made a harsh sound in his throat. "It seems my sister has become tainted by the company she keeps! I never expected to hear such cowardly, traitorous views from a d'Alban.''

"Not traitorous," whispered Philippa, "nor cowardly, but sensible. I have had time to think these last weeks." Despite her best efforts her voice broke, and she began to plead with her headstrong brother. "Think, Roger! Think of the consequences if you are taken! Remember Mary and the children—''

"Enough, sister! Would you make a coward of me, too? I pray you to remember our father, who lies stricken—''

"Stricken still?" Philippa gulped. "But Giles has received reports of his recovery—when did you last see our sire?''

"When he was taken from Alban Castle by litter. I kept my eye on things there until the family left, then followed them and their escort to Fishacre. I managed a brief word with my wife before I set about gathering a force of men with loyal hearts who were willing to fight for their King.''

''Then you do not know that he is making a good recovery!'' exclaimed Philippa in relief. ''His speech is slurred and he cannot use his left hand, but otherwise he is almost fit again!''

She saw her brother's shoulders move in a shrug. ''That is as may be. But the Earl our father would have challenged Bolingbroke, and I must do likewise.''

''Did you raise a force?'' asked Philippa faintly. There seemed no arguing with him.

''A small one, sufficient for our purpose. But I waste time, and I believe your husband comes. Farewell, sister.''

He was gone. Dissolved into the shadows like a wraith. Philippa could hardly believe he had been there, except for the new pain in her heart. Deservedly or not, she was now branded traitor by her sibling. And by her father, too, if and when he found out about her change of heart.

Chapter Nine

"**W**ho was that? Was someone bothering you?"

Philippa jumped guiltily. Giles's sharp tones brought her back to an uncomfortable reality. She had to cover for her brother.

"No one," she answered, turning quickly to meet her husband, moving away from the place where Roger had disappeared. "Just a groom searching for his master. He wasn't bothering me."

Giles's eyes glittered in the darkness and he took her arm in a firm though gentle grip. "Come, let us seek our pavilion." His voice held a degree of barely suppressed annoyance. "I would have thought you had learnt not to wander the camp at night, my lady."

Philippa realised that his manner cloaked concern, but nevertheless resented his tone. "I had Ida with me!" she flared.

"Aye, so you did." Much of the tension she sensed in his body went, but she knew his eyes were searching her face in the gloom. She suffered his scrutiny as calmly as she could. It was difficult not to show her feeling of guilt. But he seemed satisfied. He dropped her arm to drape his own around her shoulders. "I worry too much, my sweet," he admitted, pulling her to him, "but I want no repeat of that cursed incident when your hound was killed."

Philippa relaxed in the haven of his hold. "Nor I!" she assured him, in such heartfelt tones that he chuckled.

"Dismiss Ida," he whispered.

In their pavilion, by the light of the guttering candle in the horn lantern, he turned her to face him, his expression intent but gentle. He brushed the back of his hand across her flushed cheek, then let his fingers slide round to bury themselves in the escaping tendrils of hair at the nape of her neck. His other hand dealt with her circlet and the pins holding her braids in elongated coils on either side of her face. When they hung free and he had teased the plaits out with his long, deft fingers, he drew a deep, unsteady breath and moved to undo the large carved wood buttons fastening her cote-hardie.

Philippa began to tremble. He had never wooed her in quite this way before. He had always prepared for bed elsewhere, with Wat to attend him, arriving in their pavilion after Ida had left, and she waiting naked in their bed. But now his every move, nay, his very nearness, brought with it a new, tingling awareness. He had only to look at her with that special light in his darkened blue-grey eyes for her knees to melt, her breathing to become difficult...

But why? His touch was by now familiar, his close presence an admitted source of pleasure. He had regarded her in similar fashion before. Why, then, should she suddenly begin to tremble like the virgin she no longer was, to weaken and melt, wanting to lose herself in the body of this man who was her husband?

She knew why. Her brother's casual shaft had struck a target she had not known existed. The pain in her chest clutched at her heart anew. She loved Giles d'Evreux.

But she could not! Despite her new understanding of all he stood for, still he had neglected her for years, caused her father to act in a way that had brought about his illness, had carried her off by force to a reluctant marriage. And had used her ill that first night.

She stiffened in his hold. Giles, lost in the exquisite joy of at last making real and leisurely love to his wife, felt the rejection and jerked his gold-streaked head from the thyme-scented warmth of her neck, where he had buried his seeking lips. His arms tightened round her like clamps. "Pippa?" he demanded.

She felt the steely strength, the hard possession, heard the sudden arrogance in his voice. And realised something that until then had remained a mystery to her. Since that dreadful night when she had almost killed a man and Spot had died, Giles had shown her nothing but gentleness. Strength, yes. Determination to protect, to possess, yes. But force, hurtful mastery, no.

Yet now... She could feel the beginnings of that intolerant tension in him which would call forth the domineering male. And she was bringing it upon herself. As she had brought it on her bridal night.

The shock of understanding was like falling into cold water. She had evoked some primitive emotion in him which even Isobel had known to be alien. She realised now that she could not deny the desire he had for her without rousing the other, demanding side of his nature. He was too chivalrous, too self-controlled, too nice a man to do her real physical harm. To beat his wife into submission as other men thought it their right to do. But she would be hurt just the same. Because she did not want to be taken in anything other than love.

But that was stupid! She did *not* love Giles d'Evreux! And if she did not love him, then to be taken with tender strength and passion must be what her body and heart desired. She could not deny her husband. Because to do so would be intolerable; she wanted him too desperately.

She shut her eyes to avoid the growing anger in his, and let herself relax. A smile spread across her face, springing from the wells of...of affection...and desire buried deep within. She sighed, and rested her cheek against the cool texture of his satin cote-hardie.

"Nothing," she murmured. And then, with unconscious pleading, "Love me, my husband."

Giles groaned, crushed her slight frame against his chest, hurting yet not hurting, thrust a muscular thigh between hers so that she could feel his hard body pressing against the entire length of hers. "What else do you think I am doing, woman?" he demanded huskily.

Philippa giggled. Reaction from all her secret meditation set in. She did not want to think, only to feel. "You are being terribly slow," she teased, echoing yet not echoing that disastrous demand of their first night.

Her fingers went to the wrought-silver buttons decorating the front of his cote-hardie and began to tease them open. In deference to the temperature he wore no tunic beneath. She felt him catch his breath as she slipped her arms inside the opened garment, revelling in the warm strength of his body, which the thin chaisel shirt did little to shield from her touch. "You have fewer layers than I," she murmured, running her exploring fingers over the bunched muscles of his back.

"Pippa!" groaned Giles. "Stop that, my love, or we'll never reach the pallet!"

She realised the truth of his protest as his body hardened against her stomach, potent with his masculinity despite the layers of clothing still separating them.

"Then let us disrobe at once!" she suggested demurely, releasing him and preparing to step back.

But Giles was not ready for that yet. He let her go, but only so that he could frame her flushed face in his hands. He gazed deeply into her dark eyes, black in the dim light of the lantern, yet full of an emotion he had not seen in them before. He could scarcely believe it! And that secret, seductive smile which had so thrown him earlier! It seemed that his reluctant bride desired him at last!

He heaved in a great breath. Triumph, laced liberally with unbelievable tenderness, welled up in Giles. His dearest wish was about to be realised! This night he would hold a willing and responsive wife in his arms.

But, however much she teased him, he must not hurry. He must woo her anew, rouse the romantic, passionate nature he knew had lain dormant too long in his bride. And the fault had been his. That she had resisted him so long was understandable. She had fought with the same passion he hoped she would now bring to her loving.

He drew another steadying breath. God's blood! 'Twas difficult to leash his need! He had never desired a woman more. His lips descended slowly, tender and teasing before they firmed into demand, clinging to hers, the only contact between them apart from the whisper of his fingers as he drew off her over-garment and began to unlace the ties down the back of her gown. He stroked it from her shoulders, but could not remove it entirely, because her sleeves were buttoned too tightly.

Reluctantly, he took his lips from hers while he dealt with the offending fastenings. While he was working on one arm, Philippa used the other to tug at the strings on his braies, pushing the loosened garment down over his hips. She did not question where her courage, where the instinct to use her hands to discover him, came from. It was just there, in every nerve, every sinew of her quivering body.

Giles shuddered as her fingers touched him. With a protesting groan he caught at her hand and began to unbutton that sleeve. Philippa used the arm he had just freed to drag the cote-hardie from his shoulders.

"Patience, my love!" he muttered hoarsely. "How can I deal with your buttons with my arms tied up?" He stopped work for a moment while he flung off the garment and kicked off his braies, and with them the hose tied to them and his pointed shoes. His shirt followed, landing on the pile of other discarded clothing, a white marker on the turf.

He really was magnificent. Instead of shyly averting her eyes, Philippa gazed boldly at the figure of her husband, admiring the breadth of his shoulders, the narrowness of his waist, the flatness of his stomach, the strength of his thighs. There was scarce a grain of surplus flesh on him; she could count his ribs, an she tried. She reached out to trace the rippling lines spreading from his breastbone, and Giles moaned as he undid the last button and eased the kirtle from her body. Her undergarment was an altogether simpler matter to remove. He lifted the embroidered hem over her head, and threw the finely embroidered linen smock down on the growing mountain of their clothes.

Now she, too, was naked—apart from her pale saffron hose, kept up above her knees by blue ribbon garters. Reverently, he pulled the ends of the bows and slid the stretchy silken material down over her ankles and feet, taking her shoes with it.

Then he simply stood and looked. And she looked back.

"Well, wife."

He was having difficulty in speaking. Philippa opened her mouth, but no sound came. Her throat was parched as a brook in a drought.

But she had no need to say anything. Giles drew their naked bodies together, and held her fast. She could hear the thunder of his heart under her ear, echoing the pounding in her own chest. His desire pulsed against her stomach as his mouth caressed her ear and his tongue explored the intricate contours of the orifice. She shuddered, and found his small, hard nipple, almost lost in its bed of fine hair, and teased it with her fingers, making Giles jerk and suck in a breath like someone gasping for air.

He tore his mouth away and reached up to pinch out the candle in the horn lantern. Darkness enveloped them. Philippa became aware of the background sounds of the camp: the carrying voices, the occasional guffaw of lusty laughter, the clank of armour, the sweet notes of a pipe, the distant shrill of a horse's neigh.

Then everything outside their two selves was forgotten again as Giles ran his hands over her, caressing her shoulders, cupping her breasts and brushing their peaks with tantalising delicacy. Finding the hollow of her slender waist, his hands lingered a while, before travelling over her hips to mould her small buttocks in their palms.

She let her hands wander, too. She marvelled that she had never wanted to touch like this before. She had been content to take. Tonight, she wanted to discover every hidden secret of his beautiful body, to give him the pleasure he was giving her. She slid her fingers along his backbone, feeling the bumps of his vertebrae, up to those wide shoulders, down past the narrowing at his waist to the tight, lean flanks until she held him as he held her.

Mouth to mouth, chest to breast, thigh to thigh, they stood savouring each other's perfection, their breathing fast and uneven. Philippa was drowning in new sensations, Giles wondering how he had ever found pleasure in any other woman. He kept a clear head by sheer strength of will. He must not hurry. Must not frighten away this new and oh, so exquisite response.

He rubbed himself against her, renewing her knowledge of his desire. Then, gently, he lowered their bodies to the pallet. The night was warm, even sticky. They had no need of coverings. His eyes had become used to the darkness; he could feast his eyes on her delectable figure. He began a slow, arousing exploration with fingers, lips and tongue and, to his delight, his wife responded with sweet caresses of her own. She seemed to know instinctively what would please him. But, when she formed a sheath with her hand and held him *there*, he was forced to call a temporary halt. He could not delay much longer. He probed with his fingers and found her ready. But the instinctive arching of her hips had already told him that.

"Sweet wife," he murmured, and slid inside her warmth.

Philippa thought she would shatter into small pieces as the shimmering waves of sensation rippled through her body. She held him fiercely, twining her arms and legs around him so that he should not escape. The waves were just receding when he began to move. She moaned and cried out, thrusting her hips up to meet him, demanding...demanding...

And Giles did not let her down. Not until he felt her muscles contract, felt the shudders begin, did he allow himself release.

Philippa knew she must be dying, floating upwards to the azure heavens above the clouds, and Giles must be dying too, for she was just barely conscious of his racked body and the muffled groans which sounded like pain and anguish...

But were ecstasy.

Philippa's mind rejoined her lax and sated body to find her lord sprawled over her, the groans diminished into harsh breathing and the spasms reduced to occasional shudders. He was still inside her. She tightened her arms and legs around him with renewed strength, determined to keep him there for as long as possible. And smothered his shoulder with hot, tender kisses. She knew she had given him more pleasure than ever before. And, in return, had received it.

Giles lay very still, caught in the tendrils of his wife's allure. He could not have moved, even had she not entwined herself around him as though she were the ivy to his oak.

The simile disturbed him somewhat, for ivy eventually killed the tree it wound itself about. He must not allow himself to become so bound by this woman's seduction that he forgot duty, neglected prudence, was led into actions he would later regret. He must remember that she still regarded him as a traitor.

The following day most of the nobles and knights proposed to go hunting while Henry attended to his business. Breakfast was over, and they were already mounting up.

"You wished to go on the mere, I believe?" smiled Giles.

"Aye, but are you not hunting?" asked Philippa doubtfully.

"Nay, love, I can do that any time—unless you would prefer to join the chase?"

"Oh, no! I do not like hunting, even though it is for meat. I hate to see any wild creature killed."

"Then let us take a boat out on the water." He grinned, expansive and content after the delights of the night. "We will count today a bridal day, my love."

Philippa blushed, knowing why he had chosen that day to be alone with his bride. Until last night they had not been truly one flesh.

"Do we go now?" she asked.

Giles studied the sky from an east-facing window of the Hall. The sun had risen enough to throw its rays across the surface of the water, spangling the breeze-ruffled surface with gold.

"Why not? If it is not warm enough we can always come back and try again after dinner, when the sun will have gained its strength."

"We can wear mantles," suggested Philippa eagerly.

"Aye, 'twill be as well. Come, then, and I will try to borrow a fishing net. Unless you object to killing fish?" he asked teasingly.

"Oh, but I shall not kill it if I catch one," protested Philippa. "You can do that!"

"You eat meat and fish willingly enough." Giles pursued his train of thought with some determination. This was a facet of his wife's nature he had not appreciated.

"Well, 'tis natural. Man has always eaten the flesh

God provides. 'Tis just that I cannot bear to see the killing.''

"So you allow others to do it for you!" he scoffed.

"Aye, those who do not mind. But I snare conies and net fish at home." Home? Alban was no longer her home. Philippa thrust the momentary chill of that thought aside more easily than she would have believed possible only days ago. "I would kill if I were starving or threatened," she admitted defensively. "I think I have proved that!" she added, remembering with a shudder that she had been willing enough to kill a man who attacked her.

Giles chuckled. "You do not make sense, my sweet."

"I do! Men do not like seeing babies born, but they are willing enough to beget them!"

"'Tis women's work to deliver their issue!"

"As providing meat is men's!"

For a moment Giles looked quite struck. Then his features warmed into a beautiful smile that turned Philippa's heart in her chest. His eyes danced, his shapely lips parted to reveal those slightly crooked teeth as he pulled her hard against his side. "Your logic is unanswerable, my sweet," he admitted cheerfully, planting a quick kiss on the tip of her nose.

Having obtained a net and the use of a small rowing boat, they passed to the water's edge through a small doorway near the gate-tower which led to the causeway. Since the latter doubled as a tilt yard, it was even then being used by several knights to practise their skills. The sound of thundering hoofs and splintering wood echoed across the expanse of the mere.

While a churl held it steady, Giles helped Philippa to step aboard the flimsy vessel. She held bunches of her voluminous azure skirts in one hand and gripped his steadying fingers tightly with the other. She sat quickly on a thwart near the stern, while Giles took his place facing her, and bundled his mantle on the tiny bow thwart before pushing off with one of the oars. Manoeuvring expertly, he soon had the boat pointing the way they wanted to go, and then moved it through the water with strong, steady strokes.

Philippa couldn't help admiring the play of his shoulder and arm muscles, clearly visible through the fine material of his close-fitting tunic. Or the movement of thighs straining against the confines of azure tights. Her stomach tightened as she remembered the feel of his flesh against hers. Last night had been heaven—or almost heaven. If only he loved her...But that was a foolish, romantic dream fit only for a minstrel's tale. Though it did happen. Even Giles admitted that.

But he hadn't said he loved her. So love hadn't grown for him. And her own notion that she loved him was surely born of that same romantic folly. She had already decided that for her to fall in love with him was an impossibility.

The sun rose higher in the sky, hot and bright. Philippa cast off her mantle and dipped a finger in the passing water. The sleeve of her gown caught a ripple, and she brought it out, dripping wet. She shook it, gurgling with delighted laughter, then dipped her whole hand, sleeve and all, into the cool depths.

"This reminds me of my school days at Evesham," she told Giles happily. "The nuns used to watch while we paddled in the river. Some of the younger ones, and the novices, paddled too. I always enjoyed those afternoons."

"Did you swim?" asked Giles with interest, imagining a clutch of nubile maidens sporting in the water.

"Nay! 'Twas not allowed. So I did not learn. Can you swim?"

He grinned. "Oh, yes. So you are quite safe. I'll save you if you fall in."

"I thank you, but I shall not fall in!" asserted Philippa firmly.

Giles made a circuit of the lake, and finished in the middle. He shipped his oars and let the boat drift. "Methinks this will do. Have you seen any fish?"

Philippa peered into the somewhat weedy and murky depths, and shrugged. "No. But they must be there."

"Here, take the net and try."

Philippa shifted, and the boat rocked alarmingly. But she grasped the long handle he held out to her, and leaned over the side, dipping the mesh into the water, and scooping. Giles watched, amused.

Suddenly Philippa squealed in delight. "There are fish! I saw one!"

She began trawling with even more enthusiasm. And caught something heavy. She leapt up to heave it in, and went sprawling over the side of the boat, landing in the water with a mighty splash.

Giles, left alone in a wildly rocking boat, was quick to react. He knelt in the bilge-water and leaned over the side, ready to offer his hand the moment Philippa's head bobbed up again. She clutched thankfully at rescue, spluttering the water from her nose and mouth, blinking it from her eyes.

"I thought you weren't going to fall in," he accused, his eyes dancing blue delight.

"I didn't intend to," gasped Philippa. "Giles, help me out!"

"You'll fill the boat with water," he objected.

"Wretch! Giles, my clothes are dragging me down, and I'm getting cold!"

He pursed his lips and reached for the painter with his free hand. "Here you are. Hold on to this rope and I'll tow you in."

"Giles!" she wailed. "You wouldn't!"

"Why not?" he enquired blandly. "You'll be quite safe." He offered her the rope again.

But Philippa wrapped her chilling fingers round his wrist and clung on for dear life. She knew he didn't mean it, and yet... There was that mischievous look in his eye...He might...

Tears gathered and, instead of cold pond water, warm moisture washed down her cheeks. She stifled a sob. "Please? Giles?"

He relented abruptly. He hadn't meant to make her cry. But the impulse to tease had been irresistible.

"Don't cry, my love!" Contrition made his voice husky. He offered his other hand.

Philippa grasped it, and he heaved. The boat rocked again and almost tipped up, but she was safely in, sprawling in a dripping azure mess in the bottom. Giles wrapped her mantle about her and smoothed the sodden hair from her eyes, removing several fronds of weed in the process. He grinned. "Stay where you are, love. I'll row back as quickly as I can."

Philippa lay where she had landed, in abject misery. She knew she had made a fool of herself. Giles was laughing at her, God rot his soul! And she was cold to the bone.

Good as his word, Giles made the bank in moments, though it seemed an age to Philippa. The churl helped her out, and whined over the loss of the net, which she gathered he would have to replace. Giles promised to pay for it. Then he scooped her up in his arms and carried her back to their pavilion.

He waved aside Ida's twittering concern. "Just find a large dry towel," he ordered brusquely.

He was almost as wet as Philippa. He stripped off her clothes, knowledgeable now about the intricacies of her dress, and swathed her in the soft linen cloth. Then he threw off his own wet things. Philippa's teeth were chattering. Part cold, part shock, part resentment. Giles began to rub warmth back into her limbs, first of all briskly, but as her chill abated so his touch gentled until the act of drying became an erotic massage. She forgot her resentment.

His own body had dried while he worked on hers. He threw the towel aside and lifted an uresisting Philippa into his arms.

"Bed," he decreed, his voice husky. "That will warm you up."

He laid her on their pallet, and threw a light covering over her. Then stretched out beside her, and drew it over himself.

He gathered her to him, burying his nose in the damp hair spread over the pillows. "You smell of pond weed," he told her with a soft chuckle.

Philippa knew she would not remain cold for much longer. But it was not the blanket which would produce the warmth...

Chapter Ten

When the journey resumed the next day Philippa could not prevent a certain nervousness. Hiding it proved an effort. She had seen no sign of her brother since he had disappeared into the darkness, and had successfully managed to forget him during the previous lovely, eventful day; but now she remembered again. He would not be far away.

Plotting.

So what would he do? What *could* he do, without a huge army? Mount a diversionary attack while the King escaped? Try to reach the King at night and spirit him away? Either possibility seemed doomed to failure. But, knowing him as she did, she was certain of one thing. He would not be deterred. So Philippa travelled a prey to apprehension and torn loyalties.

She could not give Roger away. She had promised. Yet she felt guilty at not warning Giles of a possible attempt to free the King, who, although still treated with the greatest reverence and respect, was now quite openly regarded as a traitor to England and its people.

But nothing happened. For days the progress continued without major incident. Philippa relaxed. Mayhap Roger had thought better of his intention after all.

Then, suddenly, some few miles north of St Albans, her worst fears were realised. Out of the blue came the Alban war cry, and a tight body of armed horsemen charged ponderously from the cover of a copse, scattering grazing sheep and cattle as, in a welter of flying turf, they headed across the wide swath of green fringing the highway, cutting straight for the point in the column where the King's standard flew.

Philippa gasped, her shock all the greater for her having been lulled into a false sense of security by Roger's lengthy delay. She glanced quickly in Richard's direction, and caught a glimpse of him between the heads of his mounted guard, attempting to wheel his horse towards the commotion, his face grim and determined. Roger's message had got through. Richard had known what to expect, and when.

While Philippa sat stunned with dismay, Giles reacted instantly. "To d'Evreux!" he roared, and wheeled Majesty from the column.

No one had seriously expected a challenge at this late stage. Roger had behaved with unexpected caution and deviousness. No word of any planned resistance had reached Henry's ears. Lacking the warning she could have given, Giles was only lightly armoured.

Sir Malcolm and Sir William shouted orders, and all the d'Evreux command swept aside. Except Walter Instow, who, cursing loudly, found himself trapped on the far side of Philippa's and Ida's mounts.

The King's guard, far from being diverted, closed in about Richard. His desperate attempt to force his way past the barrier of men and horseflesh failed.

Giles pounded Majesty at an angle towards the approaching attackers. The open swath between highway and screening trees, more than an arrow's flight in width, was maintained by law to prevent ambush. Roger had had no choice but to risk an open charge. He rode at the head of the King's would-be rescuers, his surcoat proclaiming his identity for all to see. He was armoured cap-à-pie, and armed to the teeth. The two men would clash at any moment, and Giles was vulnerable.

Wat had managed to wheel his horse about and pass behind her as space was made by the departure of others. Philippa woke from her momentary trance as he whooped past. There was no time to think. It had all happened in the space of less than ten heartbeats. She dug her heels into the gelding's flanks and put him into a mad gallop which might just overtake Giles before he reached Roger. Majesty was slow and ponderous, heavily laden, Blaze fleet of foot and with only her slight weight to carry.

She had to stop the two men meeting. Had to turn Roger aside and protect Giles. It was her fault he was in danger. She was gaining. But other horsemen were in the way.

Frustration ousted deadly fear until she spotted a gap between two heavy horses and put Blaze through it. Now she was streaking up on the outside, could see Roger clearly, lance aimed straight at Giles. Wat had been carrying Giles's lance, and shields were used only in the joust. Giles had only a sword with which to defend himself.

Fear clutched anew at her stomach, threatened to paralyse her breathing, but she managed to find enough breath from somewhere to shriek at her brother.

"Roger!" she screamed, "Desist! Flee!"

All Giles saw as she shot past was streaming black hair, come loose from its braids, and billowing green sendal. He heard her shriek her brother's name. Whatever it was she was trying to do, she was succeeding in getting in the way and putting herself in danger. And then he had no more time to worry because as she drew level, with her brother only yards away, she jerked Blaze's head round and charged straight in front of Majesty, who, war-trained though he was, shied and almost threw his exasperated, furious rider. The little whore! She had tried to unseat him, to render him helpless before her cursed brother!

Roger, seeing his sister riding straight in front of his levelled lance, swerved violently aside, emitting a heartfelt curse and throwing his following train into confusion. And then they were surrounded by a large section of Bolingbroke's army, led by d'Evreux's men.

It was no contest. The small force of attackers had relied on surprise to spring the King from his human prison cell, so that he could join them and together they could flee, ensuring his escape. The plan had failed and, although some fighting ensued and some of the men evaded immediate arrest, only to be chased over the fields by screaming hordes of Henry's forces, Roger and most of his supporters were captured.

Philippa sat on Blaze's back, weak and shaking, sweating and blowing almost as much as her mount. She had prevented disaster. Giles was safe. But Roger was captured. She didn't want to think what the penalty for his rash behaviour might be. Or why, when forced to choose, she had saved Giles and delivered her brother into his enemies' hands.

Though she had tried to save him, too. Told him to retreat. Had warned him in the first place not to attempt the impossible. He would have been caught whether she had intervened or not. The thought did little to console her uneasy conscience.

She became aware that she was surrounded by horse-soldiers. Lifting her drooping head, she met Giles's gaze. He sat erect on Majesty's highly deco-rated fighting saddle, staring at her with an expression she could not fathom. Philippa tried a smile, though relief and confusion made it waver, and the ice she saw in Giles's eyes wiped it completely from her face.

had dried, and, though creased and somewhat shrunk, was cleaner than the one she had just removed, and did still fit. With her hair tidied, Philippa began to feel better. This nightmare could not last! The truth must become clear before long. No one had questioned her yet, but she was bound to be interrogated. Surely they would believe her when she told them that she had not intended to aid her brother, but her husband?

"Ida," she wondered, "will they believe me?"

"Believe what, my lady?"

"Why, that I did not intend harm to Henry's cause! That I was but trying to protect Giles! Roger would have killed him!"

Ida's face relaxed. "Is that what you were doing, my lamb? 'Twas difficult to make out what you intended, it all happened so quickly!"

"Ida! You did not think I was aiding Roger?"

"Well, it did look like it. And he is your brother."

"Oh, Ida! How could you think such a thing? How could Giles? He knows I lo—I like him, have forgiven him his high-handed treatment of me! God knows, I wish him no harm!" Quite the reverse, in fact. She reluctantly acknowledged the fact that, if anything happened to her husband, life would scarcely be worth living.

Philippa sank down abruptly on the stool. When had she made that discovery? It must have been in the same instant she had plunged so recklessly to his aid. And caused nothing but chaos and heartbreak.

For Giles thought her still against him and his cause. Condemned and hated her.

Would he visit her? Surely he must! He could not abandon her entirely! She was his wife!

Aye, and looked likely to bring disgrace on the name of d'Evreux. He would never forgive her that.

Giles paced his chamber in the lodgings at Westminster Palace, prey to a completely alien indecision. There must be some other explanation for his wife's action! He simply could not believe that she had tried to have him killed, even in a misguided attempt to release the King. She had softened of late, been a willing partner in their delightful lovemaking. And surely she had come to see Richard for the unstable, extravagant despot he really was?

Was she what she seemed: an honest, impulsive child just emerging into rational, entrancing womanhood? Or a treacherous whore who would pretend a passion she did not feel in order to allay his suspicions while she plotted against him?

He really could not believe the latter. She had been virgin on their wedding night. And had fought long and hard against admitting to even her first childish liking, let alone the adult attraction which had flared between them on that first day at Alban. She did not have the experience to fool him into believing a pretended passion genuine.

So why had she intervened? To save her brother, mayhap? That could be. She felt strong family loyalty, for which he could hardly blame her. But now she was married to him—she owed *him* her first loyalty!

Northumberland had witnessed the incident and ordered her arrest. He himself had believed the worst at the time, and done nothing to protect his wife. But now? What did he believe? And surely he owed his wife the same loyalty he demanded from her?

He must talk with her. Resist the undoubted influence of her beauty and the memory of passion, and search out the truth. Only then could he sleep in peace.

He strode from the room and made haste to the river, where the royal barges were moored.

It was almost dusk. Philippa sat by the small window, watching the busy traffic still plying the river below. Little ships from the ends of the earth brought their merchandise to London, ships which looked neither strong nor large enough to venture out into the vastness of the ocean, which she could only imagine, because she had never seen it.

Giles had described the risky crossing from Boulogne to Pevensey, made in one of the small ships Henry had seized to carry his friends and the fifteen lances brought with him from France, and the subsequent trip north to Ravenspur on the Humber, where they had arrived on the fourth day of July. To make for the south coast had been a clever feint on Henry's part. William Scrope had led a royal force to

Dover to intercept the landing and, finding his quarry gone, had returned to St Albans to try to raise an army to cover the approach to London.

St Albans. Why had Roger gone there? He might have thought to rally support more easily in a town that bore his name. Mayhap it was some of the men Scrope had tried to raise that Roger had won to his side! Poor Roger. She dared not dwell upon his predicament; her own was bad enough. Resolutely, she turned her mind back to the train of events Giles had told her of, and which had led to the present confinement of the King.

Only when the Council had realised that Henry was making for the Severn and Wales had they ridden west, where three of them, including Scrope, had met their death.

Philippa shivered at the memory of that day, wishing she had not allowed her thoughts to travel that far. Yet she couldn't have stopped them, and tangled with the horror lingered the memory of the strength, the peace and comfort she had found in Giles's arms. And she had been so determined not to yield an inch to his persuasive charm!

She let out an unconscious sigh. If only he were here now. 'Twas getting late. He would not risk travelling the streets of London after dark. She nibbled fretfully at her thumb nail. He could read. If he did not come tomorrow, she would ask if she could write him a letter.

The daylight was fading fast. They would have to

light their single tallow candle soon. Not that either she or Ida had much to do that needed light. Ida had already done what she could to mend the once splendid new gown, so torn and tattered by the time Philippa had arrived at the Tower. But even a small glimmer of light would help to disperse some of the shadows in the room, shadows which seemed to invade her very heart.

She turned from the window with another sigh. Seeing so much activity going on all around only emphasised her own loss of freedom. People spent their whole lives in prison. Would she be left to moulder into an ancient crone, denied the right to life and love and children? She had begun to bleed again that day. So she was not yet pregnant. She did not know whether to be glad or sorry. They might not behead her if was with child. Yet to bring a child into the world in captivity—that was unthinkable. So mayhap 'twas as well she was not yet carrying the heir Giles would have cherished.

How long she sat in the twilight, sunk in her gloomy thoughts, she did not know. When she glanced out of the window she could see the lanterns gliding across the water of the Thames. The echoing sound of roars and other strange cries from the Royal Menagerie, housed somewhere in the Tower, did little to calm her frayed nerves.

Ida's soft voice broke into her reverie. "Shall I light the candle, my lady?"

Philippa stirred. "Aye, 'twill seem less dismal

with a little light. Poor Ida! What have I brought you to? But you are a free woman. If you wish to leave me to join your lover I shall not ask you to stay.''

"Leave you in trouble, my lamb?'' Ida looked up from striking flint against steel to fix Philippa with an indignant eye. "Of course I will stay! You will not be here for long, you mark my words. Sir Giles will not allow it! Then, mayhap, when you are settled with him and his family, I will seek to join Wolfram Root in Northumberland. He has asked me to be his wife. He is widowed, and his three young children need a woman's hand.''

"And besides, you like him,'' smiled Philippa, cheered by her tiring-woman's happiness despite her own predicament. "Did you not accept him when he asked?''

"I told him I would consider his offer. I did not know whether you would object to my leaving you, my lady.''

"To find your own happiness? Of course not, Ida. If that is what you truly want, you must get word to him, so that he does not leave London not knowing your intention.''

"Aye, though I doubt he can read. 'Twill have to be word of mouth I send.''

"I intend to ask if I can write to my husband. They cannot deny me that privilege. I will request him to send word to your Wolfram Root.''

"Thank you, my lady. 'Twould be a load off my mind.''

"Will the tinder not catch?" asked Philippa, noticing that Ida was still striking sparks without much success. "Let me try."

She jumped up with sudden energy, glad of something practical to do. She had taken only two steps towards the table where Ida was wrestling with the flint and steel when the key grated in the lock and the heavy door began to swing open. Light from a single candle threw a beam across the straw-strewn boards. A flickering glow spread upwards to light the Lieutenant's heavy jowl and ruddy face. He had a deep barrel of a chest and a throaty voice which went with his gross stature.

"You've a visitor," he announced gruffly, and stood back to let his companion past.

The candle flared as the men moved, and Philippa gave a glad cry as she recognised the tall figure who stepped from behind the Lieutenant. Her hands went out in an unconscious gesture of appeal.

"Giles!"

He took the candlestick from the Lieutenant's hand as he passed. "I shall have need of this. It seems the ladies have no light."

"There is a candle on the pricket," rumbled the Lieutenant sourly. "'Tis no fault of mine if 'tis not alight."

"Except that the tinder is damp!" put in Philippa with sudden spirit. Seeing Giles had brought back much of her lost confidence.

"Leave us," ordered Giles curtly. "And mayhap

you can find a place by the kitchen fire for Mistress Ida?''

''Aye, if that is what what your lordship desires. Come, mistress.''

Before obeying the man's summons, Ida looked a question at Philippa, who nodded. Ida bobbed a curtsy at Giles before the door closed behind her and the Lieutenant. The key turned again in the lock.

Before putting it down, Giles lit the candle on the pricket from the one he carried. The twin flames illuminated the small chamber with a golden glow, casting long, shifting shadows beyond everything their rays touched.

He stepped back, and turned to look at his wife. The moment he had entered the room he had been aware of little but her slight figure, clad in the crumpled azure of that mere-soaked kirtle. He needed no such reminder of that day to divert his purpose. His expression hardened as he scrutinised her pinched features.

Philippa stood where she had been when the door opened. Her husband had ignored her outstretched hands, had barely glanced in her direction.

But he was here. And now he *was* looking at her, searching her face as though he sought the answer to some worrying problem. She tried to reach him again, taking a step towards where he stood, though the chamber was so small that the distance separating them was not great. ''Giles, husband,'' she whispered.

"I am so thankful you have come. I had planned to ask to write to you..."

She couldn't see his face clearly in the flickering light, but enough to know it was set in harsh, forbidding lines. Gone was the amused lift of smiling lips, the quizzical quirk of a bushy brow, the warmth in laughter-filled, almost-blue eyes. Back had come the haughty lift of the brows, the ice-chilled stare of purely grey eyes, the grim, tight line of a compressed mouth. This was an angry man—the arrogant, domineering Giles who had met her rebellion in their early days. Her heart cried out for the generous, charming, passionate bridegroom of those nights—that day at Kenilworth.

Giles's lips were white. She saw his jaw muscles clench and unclench beneath his beard. "Why, Philippa?" he demanded urgently, "Why did you betray me?"

"But I did not!"

The cry came from her very soul and was echoed by the howl of some captive animal near by. She had had enough of pride, of torn loyalties. She cared not what happened to Roger; her brother had chosen his own path. She knew where she wanted to be. In her husband's arms. To find again the security and peace she had discovered there in the past.

"You say so? How can I believe you, my lady?"

"Ask Roger!" she appealed desperately. "He will tell you that I refused to aid him! He cursed me as loudly as you did when I came between you by the road!''

Giles eyed her sceptically. He had heard d'Alban using some choice language—had it been directed at his sister? ''Why, then, did you attempt to unseat me?'' he demanded, his frigid tone not one whit modified by her pleading.

''I did not! I know it looked like it—Ida said as much; but, oh, Giles, you must believe me! I did feel guilty, I admit that. I should have warned you that Roger was attempting a rescue, but he had made me promise not to! I could not break my word! So you were not prepared for his attack, and I thought he would kill you! You wore only your breastplate... I tried to save you,'' she finished miserably.

''Then why did you not say so at the time?'' His voice had softened, his face reflected his uncertainty. Philippa took heart.

''I was given little chance,'' she reminded him grimly. ''I was put under guard, and no one even asked me why I had done what I did. Even now, you are the first—''

''Henry had other, more important matters on his mind,'' snapped Giles. ''You are to be questioned to-morrow.''

Philippa swallowed. ''By whom?'' she got out.

''Northumberland. He saw the incident and ordered your arrest.''

''Sir Henry Percy.'' Philippa closed her eyes, picturing the tough, fierce northern Earl, and finding little comfort in the recollection. "He will not believe me."

"If you speak the truth he will. He is not an unreasonable man." Giles paused, then took that all-important pace which brought him close to her, so close that she could feel his body-warmth envelop her like a cloak. "Pippa." He lifted her chin, the steel of his fingers more gentle than she had expected. "Did you speak truth? Were you trying to stop Roger's lance?"

She lifted her eyes to meet his squarely. She imagined they had some blue in them again. "Aye," she affirmed. "I spoke truth. I refused to deliver a message to someone near enough to the King to pass it on. But the message got through. Richard was expecting the attack."

"Aye, I know. I wonder who—some page, I suppose, for reward…" Giles abandoned his speculation. Her large, dark, dark eyes shone up at him without guile. He knew suddenly that she was telling him the truth. Relief and anger surged through his body in a hot tide. He longed to clasp her to his breast, to kiss her until they were both dizzy. To shake her senseless. To thrash some sense into her addled brain.

He resisted all three of his conflicting impulses. "Well, lady," he bit out scornfully, "you might have deflected your brother's lance, but you have managed to embroil us both in a wasp's nest of trouble in the process! Did you think me incapable of defending myself?"

"I did not stop to think! Afterwards, I realised you were too experienced to fall to Roger's attack. But...all I knew was that I couldn't bear for you to die. Especially at my brother's hand."

Giles's heart knocked in his chest. She couldn't mean that she cared what happened to him? "So now we come to the nub of it!" he snorted. "'Twas Roger you wished to save from a charge of murder!"

"You twist what I say! I did not even think of that!" protested Philippa desperately. "Giles, sometimes I absolutely hate you! Can you not see that I am innocent of the charge Northumberland has brought against me?"

The lion roared into the silence before he shrugged and answered. "Mayhap," he admitted, "but my opinion is not what matters." Would Percy believe her? That was the important thing. Would Henry Bolingbroke, if Giles sought him out and told him the story? Once an accusation had been laid it was so cursedly difficult to disprove it. It was her word against what Percy thought he had seen... "Pippa," he went on fiercely, "you must stop behaving like some beardless youth. You are my wife!" he finished on a sigh of exasperation.

Philippa flinched as though he had struck her, and the fingers on her chin tightened. "I had begun to doubt you remembered that!" she shot back.

"Oh, I remember." He bent his head, and his lips claimed hers in a brief, hard kiss. "I will visit again on the morrow," he promised, then released her chin and, in the same flowing movement, rapped on the door with the hilt of his sword.

The guard must have been waiting just outside. The key turned, the door opened and Giles left without a backward glance, leaving the second candle behind. She had forgotten to ask him to deliver Ida's message. Never mind. There was always tomorrow.

Tomorrow. What would it bring? Hope of release or condemnation?

Whatever else, it would bring Giles. The ache in her heart, the depression bearing down her spirit, lifted slightly. Philippa stretched out on her pallet and, for the first time since her confinement, allowed her thoughts to roam over their brief marriage.

It hadn't been all grief. But if things went badly tomorrow, she might never know the full joy of being wife to Giles d'Evreux, the mother of his children.

When Ida returned she found her mistress lying with her face to the wall, weeping quietly.

Chapter Eleven

Giles paced the ante-room to Henry's chamber. He had sought audience half an hour since. Such a wait was unusual. Henry was normally quick to admit him to his presence.

Could Henry possibly suspect him of being in collusion with his wife? He had detected a slight remoteness in his liege-lord's manner over the last days. But surely he was the last man Henry Bolingbroke would suspect of treason against his cause? Had he not suffered exile for his lord's sake?

Curse Philippa and her scatter-brained attempt to prevent her brother's doing him an injury! If she had harmed his relationship with Henry Bolingbroke, then he could wish he had never gone to Alban Castle, let alone forced the wench into a marriage against her will.

Yet—he would not be unwed. He could not deny the attraction which had flared in him the moment he had set astonished eyes on his amazingly improved betrothed, standing defiantly in the courtyard of her home. Nor the way she had changed from spitting kitten to affectionate, purring cat, the outpouring of her passionate nature diverted into new channels under his tutelage. He had always liked cats, he mused. A wry twitch of a smile momentarily softened the grim set of his lips as he absorbed the aptness of the comparison. Infuriating, independent creatures!

The thought of her suffering twisted his gut. He halted abruptly, staring sightlessly at one of the brightly patterned heraldic shields hung on the wall. The mere hint that she might lose her life over this affair tore at something much deeper in his emotions, something he refused to acknowledge.

At that point in his cogitations the door opened and a groom of the bedchamber indicated that Giles could enter. It was late, and Henry was abed, though sitting up, propped on billowing pillows which reminded Giles uncomfortably of his nuptial couch.

"Giles! 'Tis good to see you!"

His greeting sounded sincere. "Your Grace." Giles bent his knee as he always did when entering Henry's presence. "I am grateful to you for granting me audience."

"Forgive my neglect of late." Henry made a wry grimace. "I have had weighty matters of state on my mind." He indicated the parchments scattered over the coverlet of the bed.

Giles nodded. "Aye, lord. The fate of this nation

rests on your shoulders. But I crave your attention on a personal matter for a few moments.''

"Doubtless the Lady Philippa, your wife," remarked Bolingbroke, his expression of wry regret replaced by a rather grim frown. "I confess her behaviour puzzles me."

"As it did me, my lord. But I have just spoken to her in the Tower—''

"Is she lodged comfortably? I have no desire for her to suffer unnecessarily. I did not see what passed, but Henry Percy is convinced she attempted to render you helpless before her brother's lance, and thus aid his attempted rescue of the King. Not that my cousin required rescuing," he added grimly. "An he is reasonable...But that is yet another matter. You have seen your wife, you say?"

"Aye, lord. And I am convinced that, although she acted rashly—I am learning that many of her actions are rash—'' Giles admitted ruefully, "she meant neither me nor your cause harm. She wished to prevent bloodshed between her brother and myself. A not unreasonable objective, I believe, though her manner of achieving it left much to be desired. And," he added with a gesture of lofty dismissal, "her concern was quite unnecessary." He paused to look Henry straight in the eye. "But I do not believe she deserves further punishment for her foolish action."

Henry peered at him from beneath knitted brows, and waved an enquiring hand. "What does Percy say?"

Giles shifted his stance. His spurs jangled in the quietness of the bedchamber. "I have yet to speak with him, lord. But I did visit Roger d'Alban before I left the Tower." He gave a mirthless laugh. "He is in a sullen and truculent mood. He greeted me with invective, which was directed as much against his sister as it was against me. He confirms that he attempted to enlist her help for his scheme, which she refused. And then inserted her person between himself and his target—which at that moment happened to be me."

Henry's face relaxed, and he broke into a chuckle. "Always in the van, eh, Giles?"

Giles responded with a quick smile before he went on quietly. "He considers himself justifiably incensed by his sister's behaviour. Had another led the counter-attack, I doubt my wife would have taken action. She vows she was afraid for my skin, and feeling guilt because she had not broken the promise of silence he had exacted from her and warned me of her brother's intention."

Henry gazed intently at his uneasy courtier for a moment. "Who does she support?" he rapped. "Richard, or me?"

"My lord, I do not think she actively supports either party. Richard is her anointed King, and her family has always been loyal to the throne. As have we all," he pointed out smoothly. "She has now had opportunity to study Richard, and knows you to have been sorely wronged. She is content to let you work things out between yourselves. But," went on Giles firmly, lifting a determined chin as though to challenge any possible rebuttal, "her first loyalty is owed to me, her husband." He stepped forward, and lifted Henry's capable hand from the parchment on which it rested. He knelt and carried it to his lips. "And my loyalty is yours," he affirmed quietly. "My wife will follow where I lead."

"Can you swear to that?" enquired Henry, a sardonic gleam of amusement in his eyes. "But I accept your allegiance gratefully; I have never for a moment doubted it. And I hear what you say. I will speak with Northumberland in the morning, before he leaves for the Tower. Your wife appears to be guilty of nothing but misplaced good intentions. She has a loyal heart, which should serve you well in the future."

"My lord, that is my hope."

"She will be freed. But—a certain amount of questioning, of uncertainty, may prove a salutary lesson to guide her future conduct. Do you not agree?"

Giles smiled his relief and sprang to his feet.

"Aye, and I thank you, Your Grace. You have my deepest gratitude."

"I am glad to see you happy in your union, Giles. Make sure you guard such felicity. I wasted my chance," Henry admitted with a sigh. "I wore my poor Mary de Bohun down with too much childbearing and too little companionship. Yet I loved her, and miss her now she is gone."

"You are in treaty to marry the daughter of the

Duc de Berry. Mayhap you will find new happiness there, lord.''

"Mayhap." Henry sounded doubtful. His would be a political alliance if it matured. "Thank God Mary was able to give me Harry and the other children, though I should have realised how frail she was, and desisted..." He sighed. "But young Harry will be here soon! I have seen too little of my son and heir over the past years. He must be grown almost to manhood! I pray I may have the opportunity to make up for my past deficiencies as a father!" He held out his hand. "Rest easy, Giles. Your wife will be safe with you on the morrow."

"I thank you again, lord." Giles took the proffered hand, and hesitated, reluctant to ask another favour, but knowing he had little choice. "I would like to take her straight to my parents, at Acklane, in Oxfordshire. Will you grant me a few days in which to make the journey and see her settled?"

"Aye, Giles. But do not delay too long. I fancy there will be much to do over the next few weeks before Parliament meets. Negotiations...changes in the highest offices of state... Richard must be made to right his wrongs. And I shall need all the support I can muster."

"You may rely on me, lord. I will make the journey with as much haste as possible."

"Then go in peace, my friend." Henry grinned, looking suddenly much younger. "And good luck in your affairs matrimonial!"

* * *

The inquisition was harsh. Philippa, summoned from her chamber to the presence of Henry Percy, Duke of Northumberland, hid her trembling hands in the crumpled folds of her azure kirtle and kept her chin high. She would *not* be intimidated! She had done nothing wrong! Except to act recklessly in defence of her husband.

Giles, hidden behind an arras, silently cheered his wife's courage, the common sense and honesty with which she countered Percy's persistent questioning. Had he not known that Henry Percy was merely putting on a show he might have trembled for his wife. Though she seemed to be holding her own. The old man's tone had softened despite himself.

Percy harrumphed. "So you do not support your brother, eh?" he enquired, in a voice which said he didn't believe her, and if he did she was wrong not to.

Philippa bristled at his tone. "I cannot support my brother against my husband! Believe me, my lord Duke, I desire nothing but peace between them, and in this land!"

"Hmm, well, I am inclined to believe you, Lady Philippa. Mayhap I was wrong to accuse you as I did. But appearances were against you. You may go," he ended abruptly.

"'Go'?" For a moment Philippa felt bewildered. Was she free? Or merely being allowed to return to her prison chamber? "You mean I may leave the Tower?"

"Aye. All charges dropped. Your husband is waiting near by. He will escort you from here."

Relief made Philippa weak. She concentrated on Northumberland's weathered face as the room swung around her. "Thank you, Your Grace," she managed. She turned and forced her legs to carry her steadily towards the door. Her brain seemed numb with relief, yet before she reached the exit she stopped and turned again. "What will happen to my brother?" she enquired tightly.

"He will be tried."

"On what charge? He was attempting to aid the King. That can surely not be counted treason?"

"The King did not need his aid," snapped Percy irritably. "Do not concern yourself with Roger d'Alban. In due course he will be dealt with fairly and justly. Meanwhile, he is not uncomfortably lodged."

"May I see him?"

"It would be unwise. Go with d'Evreux, child. Thank God, Henry Bolingbroke, and your husband for your release. Do not become further embroiled in your brother's fate."

Philippa nodded. A modicum of warmth began to spread through her body. So Giles had had something to do with her aquittal. She left Northumberland's presence and returned in a daze to tell Ida the good news.

Giles stepped from behind the arras and frowned

grimly at Henry Percy. "You did not spare her, my lord," he accused.

"I was instructed otherwise! She is a taking filly, d'Evreux; you are a lucky man. But do keep her on a leading-rein in future! Otherwise, you are liable to find both her and yourself in deep trouble!"

Giles allowed his relief to surface, and chuckled. "She is too spirited for a leading-rein, Your Grace. And I could not bring myself to whip her. So I shall have to use gentler methods. Treats, and kind words and…ah…the occasional soothing pat and stroke…?"

Both men broke into gusts of laughter, and Giles was still grinning when he tapped and entered his wife's chamber.

Philippa, waiting expectantly for his arrival, observed the amusement on her lord's face and something inside her snapped. She could see absolutely no reason for mirth; her situation had been uncomfortable to say the least—terrifying, if the truth be told. And Giles had not helped the previous evening by his unsympathetic, critical manner. He must have been instrumental in gaining her release, but now he had the gall to laugh at her!

The candlestick, with its burnt-out stub of wax, was to hand. Without considering the wisdom of her action, she snatched it up and threw it into his mocking face.

Giles's reflexes were honed to perfection. He caught the missile easily, and stood looking from it to his wife in pained astonishment. "What did I do to deserve that?" he enquired mildly.

"You...you..." Philippa searched for a bad enough word to use "...you smirking cretin!" she spat. "'Tis no matter for amusement! I was unjustly accused, I have suffered most grievously, and all you can do is laugh!"

"Pippa! I was not laughing!" he protested somewhat guiltily. "I know you have had a miserable time! My love, I am just happy that you are free!"

"Ha!" she scorned.

He stood there with the candlestick in his hand, looking as though he didn't know what on earth to do with it. Suddenly he looked comical, the situation was comical, and Philippa broke into hysterical laughter.

Giles acted instantly. He thrust the candlestick into Ida's ready hand, strode over to his wife and took her by the shoulders. Now he could shake her with good excuse, and he did so.

"Stop it, Pippa! Stop it, do you hear me?"

The laughter turned to great, gulping sobs, and Giles gathered her to him. "My love, it is over! You are safe!" he murmured tenderly.

Philippa rested against him, her hands spread against the solid wall of his chest while the shudders racked her body. She felt his hand stroking her hair, the soft touch of his lips on her temple, gave a last convulsive hiccup, and buried her face in his shoulder.

"I'm sorry," she whispered.

"Nay, wife! 'Tis I who should apologise, for my harsh treatment over the last days. I should have known that you would not betray me. But—you had been so fierce in your father's cause."

She lifted huge midnight eyes, still swimming with tears, to scrutinise his face. "Your doubt did hurt me, husband. After all we had shared... I could not understand how you could question my loyalty."

"I shall not do so again."

He lowered his head and touched her lips with his. Fire seared between them, and Philippa's arms reached up to wrap themselves about his neck. Giles's hold tightened, his lips firmed, and the kiss went on and on until they were both breathless.

They broke apart and stood looking at each other. Something new had happened between them during that embrace, but neither quite knew what it was.

"Come, wife," murmured Giles at last. "Let us remove ourselves from this place. I am taking you to my parents, at Acklane. You will be safe and cherished there."

Philippa gulped as a sudden chill swept over her. "But—cannot I remain with you?"

"'Twill only be until Parliament meets. Until then I shall be kept busy with Henry's affairs. You would be lonely at Westminster, sweetheart, and you need time to recover from your ordeal. After that, I shall have more time, and shall know what the future holds. Then we can be together again."

"Very well." Philippa knew it would be useless to plead further. He did not want her at his side. Would probably find her presence an embarrassment. Mayhap, in a month's time, the scandal of her arrest would be forgotten.

Their arrival at Acklane two days later caused a considerable stir. Giles had sent a messenger ahead to warn of their coming. Philippa passed the great oak which gave the manor its name, rode steadily beneath the leafy branches of an avenue of wych elms, and emerged to rein Blaze to a halt before the gracious manor house Richard, first earl of Wenstaple, had built in the first half of the century, and later given to his half-brother Thomas, Giles's father. The place was alive with servants and dogs. A new wing, built of the same warm, cream-coloured stone, had recently been added to the original building, and it was from there that a man in thick leather buskins and a plain russet tunic appeared on the step to greet them.

"John, my brother," grinned Giles, leaping from Panache's back and helping Philippa to dismount while one of the grooms rushed to hold the horses' heads. Two women had appeared behind his brother, one youthful and comely in a blue linen kirtle with matching velvet bosses holding her abundant chestnut hair, the other older, in a simple grey gown and white kerchief, bearing a baby in her arms. "Constance, his wife," Giles went on informatively, "and that must be the latest addition to their brood in the nurse's arms! The older ones are away for schooling, the younger no doubt occupied in the nursery.''

Ida and Wat dismounted too, while Eadulf brought up the rear, shepherding a pack-mule bearing their coffers. Meanwhile John d'Evreux strode across the neat courtyard to greet them.

''Giles! 'Tis good to see you, brother, and looking well, too! And this must be Lady Philippa, your wife!'' He turned to scrutinise her with searching interest, his serious grey eyes warm with sudden admiration. ''My dear, we are glad to welcome you to Acklane. Giles, you appear, as usual, to be a lucky dog!''

Philippa found herself blushing. ''Thank you,'' she murmured.

Constance, on closer inspection, proved to be less striking in her features and rather older and plumper than the distant glimpse had suggested. Yet good nature shone from her rather pale blue eyes, and she appeared comfortable in her matronly role.

''Where are our parents?'' enquired Giles as they all made for the main entrance to the house, set in an embattled tower, the only sign of defensive fortification visible in a place where doves flew in and out of a cote set at the apex of the thatched roof. ''Well, I trust?''

''Father rode out to inspect the harvest; he had expected to be back before now. Mayhap he has uncovered some slackness,'' grimaced John. ''He does not yet completely trust my stewardship! And our mother is resting. She tires more easily these days.''

"There is naught wrong with her?" demanded Giles anxiously.

"Nay, brother, do not distress yourself! She has been busy this morn preserving fruit from our orchard, and decided to rest before supper, that is all.''

But Lady Marguerite had heard the commotion of their arrival and, as they moved through the screens to enter the Great Hall, a large chamber made light by the tall, mullioned windows lining one side, she came down the stairs from the solar.

Marguerite de Bellac had aged well. Never truly beautiful but always attractive, her bone-structure had stood the test of time, and her finely drawn face was as well-sculpted now as had been that of the woman of four and twenty years who had captured the love of Thomas d'Evreux.

Her hair, braided and coiled, half hidden under a circlet and veil, was almost entirely grey. She must be—what? Philippa asked herself as she curtsied to the Countess. Well past her fiftieth summer. And thin and straight as a lance. She held herself with dignity and, though blotched brown in places, the hand she extended to Philippa was shapely and strong.

"My dear daughter! Welcome!" She drew Philippa to her and kissed her cheek. "And my son! A married man at last! I had despaired of ever seeing this scoundrel honouring his contract and brought to the church door!" She laughed joyously, and took her second son into a warm embrace, which he returned with a great hug.

She had still not lost the attractive French accent with its Spanish intonations that Philippa remembered from her betrothal visit. She stared in renewed fascination at the French Compte's daughter who had defied convention to marry a base-born Anglo-Norman knight. John had arrived in the world a scant seven months after their marriage. He had not been premature. Philippa had heard only echoes of the scandal which had rocked the Lancastrian court, where Thomas had served John of Gaunt faithfully for most of his life, but she knew the couple had weathered it, and been blissfully happy in their union. As well as their two sons, they had two daughters, who were both now married with children of their own.

She and Giles were escorted to a guest chamber. Philippa gave a crow of delight.

"You had my coffers brought here!" she exclaimed. "Ida! Find me a decent gown to wear!"

Giles chuckled. "I thought you might need a few more things than those you were able to take on the journey."

"But how did you know...when did you know we were coming here?" demanded Philippa, suddenly suspicious.

"I knew we were destined for Westminster. I ordered your things brought here when we left Bristol.

I would have sent for them had you remained in London.''

''Handy,'' sniffed Philippa, suddenly less pleased to see her possessions. ''You managed to avoid that necessity by banishing me here.''

''Pippa, you have not been banished! Do you not want to know my parents? My brother and his wife? They are your family too, now. Your stay here will allow you to forge links which will last a lifetime. Sweetheart, I will come for you the first moment I am able.'' He drew her to him, holding her fast against his warm, vital body. ''You know I will burn for you while we are apart,'' he murmured deeply. ''I do not leave you here from choice.''

His lips covered hers with fierce possessiveness, and Philippa knew that he meant what he said. As the heat between them intensified she cursed her monthly showing, which would prevent their full union for several days yet. If only she could have sent him on his way with the delights of passion freshly imprinted on his mind and body! But she could still make her mark on his awareness. She vowed he would remember the coming night throughout their separation.

She left his arms reluctantly, running her finger down his cheek in a gesture of tender submission. ''Do not doubt that I shall miss you, too,'' she told him softly. ''Thank you for your thought for my comfort, Giles. I was foolish to doubt your good intentions.''

Giles, still breathing rather heavily from the passions aroused by that kiss, lifted her chin and touched her swollen lips again with his, cherishing and soothing them to assuage the effects of his previous assault. "Where you are concerned, wife, all my intentions are good ones," he assured her, "even if a little primitive at times…"

She chuckled contentedly. "So I have noticed! And now, my lord, please allow me to bathe and change, so that I may present a more respectable appearance at supper!"

The Earl of Acklane was not one to stand on much ceremony at the best of times, and kept a modest establishment now he had retired to his estates. His ego needed no boost from the lavish ceremonial some of his peers thought essential. So a single herald trumpeted the news that supper was about to be served.

Thomas, dressed still in his riding clothes, rose from his chair on the dais to greet his son and his wife as they appeared. Philippa noticed that he winced with pain as he pushed up on the arms, and limped slightly as he moved stiffly towards them. The joints of the strong swordsman's fingers which gripped her hand were knotted with rheumatism, and she guessed his knees were similarly afflicted. Otherwise he appeared fit and well, his lean face still remarkably attractive under the abundant grey hair and lavish beard which went with his advanced years. He had been the same age as John of Gaunt, whose death earlier that year had precipitated the present crisis.

He greeted her courteously, then gripped his son's shoulders. They were of a height, though possibly the father had lost an inch with age. They smiled at each other, and Philippa thought how alike their lively eyes were, apart from their colour. The Earl's were quite grey. At that moment Giles's looked almost blue. "'Tis good to have you home again, my boy," said the Earl heartily, releasing his son's shoulders to clap him on the back. "And Henry? How does he?"

"Well enough, I believe, sir." Giles returned the affectionate gesture, and then shrugged. "Though he is in two minds as to the King's intentions. Richard promises much, but—"

"Aye. Poor Lancaster had the devil's own job guiding the boy over the years. He was ever devious, and seemingly quite oblivious to the feelings of his subjects. What a tragedy for England that his father died so young." He sighed. "John did his best to keep his nephew in line, but now that he is dead…"

"Richard has run amok," said Giles grimly.

"Aye. Mayhap Henry and their uncle of York, the Percys, and others, too, can instil some sense into his head before it is too late."

"I think it may already be too late. People have had enough," said Giles soberly. "Everywhere I hear the same prayer. God give us a new King."

Thomas looked at his son in alarm. "'Tis that bad? People are openly speaking treason?"

"Aye."

"And Henry Bolingbroke?"

"Is next in the male line. He would be willing, I believe," said Giles quietly.

Philippa smothered a gasp. When she had voiced such a possibility Giles had jumped down her throat. Yet now he was airing the idea to his father!

Thomas frowned. "Be careful where you speak words like that, my son. Should Richard prevail, there are those who would have your head for treason—"

"But here, sir, in the privacy of your manor, I believe I can speak my mind without fear. Henry would make a good King."

Both men ignored the swarming churls and varlets serving and gathering for supper. They would not hear what was said, and if they did would not betray a master they respected, probably loved. Philippa knew the same could have been said of the manor folk and servants at Alban. And the men clearly trusted her not to repeat what she heard. She moved closer to Giles, allying herself with her husband. Never again would she give him cause to doubt her loyalty.

"I have known Henry since he was a babe," smiled Thomas. "Aye, he would make a good King. He has ambition, as had his father, and a wise head on young shoulders. He is shrewd, energetic, an excellent tactician and soldier, a great defender of the nation's rights. John would never have challenged his nephew himself; he had too much sense of the sanctity of an anointed King." He paused in fond and respectful remembrance of his old lord and friend, then sighed. "But things have come to such a pass that I believe he would applaud Henry's stand. And he would be gratified to see his son King. Two of his daughters are Queens, albeit of foreign lands. To have Henry King of England...'Twould delight him greatly."

"You knew him better than most, Father. I am glad to hear you say so."

Thomas nodded soberly. "And you, Giles." He pursued the subject on a more personal note. "You would not lose by his accession. You have been a faithful retainer and companion for many years. He would surely reward you well."

Giles shrugged, while Philippa studied her husband's face with renewed interest. That thought had not previously occurred to her. But mayhap Henry would appoint him to one of the great offices of State. Or grant him a title of his own.

But Giles was shaking his head. "I have no ambition for high office, sir, nor to be tied to the King's Court. Lands would be welcome, mayhap, though those my wife brought me would suffice for our needs, I believe." He drew Philippa into the crook of his arm. "We require little more than we already have. Do you agree with me, wife?"

Philippa smiled up at her husband, and the Countess, arriving at that moment, felt a sense of deep relief sweep over her. Margot loved all her children, and their happiness was important to her, but this second son of hers was perhaps more dear than the others, for he was so like his father had been in his youth. Her first-born, John, had become studious and earnest as he'd grown into manhood. At times Margot wanted to stir her eldest from his preoccupation with estates and family, make him seek honour, fun and adventure. But such pursuits were not in his nature, and he seemed happy enough.

Although Giles had undoubtedly fulfilled all her dreams of breeding a courageous, honourable, compassionate son just like his father, embodying all the best attributes of chivalry, he had troubled her of late. So devoted to Bolingbroke, always battling for honour in some joust or another, skipping from one romantic attachment to another, he had appeared reluctant to fulfil his obligations and ignored his young betrothed, who had perforce waited for him these many years.

Margot drew nearer and studied his dear face anew. It held a new expression of contentment as he smiled down at his wife, and her heart lifted. Her son needed the stability an affectionate wife and family could give him. Above all, he needed love. Just as his father had needed love, though he had not known it until it had hit him in the face like the low-hanging branch of a tree slapping a careless rider galloping beneath its boughs. She smiled at the memories, and regarded her daughter-in-law with new affection.

Philippa loved her husband, perhaps without fully realising it, but Margot was certain. That look in her eyes could mean nothing else. As yet Giles was not aware of his wife's deep attachment, and showed little sign of returning it. But he would. He appeared fond and protective, and passion lurked in the depths of his eyes. Love would grow. Margot joined the little group happier about her favourite son's future than she would have thought possible only moments before.

"Nay, husband," Philippa was answering, "I have no desire to become part of a Royal Court. I have seen enough of the scheming and treachery, the dangers which seethe beneath the surface, and I want no part in it."

Giles squeezed her waist affectionately. "We may have no choice, sweeting. An Henry orders, I must obey!"

"But he will respect your preferences, Giles, make them known to him." Margot's throaty voice joined the conversation for the first time, and Thomas smiled a welcome to his wife while Giles and Philippa bowed and curtsied.

The idea of Henry's becoming King was no new one to the Countess, Philippa noted. She had immediately understood the tenor of their conversation.

John and Constance arrived at that moment, and they all took their places for supper.

"We heard from Dickon today," Margot informed Giles once they were seated and Grace had been said.

"He will bide here on his way to Westminster for the Parliament."

"And how does my cousin Richard, the second Earl of Wenstaple?" asked Giles with a grin. "He is getting rather old to be chasing about the countryside attending Parliament, I'd have thought!"

"My dear boy, he is eight years younger than your father, and still fully active! They intend to travel to Westminster together."

"He comes alone, then?"

"Aye. Wenfrith and Wenstaple, not to mention both the Countesses, will be in his son's safe hands while he is away," his mother informed him. "'Tis a pity Matilda is not strong. I know it distresses Dickon greatly to see his wife so weak since the birth of their last child."

"Aye, it must. How is the old Countess?" asked Giles. "'Tis many years since I last saw her—"

"'Tis the same for us. Devon is so far distant," interjected Thomas sorrowfully. "I cannot ride so far these days, and neither, of course, can Eleanor. She was like a mother to me, and I much regret that we are so far apart."

"But to answer your question," said Margot, "she is indomitable as ever, though frail, which must be expected in someone who has just celebrated the seventieth anniversary of her birth!"

Philippa, listening to the chatter, relaxed into the embrace of the d'Evreux family while wondering, somewhat belatedly, what was befalling her own.

Chapter Twelve

Giles departed early the following morning. Before he left he presented his wife with a puppy from the kennels' latest litter.

"He's beautiful," whispered Philippa in gratitude. Giles had remembered his promise, and the realisation brought her more comfort than the actual possession of the tiny creature snuffling and whimpering in her arms.

"Something to remember me by," he grinned, but his voice held a deep note which stirred Philippa's pulse anew.

"I need no such reminder," she told him breathlessly, "but I shall be grateful for his company during your absence." Her colour rose, and she hid her face in the puppy's velvety fur. "Do you remember *me*, husband!" she bade her spouse gruffly.

He took hold of her chin and lifted her eyes to meet his. "Do not doubt it, my love," he assured her softly, and sealed the promise with a kiss both would remember for many a long day.

September had brought an autumnal bite to the air, and a mist lay hazily over the demesne fields as Philippa watched his departure from an embrasure in the battlements above the entrance. The turning leaves were still thick enough on the trees to obscure his figure as he cantered off, azure velvet mantelet flying behind him, Walter Instow in faithful attendance.

Eadulf had remained at Acklane to act as her escort should she wish to ride abroad. Not that there were no horse-grooms at Acklane, but Eadulf was a familiar servant and friend, and Giles, she was increasingly aware, a thoughtful husband.

Philippa lifted the soft furry creature in her arms to kiss its little head. It squirmed round to lick her face, and found the single tear which had escaped to trickle down her cheek.

She swallowed hard, and turned to descend the stairs, heaving a sigh. Despite the company of the d'Evreux family and her new pet she would be lonely while Giles was away. Mayhap he would manage a quick visit before the end of September. Memory of the ardour with which he had promised to return to her bed with all dispatch brought colour to Philippa's pale cheeks. She had astonished—nay, embarrassed—herself with her wanton behaviour during the night, but Giles had not complained. A reminiscent smile curved her lips. She had instinctively found ways to give him all the release and joyous satisfaction he needed despite her condition. And in return had received exquisite pleasure from her husband's caresses.

She prayed he would not wish to bed other women while he was away from her. She would not be able to abide other than her husband's touch, but mayhap men were different. Most wives seemed to think so, and accepted their spouse's faithlessness with resignation. But perhaps most of them did not give their husbands incentive to remain faithful. And mayhap they did not love them.

She tossed that last thought aside as she winged fervent thanks to Isobel, who had been her first instructress on the importance of giving pleasure to one's spouse.

"What shall I call you?" she murmured as she set the puppy down on the rush matting in her chamber. Tail high, yelping excitedly, he immediately set about sniffing into every corner of his new surroundings. "What do you think, Ida?"

"'Tis not for me to say, my lady. But mayhap Ears would do."

"Ears?" asked Philippa in surprise. "Why Ears?"

"They are so big and floppy," grinned Ida.

Philippa laughed, but said, "No, I don't like that idea." She caught the puppy and ran one of his long appendages through gentle fingers while a frown of concentration marked her smooth forehead. Suddenly she exclaimed, "I know! Paws!"

"Paws?" echoed Ida with raised brows. "Is that so very different from Ears? And why so?"

"Because they are big and white, while the rest of him is dun, and it has a better ring. Don't you like it?"

"Of course, my lady!" Ida chuckled. "Paws he must be! Though they won't look so large when he has grown!"

"I know that, but they will still be white!"

The days passed quietly but pleasantly. When it was fine Philippa rode out on Blaze, discovering the extent and beauty of the Acklane estate, but as the month progressed rain became more frequent and she was confined much of the time to the house.

Philippa adored Giles's parents, and liked his brother and his wife, though aware that, content in their marriage as they were, John and Constance would never reach the heights of conjugal bliss that the Earl and his wife had found. *Their* delight in each other, even after more than thirty years, was encouraging to see. It gave her hope for her own marriage, for undeniably Giles was very like his father. And if he should learn to love her...

She spent time with the children and cooed over the baby while the desire for one of her own grew. A dog was not enough, sweet as Paws was. She did not think she was particularly maternal, but to give her husband heirs was her duty. And she had become quite attached to the idea of a small replica of Giles to love.

But she could not curb her restlessness. The thought of her brother in the Tower, his wife and children bereft of his guiding hand, distressed her more every day. She had time to think now. To consider the plight of her father and sister-in-law, banished from their home. And on Giles's orders! However much she might now understand and forgive, and realise by Roger's subsequent actions that Giles's concern had been justified, the fact remained. And nothing had been done to relieve her relatives' distress.

Here she was, comfortably ensconced in the bosom of her husband's family—although John was away, visiting others of the manors which comprised his inheritance—awaiting a summons to the new King's Court. For that, she was by now convinced, could be the only final outcome of Henry's bid to regain the Lancastrian estates and bring Richard to heel.

News did reach Acklane, and they heard of concessions made by the King. The Government was still being carried on in his name, but on the third day of September he had given the Treasurership to John Norbury—another, like Giles, who had been with Bolingbroke in Paris. Philippa wondered whether the office had been offered to Giles, and turned down. Thomas grinned and shook his head, observing wryly, "Giles knows nothing of money except how to win it and how to spend it—and besides, he was here with us at the time!"

Two days later the King had ordered Edmund Staf-

ford to surrender the Great Seal, and appointed John
Scarle Chancellor in his place. Thomas knew Scarle.
He had been in John of Gaunt's Chancellery, and he
reckoned him a sound choice. But both the new ap-
pointments must have been dictated by Henry Bolingbroke, and Richard Clifford, Keeper of the Privy
Seal, had kept his office only because he had acceded
to the new administration, and vowed himself willing
to work with those appointed on Bolingbroke's in-
structions.

Eventually, Philippa could stand the inactivity, the
anxiety, no longer. She knew what she must do.
Travel to Fishacre to see her father and Mary. Why
hadn't she thought of it before? It was only just over
the Oxfordshire border in Gloucestershire—no more
than a day's journey from Acklane for a person travelling light on a good horse and with a minimum of
escort. Ida need not come. Mary's maid would see to
her needs when she arrived. Eadulf could escort her;
she need not trouble Lord Acklane for men to accompany her.

Another thought struck her, which firmed her resolve to make all speed to see her father. He would
have received a summons to Parliament. If he was
truly recovered, he would surely attend to voice a
protest, and would be leaving Fishacre any day now.
If news of Roger's incarceration had reached him he
would have sprung to his son's defence; mayhap even
now he was acting against Bolingbroke, which at that
moment would probably be tantamount to suicide. If

she was not already too late she must try to dissuade him from such a headstrong course.

She had tarried too long! In a fever of anxiety she informed her hosts of her determination.

"But, my dear," murmured Margot in some consternation, "Giles wished you to remain with us! I am certain your father is being well cared for, and your brother's family will not want. Be content, my dear. Wait until Giles can escort you there himself."

"I am sorry, my lady, but I cannot. Mayhap you did not hear the full story of my sire's sudden seizure?" Both Margot and Thomas looked puzzled, so Philippa set about informing them of the truth. "'Twas Giles's coming which brought it on! And then he insisted I leave my father's side to accompany him to Bristol to be wed! I hated him for his arrogance, and what I saw as his traitorous allegiance to Henry Bolingbroke! I wanted to break our betrothal contract, but Giles would not countenance the idea!"

"I had not realised you were an unwilling bride, Pippa! It sounds as though my son acted in a most regrettably high-handed manner!" Margot frowned slightly, remembering the soft glow she had seen illuminating Philippa's eyes when she gazed on her husband. "But he has shown his true gentleness and courtesy since, I am certain! And now, surely...?"

"I have accepted my duty," said Philippa stiffly. Not even to Giles's parents would she admit to her growing affection for her husband. "We deal well enough together now," she admitted, "but I can no longer allow him to prevent my seeing my father! I must warn my sire, beg him to show prudence in his support of the King. Mayhap I have already left my visit too late."

Margot looked her daughter-in-law straight in the eye, while Thomas frowned, troubled more by the idea that all was not as it should be in his son's marriage than by any possible difficulty Tewkesbury might get himself into.

"Giles is your liege-lord," Constance reminded her, aghast at such wifely disobedience. "You must obey your husband, Pippa!"

"But he did not order me not to leave here! And even if he had I must defy him! He has my true loyalty, but I must retain some concern for my family!"

"I agree! Thomas, my dear, I think we should provide an escort for our daughter. Will you leave tomorrow, Pippa?"

"Aye, my lady, and I thank you!" cried Philippa in relief. "But I do not need a large escort. I have Eadulf."

"Two of our grooms will accompany you," Thomas told her with a rather wry smile. "I tremble to imagine facing my son's wrath when he finds his wife gone!"

"You, my love? Tremble?" Margot gave a delighted gurgle of laughter. "I have yet to see you tremble before any man!"

"And only one woman," murmured Thomas with

a look which brought becoming colour to his wife's face.

Philippa did not miss the by-play. Would she and Giles be as affectionate towards each other in thirty years' time? So much depended on whether Giles learned to love her. At the moment he was ashamed of her, however much he might deny the charge. She vowed to become more worthy of his love.

Disobeying his wishes would scarce assist in that endeavour, but duty to her family weighed heavily upon her shoulders. Roger she could do nothing to help. However, the others' future might well depend on her intervention. Her new resolve to seek her husband's approval would have to await a more opportune moment, she decided unhappily. Resolutely, she straightened her shoulders and gave her new in-laws a grateful, rather grim smile.

"I will go and prepare for the journey," she told them. "I know you will care for Paws for me while I am away, and see that Ida does not mope. But I can ride faster without her to slow me down."

"The weather has improved today. It should be fine tomorrow. I pray you find your father and the others well," said Margot with a reassuring smile.

The journey was accomplished without incident, though Philippa arrived quite late, with the pale sun already sinking in the west. She would have missed supper, she mused, and was so hungry she could have eaten an ox!

She was not expected, and so the family did not rush out to greet her. Instead, a rather bent man of about forty years stepped out into the courtyard to see who had arrived.

"Buffey!" Philippa slid from Blaze's steaming back into Eadulf's hold, then, clutching her skirts, ran across the courtyard to the steward's side. "How does my father?"

"Lady Philippa!" Surprise echoed in the man's voice as he made deep obeisance. "We had no warning! Naught has been made ready for you!"

"'Twas a sudden decision. All I need is food and a bed. And to see my family! Father is here?" she finished anxiously, but gave the bemused steward no time to answer.

While they were speaking Philippa had led the way into the familiar manor house where she had spent many happy childhood summers, and where she supposed they might live once Giles's future was settled. Like Acklane, the building had only the suggestion of defensive fortifications, for it had been built in the more peaceful years of Edward II's reign.

A fire in the central hearth produced both warmth to dispel the autumnal chill and smoke to choke the lungs. Philippa was still breathing deeply after her exertions, and was caught in a fit of coughing.

"Pippa! Pippa, is it really you?"

Mary came hurrying forward, her homely face, as always framed in frilly white linen, alight with welcome and concern. "Are you well, sister? You are not suffering from a chill?"

"Nay!" gasped Philippa. "'Tis the smoke! After the warmth of the summer, I had forgot how it makes one cough!"

"I'm glad you are well. We had thought never to see you again! Have you news of Roger?" asked his wife fearfully. "We know he was taken; one of those who escaped came to give us the news…"

Philippa pushed the question aside with an agitated wave of her hand. "Later," she said quickly. "Mary, I must see Father. Where is he?"

"There, near the fire. He is well enough."

"Thanks be! I had feared he had left for London."

"He will not be answering the summons to Parliament, Pippa," Mary told her quietly.

Philippa frowned. "Why so? Is he not fully recovered? The last message Giles received—"

"He is well enough physically. But you will find him changed. He has a new passion. Come, he will be pleased to see you." She led Philippa across the smoky Hall to where a man sat on a stool fondling a fierce-looking peregrine falcon lodged on a low perch by his side.

Philippa stopped short. Her sire had lost weight, and with it presence. He looked his age, with added lines to emphasise the new hollowness of his face, but otherwise weather-beaten, active and fit. She ran forward and dropped to her knees by his side. The bird's chain rattled as he moved his feet and stretched his wings, disturbed by the presence of the newcomer.

"Father! I am glad to see you so much recovered!"

"Philippa?" Hugh d'Alban looked rather confused. "I thought you were with that traitor Bolingbroke."

"Nay, Father, I am here, come to see how you do." He spoke belligerent words, but in an unfamiliar, passive voice. "Mary says you have heard the news of Roger's arrest," she said gently. "I am sorry he acted so rashly. I attempted to dissuade him."

"'Twas a lost cause," muttered the Earl, his words slurring slightly. He reached out to stroke the smooth feathers of the falcon. "He should have realised it. You know, daughter, this peregrine is an excellent hunter, and I have more fine birds in the mews. I fly them every day; we do not lack for meat for the pot, do we, daughter?"

He smiled at Mary, a satisfied, lop-sided smile caused by the lingering uselessness of some facial muscles, a smile that tore at Philippa's heart. Her father had indeed changed if his main interest was now to fly his falcons and fill the pot with small game and birds. She did not know whether to cry for the man he had been or to be glad that the man he had become had taken no rash action in his son's defence and was therefore safe.

"Roger is in such trouble," she reminded him gently. "I had feared your concern would cause you to court danger on his behalf."

Her father shrugged. "He must fight his own battles," he told her irritably. "I am too old. I have done with such things. Buffey!" he bellowed. Receiving no immediate answer, "Where is that pestilential steward?" he complained to no one in particular. "Buffey!" And as the harassed steward appeared, "Bring me more wine!"

Philippa rose slowly from her knees and turned to Mary, who stood by with a sad, rather exasperated look on a face which had lost some of its healthy colour and plumpness. The past weeks had taken their toll of her, too.

"He thinks of nothing but his birds," she explained tiredly. "Even news of his son and heir's arrest did not move him for long. He seems able to shut out any unwelcome thoughts. 'Tis sad for one who was so fiery, so fierce and impetuous. But he is happy, so that is something," she added with a sigh.

"But you are not happy!"

"Oh, I do well enough," assured Mary quickly, "though naturally I am concerned for your father, and for my husband's welfare."

It took no seer to realise that Mary was always happier in her lord's absence. In the past, Philippa had noted the fact with faint censure. Now she could understand more readily how a woman could dread being at the mercy of a man she neither loved nor respected. And Mary had married from duty.

"Poor Mary!" she sympathised, feeling a new fondness for her sister-in-law, and expressing it in a swift hug. "I cannot think how to cheer you! Roger is in bad case, incarcerated in the Tower, and I cannot hold out much hope for his future.'' She shook her head in helpless regret while tears gathered in her eyes. ''Why could he not see his attempt to rescue the King was doomed to failure?'' she groaned. ''I warned him! I tried to stop his foolishness, and ended up in the Tower myself!''

''You, Pippa?'' Mary's shocked tone told Philippa that news of her part in the affair had not reached Fishacre.

''Aye, and it was not a pleasant experience, believe me! I attempted to part Roger and Giles, to deter Roger from his purpose, but my motives were mistaken. Some thought I was assisting Roger, and I was accused. Giles believed—eventually—in my loyalty and innocence, and pleaded my cause with Henry Bolingbroke, and I was released.''

The softness with which she said her husband's name caused Mary to scrutinise her sister-in-law afresh. ''You do not now regret your marriage?'' she asked a trifle apprehensively. ''I had wondered whether I did the right thing in sending Sir Giles to the Priory to seek you…''

''I cursed you at the time,'' admitted Philippa ruefully, ''but you did right, Mary. 'Twas my duty, and he is not the monster I believed then. I see now that Father brought this sickness upon himself. Just as Roger has brought his trouble about his own shoulders. Could you not dissuade him, when you spoke to him the day you arrived here?''

Mary shook her head. "Believe me, I tried. But once my husband's mind is made up no one can change it, least of all me," she admitted with a touch of bitterness.

Philippa sighed, knowing the truth of Mary's statement, and recognising rather belatedly that her brother had a touch of the despot in him, demanding absolute obedience from his wife and family. "I know," she admitted wryly. "I have been advised to detach myself from him, and I must, for my husband's sake, even if I did not now think his and Father's erstwhile loyalty misplaced. Richard is a bad King, Mary," she told her earnestly.

"He is God's anointed—" began Mary.

"I know, I know!" cut in Philippa. "But I have seen him, remember—so aloof, demanding quite preposterous reverence and respect, almost effeminate in his love of costly clothes, and so extravagant—almost every lord in the land is against him, especially since he confiscated Bolingbroke's inheritance. I came here partly to warn Father to be circumspect, but I see that I had no need to concern myself." She smiled suddenly, her sombre mood dispelled. "But how are the children?"

Philippa ate while Mary brought her up to date on her offspring's progress. How futile her journey had been! she thought. She had risked Giles's wrath to no purpose! Though she could not have known how much her father had changed, and was glad to have her fears over his possible actions set to rest.

"Where is your husband?" asked Mary when the subject of her children eventually ran out.

"Giles?" A dreamy look entered Philippa's midnight eyes. "With Henry at Westminster. Where else would he be?" she questioned rather wryly.

But Giles was not at Westminster. He was on his way to Acklane, nearing a manor hourse where he could ask for shelter for the night. He had left Westminster late, and would have a long ride ahead of him the next day, would have to push Panache as fast as the horse could go if he wanted to arrive before the family supped. A smile curved his shapely lips and his heart beat faster as he imagined Philippa lying under him once more. Frustration had made him edgy over the last days, and Henry, with wry acumen, had ordered him to seek his wife and return with her at his side.

As in the past, he had sought to relieve his needs with willing ladies about the Court, for old habits died hard. But somehow the satisfaction he had previously found in such amorous adventures had not materialised. He had succeeded only in making himself feel disgust and guilt, and knew he would not readily seek solace in strange beds again. Pippa, his fiery, independent, passionate little wife, had spoilt him for other women.

He swore softly under his breath, the smile momentarily wiped from his face. He could almost hate her for that! And yet he did not. What mattered variety, the pursuit of other female charms, when his own wife offered him so much more than the mere satisfactions of the flesh? Her body was deliciously desirable—and God knew he wanted it desperately!—yet his need for his wife went much deeper than that.

Panache's hoofs beat out a steady rhythm in the soft mud of the road, Wat's horse travelling half a head behind. The two men rode without speaking, Wat sensing his master's desire for silence.

Giles was struggling with new emotions, a new awareness of just how much he had come to rely on his wife's company, on her approval, her care. He did not just desire her, he was truly fond of her, he thought in amazement. She might spit and scratch on occasion, she might be a handful to manage, but he had known no other woman quite like her, and had fallen victim to her charm.

Did he love her? What was love? He saw it manifested in his parents, but had scarcely expected such a lasting passion would ever come to him, and had not been certain he wanted it, in any case. Such total commitment had its reverse side: greater dependence, greater anguish on separation or loss. Love wasn't necessary. Not at all.

But he could not deny the attractiveness of a future blessed by mutual love. Cold aloofness, perhaps even enmity within a household, did not appeal to Giles's warm nature. But if he admitted to his love for his wife, could he be certain it was returned? The thought that she might one day fall in love with another, if she did not already love him, brought with it a surge of such fierce jealousy that his hands tightened on the reins and Panache jibbed, tossing his head and snorting in outrage.

Giles dismounted at the manor house without having come to any conclusion in his thoughts. But, he promised himself, he would know when he saw his wife again on the morrow! And he would know, too, whether she was truly growing fond of him. He thought she was. She had softened of late, and showed some concern for his comfort. And he remembered the kiss they had exchanged in her bare lodging in the Tower, and the caring way she had pleasured him the night before their present parting. When, later, he dropped into exhausted slumber, his wife's name was on his lips.

At Acklane next day he threw himself from Panache's back, leaving the horse to waiting grooms, and strode rapidly indoors. His mother and father were sitting in the Hall with Constance and several others. The supper-boards had already been cleared away. He had been delayed because Wat's horse had cast shoe along the way.

He looked around expectantly. "Greetings!" he cried cheerfully. "Where is my wife? In our chamber?"

"Nay, my son." Margot's voice was gentle. She watched Giles's face carefully. "She has gone to Fishacre, to see how her father does."

His face darkened; it was like watching the thunder clouds gather. But pain and disappointment, not anger, filled his turbulent eyes.

"Fishacre?" he exclaimed explosively. "I told the wench not to become involved with her family's affairs! How dare she disobey me?"

"She loves her family, Giles. You cannot deny her the chance to see how they are, or to warn her father against taking action on his heir's behalf. She was afraid for him, my son. She had waited for you faithfully until yestermorn."

"She departed only yesterday?"

"Aye, my boy, with our blessing. We have become greatly attached to your wife." Thomas's voice held mild reproof at his offspring's anger. "She owes you duty and loyalty, but has a mind of her own which you will never wholly control," he observed whimsically. "So take my advice, and do not attempt the impossible! Sit down, refresh yourself with small ale, and tell us the news from Westminster."

Giles stepped forward with long, impatient strides, his golden spurs sounding a jangling note into the comparative silence which fell after his father's words. He picked up the jug and drank deeply, passed the back of his hand over his lips to remove the excess moisture, and addressed his father.

"I must beg the loan of a good horse. Panache is finished. I ride for Fishacre within the hour."

But it was several hours before Giles and Wat finally set out, against his mother's pleading, to travel through the night. Giles wanted to be with his wife by the time she broke her fast.

Philippa rose before dawn. She had developed an urge the previous day to visit Alban Castle. No news had arrived from there since the day they had been escorted from its precincts.

The place had been stripped, that she knew. It would be bare and chill now, yet it had been home. She had a longing to see it again. And the manor folk would welcome her; she could see to their welfare. Without the castle to turn to for protection, the inhabitants of Alban were at the mercy of any marauding band of outlaws or cut-throats who happened by.

She would easily find shelter for the night, either within the castle or in the village, or failing that with the Prioress Mary-Luke in Evesham. She lingered only to break her fast and to pick up the saddle-bag packed with spare linen and victuals before going out into the pale dawn to join Eadulf and the Acklane men in the stables, where Blaze and their own horses were standing ready, saddled and bridled.

Eadulf tightened Blaze's girth, and threw his mistress into the saddle. "'Twill be another fine day, my lady," he remarked as he adjusted her stirrups. "We should reach Alban well before nightfall."

They did, arriving while the sun was still quite high above the horizon. The stark walls rose ahead, outlined against its brilliance, but—

Philippa urged Blaze to increase his pace, outstripping the others as she made headlong for the home of her youth. Something was amiss. The familiar outline of the stonework against the sky looked different, but it was not until she was within arrow's distance of the walls that she drew rein and sat quite still, staring.

Much of the edifice was in ruins. The drawbridge was down over the dried-out moat, the gatehouse had gaping holes where the mechanism for its raising should have been housed. The portcullis had gone. And the curtain wall had been breached in several places.

Alban Castle had been destroyed. Tears began to course down Philippa's ashen cheeks, but she did not notice.

Chapter Thirteen

Closer inspection revealed that the main part of the original castle remained largely untouched, though some of the entrance steps had been prised loose and heaved aside, leaving a difficult scramble up to the open doorway.

Silent and grim, Eadulf helped Philippa to reach the Hall, while the Acklane men dismounted and stared about them, taking it all in, though knowing they had no part to play in this drama except to get their lord's son's wife back to Fishacre safely on the morrow and to Acklane soon thereafter.

Philippa wandered through the ancient stone building, and found only ruin and desolation. Sour, evil-smelling rushes in the Hall, where rats and mice had made their nests. In the chamber at the top of the tower she pounced upon a rag-doll kicked among the dusty straw, disturbing a rat, which scuttled to cover. She held the toy tenderly in her hands, a poignant reminder of the little girl and her brother who had sheltered here with herself and their mother on that fateful day, etched so deeply on her memory, when Giles had come riding into the courtyard on Majesty, splendid and disturbing, to turn her world upside-down.

She tucked the doll into the scrip at her waist and went on up to the battlements above. Like the curtain wall, the parapet had been breached, and here all the protective merlons had been levelled, giving the tower the strange, unfinished look which had arrested her attention at that first distant view.

In a remote, unthinking daze, she descended to the courtyard and crossed to the living quarters, there to be shocked from apathy into acute pain. Not only had the rooms been stripped, but also in places, where wood had been plentifully used in the construction, gutted by fire. She stared at the blackened walls, at the open sky striped by the charred beams of her old chamber, and tasted gall.

She returned to the courtyard sick and dismayed, crossing it with dragging steps, dreading what she would find, wandering in a daze of warring emotions from the empty but mercifully spared stables and kennels to the undercroft, with its barren granary and buttery, smashed churns in the dairy, destruction in the brewery. And as for the kitchen...blackened hearths with ashes still in them, empty meat hooks, broken spits, iron and copper utensils left battered and useless.

Marauding outlaws would not have done such extensive damage. Giles must be to blame! How could he have ordered such a thorough dismantling of her past life? Hadn't leaving the place an empty shell been enough? Why had he destroyed so much of the d'Alban heritage? There had been no need for that!

But, yes, there had! No one, now, could use Alban Castle to stand against his liege-lord, Henry Boling-broke, who had become undisputed master of the Lancastrian inheritance, and probably of England, too. That was why Giles had ordered the castle slighted!

Resentment flooded Philippa, filled her with impotent fury against her husband. She hurled a warped and split wooden bowl into a corner, watching it splinter in a burst of angry satisfaction before turning back into the courtyard.

A murrain on Giles d'Evreux! She drew a harsh breath and lifted unseeing eyes to the pinky golden-edged clouds gathering round the lowering sun. How he had deceived her! Leading her to believe that all he had done was remove her family and their belong-ings to a safe place while denying Roger shelter from which to gather an army. He had cared nothing for her feelings! Only for the welfare of his treacherous, traitorous, banished master!

All the new, tender feelings she had been nourish-ing for her husband shrivelled under the searing heat of an anger fuelled by a disconsolate sense of loss and disappointment. She had come to expect better of him. All her dreams of future happiness faded and died. For she could never forgive him this desecration.

She sank down on the chill stone of a mounting-block, and buried her face in her hands. The tears would no longer be denied.

It was Eadulf who heard the fast approach of horses and went to the ruined gatehouse to see who came. Philippa was so lost in her anguish that nothing seemed able to penetrate her misery. Even the stamp of hoofs on the cobbles failed to rouse her.

Giles took in the scene in one all-embracing glance. The destruction, the two Acklane men, strangers to him, slouched against a wall drinking from their flasks, Eadulf with his anxious, tired face. Shock and anger were quickly replaced by concern and pity and a flood of some unnamed emotion which included infinite tenderness as his gaze was drawn irrestibly to the forlorn figure huddled on the block.

He strode across and laid a gentle, comforting hand on her shoulder. ''Pippa!'' he murmured, all the shocked sympathy he felt clear in that one syllable.

Philippa did not heed it. He had wrenched her from her private grief, had forced his attention on her when he was the last person on earth she expected or wanted to see. She flinched away from his touch, and sprang to her feet.

''Go away!'' she spat. ''Have you not done enough damage, injured me and my family enough? I hate you! Go away!'' she repeated desperately. ''I never want to set eyes on you again!''

"Pippa! 'Tis not seemly for you to address your husband so!" Giles's mouth had hardened and his words chided, but his already blanched face took on a stretched, taut look, and his eyes—his eyes looked back at her with a tortured expression which tore at some corner of her heart. Yet he could not possibly be feeling sorrow, anguish, desperation to match her own. He had *caused* this shambles, this death of all the memories and dreams she held closest to her heart.

"I do say so!" she insisted vehemently. "Sir, how could you? How could you order the destruction of my home, of my family's inheritance? How can I continue your wife, when you have done this to me and mine?"

"I seem," responded Giles coldly, while his firm jaw lifted in arrogant challenge, "to have heard this accusation before. Then, I forgave you, for we did not know each other well. But now—now, when we have shared so much, have loved so well, how can you believe me capable of issuing such an order?"

"Love!" scorned Philippa. "You speak of love! Did you believe me, until I pleaded with you to trust my loyalty? No, husband, for days you left me in captivity without lifting a finger to help me. The sharing, the loving meant not *that* much to you!"

She snapped her fingers under his nose. Giles made a protesting sound in his throat, and Philippa gave a fierce snort of laughter which almost broke on a sob.

"I cannot easily believe in your honesty," she declared. "Admit it! You ordered Sir William Grafton to slight this castle! And he did his work well!"

Giles felt all the old exasperation, all the simmering anger rising to the surface again. Impossible wench! Why should he offer sympathy when she threw it back in his face?

He drew a deep, calming breath and managed to keep his temper in check. There was little point in engaging in battle. He knew only too well the searing pain of disillusion, warranted or not. Had he not felt it when he'd thought Pippa disloyal? Was not that why he had kept away from her for those agonisingly long days and nights while she travelled in captivity?

Her pinched, suffering face pierced him like a shaft in his breast. She was shaking, almost as though with an ague. He was forced to clear his throat before he could speak. "Pippa," he began gruffly, "I have apologised for that lapse. I deeply regret it. But that experience helps me to understand your feelings now. I know why you are so upset."

Philippa just stared at him. Her great eyes seemed darker than midnight, red-rimmed, the long black lashes glued together in damp clumps, her nose tipped pink. She had never appeared more vulnerable, more desirable. He longed to crush her in his arms, to erase the pain and scorn he saw writ large on her face.

"Do you?" she wondered derisively. She hardly knew herself why his unwarranted act of destruction should cause her such desperate anguish.

Giles ignored her interruption. "Wife, you must believe me.'' He held out his hands in appeal, but did not touch her, for he knew the time was not yet right. ''I did not order Grafton to slight this place. If this is his work, he exceeded his authority, and shall answer for it.''

Philippa studied her husband from near-dry eyes, seeing him in watery outline still, and distorted by her mind's distress. Yet she could not now miss the concern, the genuine anger in his voice, the sincerity mirrored in those eyes she had learned to read so accurately.

She blinked to clear her vision. 'Twas true. She knew him well enough by now to tell when he was bluffing, when he was lying, when he was evading an issue. He was doing none of those things. His gaze was clear, his eyes intent upon her face. And they held a look of such honest purpose that she could not doubt his sincerity.

''Grafton?'' she whispered. '''Twas his doing?''

''Aye, my love. It must have been, unless others have passed this way. The villagers will know. 'Twas not done on my orders,'' he repeated. ''There was no need—we are not at war, and I knew stripping the place would be enough to deter your brother from lingering here. I will discover who is responsible, and see that restitution is made. I am sorry you found out in this fashion. Had you remained at Acklane...''

He allowed his voice to trail off. Not accusing. Just stating a fact. But to Philippa, emotionally scoured, still half blaming her husband for the condition of

Alban even if he had not ordered its destruction, it came as an accusation.

"I could not!" she flared. "Even your parents saw that I could not remain obediently with them in ignorance of how my father and Mary and the children did! If Father intended answering his summons to Parliament, I had to warn him to desist from his support of the King! Had to make him understand the danger of attempting to side with Roger! Though," she choked, "my brother could well accuse us of deserting him in his time of need. Mayhap we *should* stand by him, ready to share his fate!"

"Not you, my wife. You are too precious to risk your life in your brother's lost cause."

"'Precious'?" Philippa blinked in surprise. The whole bailey was illuminated by the red-tinged light of the dying day, and Giles stood in a shaft finding its way through the ruined curtain wall. She realised anew just where they were. His presence at Alban was as unexpected as the word he had used. She frowned. "How come you here?" she demanded.

Giles held out his hand. "Come, wife. If we are to talk, let us do so sitting down. We can use the edge of that drinking trough," he suggested.

Philippa hesitated only a moment before placing her small hand in her husband's warm, strong hold. The comfort the contact gave her was instantaneous. How could it be, she wondered, that this one man's touch could set her alight, calm her, warm her, protect her, content her, bring her hope, give her peace? She sat beside him, unresisting, and allowed him to retain her hand in his.

"I went to Acklane to fetch you," he told her, once they were settled. "I have secured decent lodgings within the Palace of Westminster, and wanted you by my side." His voice deepened. "I missed you, Pippa," he admitted with a slightly embarrassed laugh. "I had not realised how much I needed you near me."

She made no response, but gazed steadily into his face. So he went on.

"I found you gone, and intended to set out immediately for Fishacre. But my mother persuaded me to rest for an hour or so, that to arrive before dawn would not be convenient. And then Dickon rode in on his way to Parliament, so my departure was further delayed. The journey took longer than I anticipated, since to travel in darkness is to travel slowly, and the horses we borrowed were not as fleet as Panache and Wat's usual mount."

"At what time did you arrive at Fishacre?" asked Philippa quietly. Her heart had leapt at his declaration, and was thudding with renewed hope, but she feared to build too much on his words.

"A good long while after Prime, with the sun already riding high, and you gone! Imagine my annoyance! Such an elusive wife I have!" He grinned suddenly, encouragd by her mellowed mood. "Independent, disobedient wench! I could have wrung your neck!"

Philippa laughed at his affectionate teasing, allowing her new-found hope to surface in a joyous burst of sound which echoed around the courtyard, causing both Wat and Eadulf to look over to where the two sat so closely together, and exchange a knowing smile. And, scrutinising her husband's face, Philippa saw the drawn lines of tiredness around his eyes, put there by days and nights in the saddle with very little rest or sleep. Put there by his pursuit of her.

Was it just possessiveness which had made him chase after her, or something more? He could have rested at Fishacre to await her return on the morrow instead of borrowing fresh horses and riding on. Her free hand went up to touch the signs of his weariness. "You are tired, my lord husband," she murmured softly, "and there is nowhere here for you to rest."

"But is that not my own fault?" he questioned wryly. "I had thought myself blamed—"

"I believe," said Philippa with a small smile, "that you were as responsible for this—" she waved an expressive hand as her lips twisted in distaste "—as for my father's seizure. Both arose from your visit, but neither was truly your wish or fault. And I do not want to quarrel with you further, husband," she admitted with a small sigh. "I would like us to be— comfortable together." She paused. "As your parents are," she mumbled low, her flushed face hidden from his suddenly intent gaze.

"But they," reminded Giles soberly, "fell in love with each other. Passionately and deeply. I truly believe that either one would give his or her life for the other's happiness."

"Aye." Philippa sounded deflated, and did not raise her face. "I...had hoped..." she began tentatively.

"That we might find a similar love?" Giles tilted his wife's face to his. His eyes were so intense, so soft, so blue. His beautifully sculpted lips curved within the frame of his beard. "Do you find it a possibility, Pippa?" he asked deeply.

Philippa's breath had got caught up somewhere in her chest. Her heart had stopped merely pounding. It was hammering so hard and fast that it had cut out every other function of her body. She couldn't answer. But her eyes were shyly eloquent as they locked with his and the small nod she gave travelled from the fingers which held her chin and on down Giles's arm to wound him anew in his suddenly vulnerable breast.

He drew a harsh breath and swore softly. "Pippa, I want to love you as we've never loved before," he growled urgently, "to tell you that you have given my life new meaning, new purpose, that I cannot imagine living without you now!" He grinned suddenly, boyishly, relieving his own tension. "Oh, I was annoyed when I found you gone from Acklane!" He sobered again quickly. "But even more was I afraid— afraid that I had lost you, that you had returned to your father's roof to escape me..."

Philippa's heart had stopped behaving like a farrier's hammer on an anvil, but the blood still coursed hotly through her veins, making her tremble.

"No," she denied breathlessly. "You forget, husband, that Fishacre is yours now. I felt obliged to visit, but went reluctantly, for I knew 'twould anger you, and I wanted to win your love, not your disapproval." She smiled with a radiance Giles had never seen before. He caught his breath in wonder.

"You desired my love?" he asked tentatively. "You have forgiven me my harsh treatment of you?"

"Aye, husband. I know you were driven by considerations I knew nothing of at the time. And I was happy in our union until…until the Tower."

She shuddered, and Giles drew her closer. "And you have forgiven me that lack of faith, too?"

"As I hope you have forgiven me, for doubting your intentions over Alban Castle."

"You cannot imagine," he told her quietly, drawing her so close that she could feel his warmth through the layers of their apparel, "how devastated I felt when I believed you had left me." He paused, then added deliberately, "I do love you so much, Pippa."

She gasped as her heart leapt anew, and drowned in the tender blue pools of his eyes. "You do?" she managed.

"Aye. I had not fully realised it until then," he admitted sheepishly. "Promise me you will never leave me again! And tell me that I can hope for you to love me, too!"

The tears began to fall again. Giles bent his head and gathered them on his tongue. Salty proof of how much his declaration had moved her. His spirits soared, and an urgent desire to show her his love in the only way open to him seized his loins.

"I did not leave you, husband," she whispered. "And I do not think there is anything could drive me from your side now! For I have loved you since…oh, Kenilworth, at least!" The convulsive tightening of his arms brought a new glow to her cheeks as she went on. "Only I would not let myself believe it! How could I love the man who had caused my father's illness, who was allied to Bolingbroke, who threatened to dethrone the King?"

"Aye." Giles's arms slackened, and he shifted uncomfortably, his eyes dropping from hers as a frown drew his brows together. "Will it concern you, wife, if Richard abdicates and Henry is acclaimed King in his stead?"

"Is that what will happen?"

"I believe so. 'Tis mooted." He lifted his gaze to meet hers again, and took both her hands in his. "Richard will not trust his cousin, and Henry holds the power. Had the King proved honourable in the past, 'twould be a different matter. But Henry would be foolish to give credence to Richard's promises now."

"I am wiser than I was a month or more ago. I can see the King's faults, and that many people suffer under his rule. He spends more money on peaceable things than he would on war!"

"Aye. He is a prodigal spender! Henry would make a just and thrifty King, and have the Lancastrian wealth to call on without recourse to confiscation! But—France would not like it. If Richard abdicates, his little Queen Isabelle will lose her throne, and her father will surely declare war."

"So the truce would end." Philippa sighed. "It seems we may jump from the skillet into the fire."

"But the die is cast now, my love. For Henry, there can be no going back."

"Well, we can do little to influence the course of events. But we *can* attempt to find shelter for the night! I had not noticed how low the sun has sunk. 'Twill be dark soon. The days are drawing in fast."

Giles stirred, tempted to kiss the lips so near his own, yet putting off the moment in a desire to savour the anticipation—and to find privacy. He sprang to his feet.

"Wat!" he bawled.

Wat came running. "Aye, lord?"

"Send Eadulf into the village to obtain victuals for us and the horses. Here—" he dug in his pouch "—give him this penny; he'll need it to buy them. And see if there is hay or straw in the stables for bedding, otherwise we shall have to ask the village to supply that, too. But first send those idle churls from Acklane to me."

"At once, Sir Giles."

Wat ran off, and Philippa stood up. "We shall need water," she reminded her husband. "Since it is dry,

Grafton must have dammed the stream which feeds the moat. There can be no shortage of water after the recent rain.''

"What of the well? Is there no water in that?''

Philippa lifted her brows and gazed straight at him.

Giles cursed. "The devil take William Grafton! We cannot know whether he tampered with the water, so cannot risk using it. Is that your view?''

"He was very thorough in other ways.''

"So he was. Ah, you there!'' He addressed the Acklane men, one sturdily built and tall, the other shorter and wiry, who had presented themselves at Wat's request. "What are your names?''

"I am Alan,'' said the wiry one, "and this is Ralph, lord.''

"You know me?''

"Aye. You are the Earl of Acklane's younger son, Sir Giles.''

"Good. Then you will not object to carrying out my orders. One of you stable the horses and rub them down. Eadulf, the groom, has other matters to concern him. I sent him into the village, since the people know him, and will be generous with supplies. The other of you must go for water—an he can find a container. The stream is yonder, beyond that line of trees.''

He pointed through a gap in the curtain wall, and Ralph nodded. "I'll go. My arms are stronger, and Alan will be better with the horses.''

"You'll find buckets in the dairy. They do not appear to have been destroyed. There,'' put in Philippa, indicating the door in question. She grinned at Giles. "I'll go and look in the stew. There may be fish still there."

Wat returned to report a cache of straw, found forgotten in the darkest corner of the loft above the stables.

"Then we may sleep soft tonight! Fetch the saddlebags, will you? Alan is seeing to the horses, Ralph has gone for water, and the straw needs bringing into the Hall—enough to make pallets for us all. Make yourself useful, you lazy varlet!" he grinned, and Wat returned an impudent grimace before running off to do as he was bidden. Giles turned to Philippa. "We will bed in the solar, I think. 'Tis usable?"

"I believe so. Just empty."

"Then come, wife." He held out his hand in invitation. "We will investigate further."

"First I must go to the stew," she reminded him "I'll take a cauldron—I saw a dented one in the kitchen, and I don't suppose we'll find a net. We shall need kindling, too, if I am to cook my catch."

"Then we will go together. I can't have you falling in!" chuckled Giles, reminding them both of her ducking and what had followed.

Philippa skipped along, fizzing like newly brewed ale, euphoric with love, her feet barely seeming to touch the ground. Giles shared her mood, and the excursion became an adventure. They returned singing loudly, Philippa with a huge armful of brushwood and Giles carrying the cauldron, heavy with plump trout.

With the supplies gathered together, Giles declared a feast, to be laid out on the only surface available— a work-bench in the kitchen—and eaten sprawled on the floor. Eadulf had done well in the village, and returned with rough brown bread to cut into trenchchers, small ale, milk, cheese, fruit, cold salt pork, a supply of rush lights and a couple of women eager to serve them.

Through it all, Philippa continued to bubble with happiness. She was with Giles again, and he wanted her. Not just for bed-sport, though he wanted that, too—she could see it in the intense, burning gaze turned so frequently on her—but as companion, lover, wife. She ate with relish, her eyes constantly meeting her husband's, so full of love and desire, each mouthful of succulent trout or tasty cheese bringing nearer the time when they could retire. And, when supper ended, she followed him up the stairs to the solar with an eagerness she did her best to hide. It would not be seemly to exhibit impatience to strange eyes.

Giles had dismissed Wat, and they served each other. A bowl of water stood ready for their use, and Giles turned her disrobing and the removal of the day's dirt into a sensuous rite. He seemed in no hurry to claim her, but intent on showing her how much he reverenced and delighted in her body.

The cleansing complete, he knelt at her feet, hands on her buttocks, moving his lips up her thighs to linger in the thick black hair at their join. Philippa held his golden head, pressing his face to her, her fingers laced in the springy waves of his hair. When he reached higher and touched her navel with his tongue, she shuddered and cried out. Giles growled in response, and drew her down to him, so that they knelt thigh to thigh and he could reach her tender breasts with his worshipping mouth.

She groaned as the thrill of his suckling pierced her through. "Giles, stop!" she pleaded huskily. His clothes still separated them. "Please wait! Let me do for you what you have just done for me!"

Giles lifted his head, his eyes heavy with desire, and succumbed to the temptation he had been denying since first she had declared her love. After all her past enmity and scorn he could still scarce believe it. He must test her response now! He would surely detect the difference if passion was now truly spiced with mutual devotion.

His lips claimed hers in a kiss tender yet passionate, a long, enervating caress that seemed to draw her soul from her body and leave her empty of all feeling but one of wondrous, palpitating, tender love. He lifted his lips. He felt drained yet infinitely satisfied. Oh, yes! There was a difference.

"Anything you want, my love," he promised gruffly.

He had often called her his love, but never before with that special throb in his voice that told her it was no figure of speech, but the true expression of the feeling in his heart.

He helped her with the buckles on his spurs, with his hose, the long boots he had worn for riding, and with his belt and points; but otherwise let her manage alone, revelling in the feel of her small hands on him, caressing as they moved, as his had caressed her. She sponged him carefully, dried him meticulously—even his most masculine parts—and Giles held his breath and clenched his fists for fear of breaking down and gathering her to him, so putting an end to this most exquisite form of torture.

When she had finished, she knelt before him and did as he had done to her until she reached his groin. As her lips whispered tenderly over his body, Giles found he could stand the torture no longer. He bent down and scooped her slender figure up, holding her close to his breast, and carried her to the pile of straw and hay which would make their bed that night.

He had spread her houppelande over it, and drew his larger one over them as he gathered her into his arms.

He had sworn to love her as he had never loved before, and he kept his promise. He subjugated his own need to give her the most exquisite pleasure she would ever know. He clung to his own control, bringing her to an exultant climax and waiting for her to spin back to earth before beginning his strokes again, coaxing her into yet another.

Returning from that high and distant plane to which he had lifted her, Philippa clasped him close, her legs twined about him, and thrust her hips upwards in an endeavour to take him into her very centre, to fill herself with him. For this was what she needed above all else—Giles a part of her, for ever. But to become one indissoluble whole with her lover she knew that she needed to give of herself, as he had given. Love was composed of give and take.

"Giles, my darling," she murmured huskily, "I love you so. Let me show you how much."

She kissed him then. Giles accepted the tribute, allowing her to make love to him, to pleasure him, to urge him to his own release. And at the end they shuddered together in a cataclysm so great that Philippa for one was surprised to find herself still alive when the blood slowed and reason returned.

But it seemed to her that they had truly become one, that they belonged together as the church bade: 'til death came to part them.

Chapter Fourteen

Margot and Thomas eyed their son and his wife with amused tolerance, exchanging satisfied glances. There could be no doubt that the couple had returned to Acklane in a state of loving euphoria—Giles proud and indulgent, gazing at his wife with that in his eyes which spoke of a bewitched adoration, Philippa starry-eyed and pliant with a new softness which only love could have inspired. What had brought about the change was a mystery into which Margot had no intention of enquiring but, as she gently squeezed her husband's hand, careful not to hurt his tender joints, she thanked the Holy Mother for her son's patent happiness. It was exactly what they had wished for him. John could manage with a stable, unromantic affection that would never satisfy the more imaginative, demanding Giles.

Richard, second Earl of Wenstaple, greeted his new cousin with affection, tickling her face with his greying beard and flowing moustache. A tall man who had once been fair, like Giles, Dickon carried his dignity without pretension, and Philippa warmed to him. He had brought his youngest son along—a lively, athletic lad of fifteen, who was to join another household as a squire. Edward had been named for the old King, and was inevitably known as Ned.

Philippa found the boy endearing, not only for his dark good looks and cheerful nature, but also for his open display of adoration for his new cousin, which shone from his ingenuous grey eyes whenever he looked at her. She was flattered by his evident devotion and encouraged his chatter, discovering that his grandam, Eleanor, was in good health despite her years, and virtually ran the manor at Wenfrith because of his mother's indisposition.

"Though she still misses my grandsire," he confided with a boyish grimace of disgust. "And him dead this ten years past!"

"You have yet to fall in love," she teased him gently. "One day you will understand."

Ned coloured to the roots of his straight black hair. His grey eyes reproached her. But he did not declare the love burgeoning in his romantic young heart.

Philippa grinned. "Go and practise your arms," she ordered him gaily. "Do not waste your time while here at Acklane! Wat will oblige you with a contest, I am quite certain!"

Giles viewed his young cousin's infatuation with tolerant amusement. "'Tis obligatory for a squire to fall in love with some unattainable lady," he told his wife with a chuckle. "He would be thought a strange lad were he not to sigh and swoon over the object of his youthful adoration."

"Do not laugh at him," chided Philippa severely. "I find his attentions warm and sweet. Remember your own youth, I pray!"

"Oh, I do! That is why I can laugh at young Ned's devotion. Were he older, I might show rather less tolerance." He pulled her to him and lifted her chin to gaze fiercely into her soft eyes. "Be warned, my love. I will not stand by and see you taken from me."

Philippa wound her arms around his neck. "You need not fear that, husband. I am entirely yours, now and for always, as you very well know!"

"Mmm." Giles tasted her eager lips, then released her, giving her a sharp slap on her rump. "Run along, wench! And behave yourself at Westminster!"

"Of course, my lord!"

Philippa executed a deep obeisance, and ran, laughing, from the room.

The family party travelled to Westminster together, arriving the day prior to the meeting of Parliament. The entire place was buzzing with the latest news.

The King had abdicated! Reputedly with a smile on his face, he had signed a document asking that Henry should succeed him, and as a token had sent Henry his signet ring! But had he truly meant to abdicate, to hand over the Kingship, or merely the administration, as he had been forced to do once before, to the Lords Appellant? *Regnum* or *Regimen*—which had he intended? The words were so similar. Opinions differed, but next day, the last of a rather damp September, when the Parliament summoned by Richard met in Westminster Hall, it was declared in his absence that Richard had abdicated and that Henry had succeeded him as King.

There were protests—even the Percys appeared uncomfortable with the turn of events—but such voices were not heeded. Three and thirty articles were read out, proclaiming why Richard had deserved deposition. Great emphasis was laid on his perjury, on his record for breaking promises.

Then Henry stepped forward and asserted claim to the vacant throne by right of descent vindicated by conquest, whereupon he was acclaimed King by the majority of those present.

Thomas and Dickon returned to the lodging accompanied by Giles, who was not qualified to sit in Parliament, but had watched proceedings from the gallery and was still fuming over the fact that a London mob had managed to gain entry to the Hall to mingle with the Members, while he had been excluded.

"He is without doubt next in the male line—but conquest?" queried Philippa. "I saw no battle!"

"God be thanked!" exclaimed Thomas and Dickon together, for, though neither would shun a fight, both had seen enough of bloody, unrewarding conflict at Najera, in Castile, some thiry years before. Dickon, in addition, had been finally disenchanted when his hero, the Prince of Wales, that "chief flower of chivalry of all the world", as the poet Jean Froissart had written of him in his *Chroniques*, had ordered the sacking of the town of Limoges. Weak and ailing, the once glorious Prince had watched the brutal scenes from his litter. Dickon had found himself defending women and children from the swords of his comrades. He had not sought honour on the battlefield since.

"The huge size of the force which rallied to Bolingbroke's banner deterred active resistance," declared Thomas, rubbing thoughtfully at a swollen knee joint, "so the succession had been achieved without bloodshed."

"What happens now?" Philippa asked.

"The proctors must renounce their homage to Richard. They will do so tomorrow, at the Tower. Then Henry will issue new writs, and Parliament will meet again, in a week's time." Thomas smiled serenely, evidently pleased with the way things had gone. "The new Parliament will proclaim Henry King, and he will be crowned in Westminster Abbey on the thirteenth day of the new month. The ceremony is already being planned."

A slight frown crossed Philippa's face at mention of the Tower, for it reminded her of Roger. But Giles quickly diverted her mind from such grim matters.

"You, my love, will require a new gown," he told her.

Philippa caught her breath. "I shall be present?" she asked in awe.

"An you wish it. Henry will squeeze us in; of that I am certain!"

"What colour shall I choose?" wondered Philippa, trouble forgotten, excitement bringing a warm flush to her cheeks.

"Azure," proclaimed Giles without hesitation. "Azure and silver, with miniver trim and acorns embroidered on the skirt!" At that moment a page arrived to summons Giles to attend Henry. "We will see about it when I get back," he promised as he settled his deep blue houppelande on his broad shoulders, set his elaborately swathed court hat on his fair curls, and went to obey his lord's command.

Philippa was determined to have the Alban knot embroidered somewhere on her court dress. Perhaps on the breast. She set about sketching the design for the embroiderers. She could draw it, but she couldn't sew it, for she would ruin the fabric. Ida could work it, given time, and the acorns, too, but perhaps it would be best to leave it all to the court seamstress and her assistants. First have the gown made to her liking!

She was happily engaged in designing when Giles returned. He was having difficulty in repressing a smile, though his eyes held a rather dazed look. Both the older d'Evreux men were present, since they were sharing the lodgings with them, and Philippa had joined them in the lower chamber. Ned had left, gone to join his new lord—a scion of the powerful Mowbray family—in his.

Philippa had been impressed with the comfort of the dwelling allocated to them, one of a terrace of two-storey, timber-framed, wattle and daub buildings built on a stone foundation and roofed with shingles. There were only two rooms, one above the other, with wardrobe and pallet chambers attached. Every window was filled with glass, and the beds had feather mattresses, satin covers and many a pillow.

"Giles?"

Philippa sprang to her feet, almost tripping over Paws, who had been brought along and was busy chewing an old shoe. She knew something important had happened. Giles held out his arms, and she ran into them.

"Giles," she repeated, "what is it, husband? You have news?"

"Aye, wife." He bent his head and smacked an exuberant kiss on her startled lips, then released her and looked around the company. "You remember Richard introduced the rank of Marquess to honour Robert de Vere?"

"Aye." Dickon answered for himself and Thomas, who merely nodded. Philippa frowned, for the reference meant little to her—the exiled de Vere had been dead eight years. "You were with Bolingbroke and the other Appellants twelve years ago at Radcot Bridge, when the King's force, led by de Vere, was routed, weren't you?" remembered Dickon.

"I was, as Henry's squire." Giles grinned. The memory of that occasion was, for him, one of glorious accomplishment. "'Twas a lively skirmish! Well, I—" he swept an arm, threw up his head and paused for dramatic effect "—God willing, I am to be Marquess of Thame!"

The exclamations of delight interrupted his flow. He gathered Philippa to him again. "How do you fancy becoming a Marchioness, my love?"

"I do not know!" she gasped.

"Will you have lands?" the Earl of Acklane asked.

"Aye, Father, 'tis not an empty honour. Some in Oxfordshire, which march with Acklane, others in several counties, a borough or two—enough to give me an income to meet our most extravagant needs!"

"And you will outrank our fathers and your cousin!" realised Philippa, still trying to take it all in.

The Earl of Acklane laughed, and came to clap a hand on his son's shoulder. "Congratulations, my boy! I always knew you would go far! Wait until your mother hears the news! I must send for her! She cannot be allowed to miss the Coronation."

"Your device will change!" frowned Philippa, fixing her whirling mind on something practical. "My gown..."

"I will keep the acorn as badge—I have always liked it—and my new heraldic coat will be impaled with your father's lozenge now, my love. We will wear coronets and ermine to the Coronation, but the rest can wait."

"I had thought to incorporate the Alban knot..."

"Of course!" agreed Giles expansively. "By George, but I need a drink!" He strode to the table and poured ale from the waiting flagon. He distributed the cups and lifted his. "The King!"

The others echoed his salute and drank.

"You are very certain of all this," observed Dickon, wiping the moisture from his facial hair. "Parliament has still to confirm Henry as King. There may be counter moves—"

"But it will! Surely nothing can prevent it now!" exclaimed Giles. "Henry himself has issued the new writs, and plans for the Coronation are going ahead. You saw the temper of the Members. Few spoke against Richard's removal, and the Londoners—damn their audacity—fairly demanded it! They have already acclaimed Henry King!"

"Aye, Henry is a popular choice," observed Thomas, "I think your doubts are unnecessary, Dickon."

"The honour cannot be confirmed until Henry is finally acknowledged King next week," admitted Giles, "but 'tis certain enough. I will call in the tailor, the seamstress and the goldsmith, my love!" he declared to Philippa.

The next two weeks passed in a whirl. Henry's accession was confirmed, and the Court gathered about him, switching allegiance with little apparent difficulty. Certain things at Westminster Palace changed, however.

Although Henry had cultivated tastes, was sensitive and intelligent, he disliked the messed-about food Richard had favoured. The cooks were instructed to provide real meat, huge roast joints, whole sucking pigs, entire fish and birds for dinner. At supper, the spiced cakes and wine were supplemented by more substantial fare—meats, cheese and fish, fruits and bread. Richard was a gourmet, Henry a hearty eater. Few at Court regretted the change.

After supper, an elderly poet called Geoffrey Chaucer read from his works to amuse the members of the Court. He had been brother-in-law to Katherine Swynford, John of Gaunt's love and third Countess. The first evening he read a new poem he had written to honour Henry, hailing him as "the Conqueror of Brutes Albioun of which, by line and free election, he is truly King". Afterwards, he read excerpts from his *Book of the Duchess*, written to eulogise Henry's mother, Blanche, after her death. On subsequent occasions he entertained them with tales told by an assorted group of pilgrims on the way to Canterbury. He had an attractive voice, and Philippa listened avidly and laughed with the rest at the capers he described.

Many of the women wore elaborate head-dresses about the Palace, some shaped like cows' horns, others like hearts, all made from costly materials, studded with jewels and draped with wispy veils. One

Countess wore a long, steeple-shaped affair, with a fine veil floating to the floor from its point, which, she informed Philippa, was called a hennin. Such fashions were fast becoming all the rage in France, a fact acknowledged by Giles. Philippa wanted a hennin.

"Remain as you are," pleaded Giles, smoothing her forehead. "I like your hair coiled into frets or bosses. To wear any of these fashionable head-dresses you would have to shave the front away to raise your hair-line." His fingers travelled upwards until they mingled with her hair. "'Twould be a grave pity, my love."

Philippa grimaced, and gave way. For the moment. But if they were to remain at Court, she would insist. She did not intend to be labelled an unfashionable dowd, even to please Giles!

They saw little of Ned, and when they did he was invariably with other squires. He always gave her a deep bow and a speaking look, but no longer sat, almost literally, at her feet all day. For one thing he did not have the time, but Philippa thought his passion was wearing off, and surprised herself by feeling disappointed. Giles worshipped her, of course, but Ned had been the first human being to do so unconditionally and without hope of reward, and the novelty had been sweet while it lasted.

To her delight she met up with Isobel again, her belly already beginning to swell, and with less enthusiasm renewed her acquaintance with Helen Cooksey.

She made other friends about the Court, and began to feel quite at home.

Ida had been reunited with her archer, and it was arranged that, when Northumberland and his retinue returned north, Ida would travel with them as wife to Wolfram Root. Philippa knew she would miss the woman who had served her faithfully for so many years, but there would be no difficulty in replacing her. In fact, as a Marchioness, she would need several serving wenches and tiring-women, as well as a court of ladies to keep her company. Giles would also have to increase the size of his household.

Philippa was entranced by her new gown. Embroidered with silver thread and pearls, edged with ermine, it had a long train at the back and trailed the ground at the front, making it difficult to walk, but that seemed a small price to pay for the splendour and dignity afforded. The short cote-hardie fitted snugly into her waist. More ermine trimmed it and formed the long tippets floating from her elbows. Its sleeves ended there, allowing the tightly fitting ones of the kirtle, buttoned to the wrist before flaring out to cover her knuckles, to show beneath. There was a mantle, too, with an ermine cape and a train which rivalled that of her kirtle for length. The Alban knot became part of the fastening across her breastbone.

Giles's white hose and cote-hardie of cloth of gold were covered by a magnificent scarlet houppelande, the sleeves of which were so wide that they swept the floor when he bent his arms. An ermine cape covered his shoulders below the high, jewel-encrusted collar of the houppelande.

"You make a splendid couple," Margot told them with a smile as they paraded before her. She herself had recently arrived to join the Earl, and was magnificently attired for the ceremony, as was he.

"And so do you!" rejoined Philippa sincerely.

On that thirteenth day of October Henry was crowned with great splendour in Westminster Abbey and anointed with the sacred oil reputedly given to St Thomas of Canterbury by the Virgin. He was now King in the sight of both God and man.

All the lords, great and small, attended. Cloth of gold combined with scarlet and purple velvet, ermine and jewelled and padded coronets to make the Abbey vibrate with colour. Henry paraded down the long, arched aisle with all the dignity anyone could require of a King. Behind him, helping to support his train, walked his sons, Prince Henry, the eldest, safely returned from Ireland to a future he could hardly have envisaged a few weeks earlier.

Heir to the throne! Philippa eyed him fondly. He, in his turn, would make a splendid King. A handsome lad, he had the air, the natural authority bred into the Plantagenets through generations of power. Which, in Richard, had turned to overweening pride and arrogance bordering on tyranny. At the moment young Henry was a bit brash, a touch inclined to feel his position and to overact his part, but with his father to guide him he would soon grow out of that.

So this was what that long and arduous journey had led to. A new King, a new heir, a new chapter in the history of England. And her own happy marriage.

Philippa was content.

Philippa, accompanied by two of her attendants, was walking in the pleasaunce of their new manor of Morton. The January snow had long melted away, the sharp, icy, invigorating cold replaced by the grey, damp chill of a dripping February, but she needed air and exercise.

Things had gone well since their retirement from Court. After the excitements of the January uprising, when John Holland and his cronies had tried to capture Henry at Windsor, where the Court had spent Christmas, Philippa had been glad to have Giles safely back from the skirmish at Maidenhead, ready to shoulder his new responsibilities in the safety of his manors.

She walked carefully on the muddy path, her feet kept clear of the mire by pattens, her gown held up in both hands, her mood sombre as she wondered how her brother was faring in France. She had been both relieved and anxious when Giles had brought her the news.

"Banished?" she had gasped. "For ten years?"

"Aye." Giles had been matter-of-fact. "'Tis better than standing trial, mayhap being sentenced to the block. He will still retain his right to inherit your father's estates and, after his own experience, Henry will not be foolish enough to recant his word on that!''

"Poor Mary!'' All Philippa's compassion went out to her sister-in-law. "I wonder if she will join him in France—I assume that is where he will go? And the children…''

"An she is wise she will remain here with Lionel and Maud, on hand to take responsibility for the Alban inheritance should anything happen to your father.''

"Perhaps so,'' she'd agreed, and shaken her head ruefully. "I do not think the separation will trouble her over-much. She manages well enough without him. Roger kept her subdued. She has more strength of character than I once believed.''

Giles had smiled and given her a brief kiss. "Then I am glad I argued for this outcome. Henry does not wish to appear vindictive, and in truth is not.''

The restoration of Alban Castle was already well advanced. Sir William Grafton, challenged, had admitted exceeding his orders, though from the best of motives to his own mind, and been ordered to contribute most of the cost. Philippa could only imagine the anger he had faced from both the King—who had not wished his march to be destructive—and Giles, whose orders he had disobeyed. He had retired to his manors disgraced, while her father, Mary and the children remained at Fishacre awaiting completion of the works.

Her companions were chattering just behind her,

but it was the winding of a horn which brought her thoughts back to the present. A few moments later Giles appeared from the gracious manor house, which was in process of restoration and extension. A frown of concern marred his normally cheerful countenance.

"Bad news, my lord?" asked Philippa anxiously as he drew near.

"Nothing to concern us too nearly," he reassured her quickly. "Come, wife, I will walk with you awhile."

Her companions were left behind. The moment they were out of earshot Philippa stopped and faced Giles, determined to discover what was troubling him.

"Tell me, Giles. I heard the messenger arrive. Was he from Westminster?"

"Aye." Giles took a deep breath. "Richard is dead."

"Richard? But—he was safe at Pontefract! Or so I was told! Giles, I always knew Henry would have Richard killed in the end! How could he? How can you condone it?"

She was both angry and distressed. Giles placed his hands on her shoulders and spoke deliberately. "I do not believe that Henry ordered his death."

"No? Almost everyone else connected with the January rising has already been summarily executed. Four of them were seized by the people of Cirencester on Twelfth Night—after two days of hard riding they had few followers left. They were beheaded in the market place the next morning. Despencer cut his way out, and managed to reach his castle in Cardiff—''

"From whence he attempted to take ship for France—''

"But the ship's master took him to Bristol, where he was beheaded by the burgesses!'' Philippa persisted.

They were rehearsing an old tale, an old conflict.

"But not by Henry!'' Giles reiterated. "Those events show how solidly behind the new King the people of the Realm were—and are! The stir in Cheshire was put down by local people!''

"But John Holland's capture at Pleshey and his execution later in January were not spontaneous acts by the people!''

"No. Young Tom Fitzalan took his revenge there. Holland was instrumental in the arrest and execution of the boy's father, the Earl of Arundel, remember. Tom is not one to let a grudge go.''

"So Henry is blameless?'' scorned Philippa. "How did Richard so conveniently die?''

"He starved himself to death.''

"So that is the story! He was starved, more likely! Or given putrid food he would not eat. Everyone knows how fussy he was, how delicate his tastes!''

"But not on Henry's orders,'' insisted Giles. "Pippa, believe me, Henry would not stoop so low! Though mayhap Tom Swynford, who governs Pontefract and so had Richard in his care, thought to help his stepbrother the King. That is not impossible.''

"All Katherine Swynford's brood have done exceptionally well for themselves, have they not? Look at John and Henry Beaufort! And Joan, married to a Neville."

"And why not? All are Henry's siblings, in one way or another. Do you blame him for seeing that his step and half-brothers—and sister—are well provided for? Or John Holland for attempting to restore his half-brother Richard to the throne? He has suffered the ultimate penalty, but I cannot truly blame him for his loyalty."

"Oh, I hate you!" muttered Philippa darkly.

"Do you, my love?" murmured Giles, gently pulling her into his arms. He stroked the bulge of her stomach, which had just begun to swell. "Then 'tis a pity we can no longer have our marriage annulled. No one would now believe it had not been consummated…"

Philippa's skirts dropped into the mud as her arms wound themselves around her husband's neck. "Why are you always so right?" she demanded indignantly.

"Because I am your lord and master," he pronounced arrogantly, his face alight with love and humour.

"Mmm…" Philippa enjoyed the rapturous kiss to the full. "Giles," she murmured as they came up for air, "I am a little chilled. Would you fetch my fur-lined mantle?"

He nipped the tip of her nose with his beguilingly uneven teeth. "Wretch! Proving your power, eh?

Why not send one of your ladies? Then we can continue with this much more entertaining occupation…"

As his lips claimed hers again, Philippa gurgled with laughter. She had not truly needed the mantle at all…

* * * * *

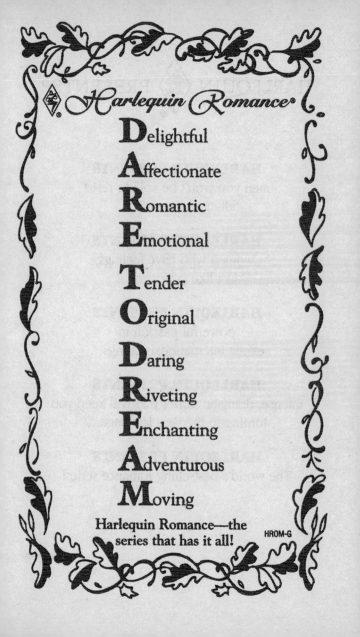

Harlequin Romance®

Delightful

Affectionate

Romantic

Emotional

Tender

Original

Daring

Riveting

Enchanting

Adventurous

Moving

Harlequin Romance—the
series that has it all!

HROM-G

HARLEQUIN PRESENTS®

HARLEQUIN PRESENTS
men you won't be able to resist
falling in love with...

HARLEQUIN PRESENTS
women who have feelings
just like your own...

HARLEQUIN PRESENTS
powerful passion in
exotic international settings...

HARLEQUIN PRESENTS
intense, dramatic stories that will keep you
turning to the very last page...

HARLEQUIN PRESENTS
The world's bestselling romance series!

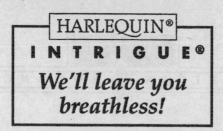

LOOK FOR OUR FOUR FABULOUS MEN!

Each month some of today's bestselling authors bring
four new fabulous men to Harlequin American Romance.
Whether they're rebel ranchers, millionaire power brokers
or sexy single dads, they're all gallant princes—and
they're all ready to sweep you into lighthearted fantasies
and contemporary fairy tales where anything is possible
and where all your dreams come true!

You don't even have to make a wish...
Harlequin American Romance will grant your every desire!

Look for Harlequin American Romance
wherever Harlequin books are sold!

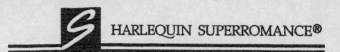